# OUR LYING KIN

## Claudia Hagadus Long

Kasva Press

Make its bowls, ladles, jars and **pitchers** with which to offer libations; make them of pure gold.

וְעָשִׂיתָ
קְעָרֹתָיו
וְכַפֹּתָיו
וּקְשׂוֹתָיו
וּמְנַקִּיֹּתָיו
אֲשֶׁר יֻסַּךְ
בָּהֵן זָהָב
טָהוֹר תַּעֲשֶׂה
אֹתָם

St. Paul / Alfei Menashe

Book design & layout: Yael Shahar

First edition published 2023
Kasva Press LLC
www.kasvapress.com
Alfei Menashe, Israel / St. Paul, Minnesota
info@kasvapress.com

Our Lying Kin

ISBN
Trade Paperback: 978-1-948403-33-7
Ebook: 978-1-948403-34-4

9 8 7 6 5 4 3 2 1

# Dedication

To my father, Ronald J. Hagadus, 1927-2020. Curiosity, Energy, Optimism

# OUR LYING KIN

Claudia Hagadus Long

# A Cast of Thousands

## or Ten Wandering Jews

ZARA PERSIL-PENDLETON — your narrator, writer of this journal. I'm short, thin, blonde (or at least I was, once upon a time.) I have a law degree and I work on my own as an employment investigator. I'm subject to hallucinations and visions of my dead ancestors, especially my mother, Aurora. I was the one who first saw her menorah, about 40 years ago. I make jokes when I'm nervous or emotional.

LILLY PERSIL — my big sister. Given name: Lilliana. She's older by 11 ¾ months, she's 8 inches taller, with long, dark hair enhanced by judicious applications of product. She's voluptuous, outgoing, and liberal with her favors and her politics. A retired teacher, she has a spectacular talent for languages and creative word usage. She had an unfortunate affair with Walter Rosen, a tough relationship with our father, Daniel, and is currently in a romance with Lev Zimmerman.

AURORA — our mother. At age 13 her life was turned upside down by the Nazi invasion of Poland. The daughter of a wealthy industrialist Ashkenazi father and a Sephardic mother, she was beautiful, plump and brilliant. Everything you can imagine a pretty Jewish teen suffered in

I

the War happened to her. She survived, orphaned and deeply scarred. She spoke seven languages, and retained her traffic-stopping beauty into her eighties, when dementia laid waste to everything she was. Forty years ago, she took me to the Jewish Studies Museum, and pointed out a menorah on display. She whispered to me, We had one just like that. Four decades later, a few years after her death, Lilly and I saw it again. And Aurora haunted me until Lilly and I got the menorah back.

DANIEL PERSIL — our father. Predeceased our mother by four long years. More about him anon.

LEV ZIMMERMAN — He's a man with a past. Dark hair, Tom Cruise smile, brilliant blue eyes. His hearing aid matches his eyes. Forty years ago, Lev's father lent a spectacular collection of Judaica to the Jewish Studies Museum. Two years ago, Lev again lent the museum much of his father's collection. Lev got into a scheme with Marie Goldberg, museum curator, to steal some of the artifacts from the display, make insurance claims, and sell the pieces. Nothing went as planned. Alas, one of the items was our menorah. Lev is now Lilly's lover. Don't ask.

SAM PENDLETON — my husband. Political Science professor at a prestigious West Coast university that has asked not to be named, and partner in the Coalition for Electoral Rights, an underground political manipulation group that also asks not to be named. We call it the Rights Coalition, and don't talk about it. He got a sabbatical to New York City two years ago, and that's when the whole menorah problem started. Also, not Jewish.

WALTER ROSEN — the bad guy. Rosen wangled his way into museums across the country, usually as "interim director", and orchestrated thefts of Jewish artifacts. Posed as a Jew, but is actually a Nazi sympathizer and descendant of Alfred Rosenberg, Hitler's art collector. Currently in Federal prison awaiting trial for art theft and Nazi affiliations, he romanced Lilly, seduced her, kidnapped her, and cut her with a knife. She broke her leg escaping him, and has not been herself since. He is also a computer genius.

MARIE GOLDBERG — no longer among the living, she was the curator that conducted the actual heist from the museum. She thought she and Lev were conducting a harmless insurance scam. She was actually Rosen's puppet, and paid dearly for it.

TRUDY ANDRADE SEMPLE — hoo boy. A pretty, elderly woman who took care of Aurora and knew Daniel for a long, long time.

JEANINE ANDRADE CRUZ — Trudy's daughter. Big trouble. Really big trouble.

## Other characters with cameo roles:

ANGIE — my grown-up daughter, married to DEREK, who's never home; MEGHAN — their 5 year old daughter, my perfect granddaughter.

JOEY PERSIL — Lilly's and my brother. Born ill, died before he was four. Not a good thing.

SHEILA MCCONNAUGH — Walter Rosen's admin at the Museum. Smart, tiny, given to funny T-shirts. We miss her. She knows everything.

ANDRES — hot Swiss-Italian retired arts appraiser.

THE LEGAL TEAM: PHIL CARAVAGGIO — not the artist. He's the Federal prosecutor in charge of Rosen's case. ALAN SESKIN — knows all the New Jersey low-lifes, and is our personal lawyer in the New York area. SIMON CREE — Lev's Criminal Defense and other general get-out-of-jail lawyer; frequently says *Simon says*.

THE LAW ENFORCEMENT TEAM: LETICIA SKORDALL — blonde ice-queen FBI agent. Has something to do with the Rights Coalition, and everything to do with investigating Nazis. Officer FAZZINGA — a popular name in the county, as there are more Fazzingas than people in some towns, she's a local Katonah cop these days. Officer BRUNO — we don't know if that's his first or last name, but he's Officer Fazzinga's loyal assistant.

# PART ONE

## CALIFORNIA

# Chapter One

# The Arrest

When my phone chimes at 5 a.m. it can only be bad news. Or someone trying to sell me an upgrade on my car warranty. It's Lilly, and the last time I got a call at this hour she was lying in the woods in Vermont with a broken leg and three-quarters of a swastika cut into her chest. "What's wrong?" I say, not even *hello*.

"Lev's been arrested!"

"He'll still be arrested at nine. I'll call you back." I hang up. You'd think after I've been in California for forty years that Lilly would understand time zones.

Moments later, Lilly's special sound chimes again. I pick up the phone and go into the bathroom so as not to wake Sam. We're sharing a room again and he's snored through the first call.

"Ok, what's the matter?" I ask once I've shut the door.

"It was terrible. Federal agents started banging on my door at seven this morning. I freaked and called the cops. Told them there was someone outside trying to get in. They show up, lights and all, no sirens thank god, and next thing I know everyone's inside my house."

I can just picture it. "Um, so was Lev at your house?"

"Of course."

I knew she'd started seeing him almost two years ago; it was a question, that's all.

"What's he arrested for? Insurance fraud?"

"God, Zara, how'd you know?" She sounds truly astonished.

"Doesn't take a rocket scientist, Lilly."

"So, I made everyone coffee while Lev got dressed, and we sat at the big table as if this were a social call. It was surreal. When Lev was ready, though, they took him out in cuffs. Completely unnecessary."

"Does he have a lawyer? I've got a friend of Sam's, lives in—I'm pretty sure it's New Jersey — I can call him."

"Yeah, that would be great, but his old lawyer got him out already. He's here."

"Wait! Got him out already? So what's the big panic?" Lilly does this, she leaves out the end until the end. Me, I start with it. But she likes the dramatic effect.

"The big panic? They threatened me too! And oh, by the way, I think I found us some more relatives."

<hr />

A little perspective is necessary. My name is Zara. Zara Persil-Pendleton. I'm Lilly Persil's younger sister by a week less than a year.

Before the Big Pause — the lockdown, the pandemic — I spent a year in Manhattan while Sam, my husband, was on sabbatical. Lilly and I had lots of sisterly adventures, not the least of which was stumbling over a menorah that had once belonged to our mother, Aurora, when she was a child in Poland. We encountered the menorah at the New York Jewish Studies Museum, apparently on loan from the *Zimmerman Collection*.

Yeah, as in *that* Lev Zimmerman, currently sitting at Lilly's breakfast table and playing footsie with the Feds.

Before we could get our hands on the menorah, though, it disappeared. Our chase across the City to get it back entangled us with a man named Walter Rosen, a crooked museum director who turned out to be a ruthless international art thief as well.

We also found the famous Rosenberg Nazi art albums, complete with lists of Nazi-looted items and photographs of what Hitler called "degenerate" (aka Jewish) works of art.

Walter Rosen had not only had an affair with Lilly, but tried to carve a swastika on her chest. Oh, and we're pretty sure he's also a murderer.

Complicated? There's more. When dealing with Lilly, there's always more...

Once we recovered the menorah, it became the subject of competing insurance claims, as well as a tug-of-war between Lilly, as the inherited owner, and Lev, as the owner of the Zimmerman collection.

Now Walter Rosen sits in Federal prison awaiting trial for international stolen art trafficking, Lev Zimmerman sleeps with Lilly, and the menorah sits on Lilly's mantel. I'm at home with Sam in the gorgeous little city of Alameda, across the bay from San Francisco, where I've been sitting out the pandemic.

Lilly did get Covid during that charnel-house March in New York City, but it resulted in high-octane antibodies and she's been giving plasma ever since. She gets to play the I-got-Covid-card at her convenience.

One of Lilly's newest obsessions is an ancestor search. The discovery of the menorah opened up a can of worms regarding our mother. With time on her hands now, Lilly has been going through all the old boxes our mother kept, and we're making a scrapbook with photos and letters from the past eighty years.

Lilly's also taken up with a vengeance the search for our family background. I refused to spit in a vial, but Lilly did a DNA test and now she frequents websites that dig up living and dead relatives to the great disruption of other peoples' lives. She loves it.

She says she's "discovered" the thread of our Sephardic ancestors, a line that ran oddly through Poland. Being Sephardic is the cool-of-the-moment among Jews. Our names are a dead giveaway: our mother was named Aurora, my sister is Lilliana, my grandmother was Leokadia. Not exactly Zara (as usual, I'm the exception) Chana or Rivka. Now, Lilly is hell-bent on unearthing third cousins.

Not satisfied with our family, Lilly's current bone to worry has been Lev's family history. Like ours, it's a mélange of observant and apostate, with deep disruptions thanks to World War II, and has the added fillip of a strong Catholic branch. French and Alsatian elements make for a spicy stew and Lilly has found all manner of indiscretions and by-blows in his family tree. Lev himself has quite the checkered past, even without delving into his forbearers.

Our dull Hungarian Jewish father's line is of no interest to her. Which is too bad, since that's where all the money came from. And as I'm learning, more than a little scandal.

## Family Scrapbook Photo # 1: 1960

*There are only a few photos of me, the second daughter. I will be followed after the requisite number of months by Joey, the little brother we never speak of, but in this picture, I'm only three months old. My father, Daniel Persil, stands very tall, a thin man with black hair and full lips, close to his wife, Aurora, who's seated on a chair next to him. Aurora's got big, deep eyes that look hard at the camera, and she's wearing a dark dress with a Peter-Pan collar. She holds the hand of a toddler in a dress with pine-tree appliqués, and though I know the child is not even sixteen months old she's already as tall as a three-year-old, and has a head full of black curls. That child is Lilly.*

*The man is in shirtsleeves with a skinny tie, and he's holding me, an infant wrapped in a long white blanket. Although the photo is in black and white I remember that the blanket has a border of embroidered pink roses. I fit on his forearm, and my little bald head peeks out near his elbow.*

*Like his wife, the man also looks intensely at the camera. His eyes squint slightly, although I know that he's not nearsighted, almost daring the photographer — or the viewer — to comment. No one in the picture is smiling.*

---

Once the sun is up and I'm fully caffeinated I focus on what Lilly is trying to tell me. Lev's arrest is no real surprise. He was the owner of the menorah. When it was stolen from the Museum he made an insurance claim. The insurance company paid. The menorah was found. The money wasn't repaid. Simple.

Walter Rosen's situation is far more complicated. A Federal grand jury returned an indictment for international art theft against Walter Rosen, and Lilly and I testified.

It was surreal, testifying via Zoom. Of course, we were living on our computers at the time so everything was surreal. Three Zoom Shivas, Zoom Passover Seder, Zoom romances — not mine, Zoom book club. So why not testify before a Federal grand jury, all of us little boxes on a screen.

Rosen was indicted. That means "charged", not "convicted." But of course, in these crazy times, Rosen still hasn't been tried.

Somehow, Lilly is caught up both as a victim and as a collaborator. That word hangs heavy over her, with its historical grotesqueness. Jews are very sensitive about that word. Maybe it would be easier if the grand jury had used the term *conspirator*. Or not.

So why Lilly?

At least, so far, there's no specific indictment against her. Lev's arrest is a big clue. Lev's more-or-less immediate release is another. They've got bigger fish to fry, and that fish shouldn't be Lilly.

Another man might have skated on this, but Lev's past seems to have caught up with him and made him more vulnerable to prosecution. Lilly has no such past. Lev may or may not be technically guilty, but unfortunately Lilly's *affaire* with him puts her at risk as an accessory after the fact. Even though she *is* one of Walter Rosen's victims in his grotesque web of crimes.

Whether that's enough to keep her safe remains to be seen.

———— ·‖≡◆○◗○◖�<‖═·‖ ·‖ ·————

Sam's up, and I can hear his low voice rumbling on the phone. He's turned the back bedroom into his office, and while some of the time he's back at his "real" office these days, he still teaches on line, and has found the lack of commute fairly appealing. I adore the guy but two years of having him home all the time has really worn thin.

My own office is a converted pantry, and behind me on Zoom calls, when I don't put up a fake background, cans of tomato puree live next to my investigation manuals. My work has been, to say the least, sporadic. Harassment claims have decreased substantially since workers have been relegated to their homes. Only now are we discovering other ways of hurting one another remotely.

I wait until I hear Sam go off his call before I join him.

"Lilly's being investigated," I say with no preamble.

Sam nods. "Accomplice of an accomplice?"

"But that's impossible," I say. "She was the victim. And we had no part in the theft itself, nor in the insurance scam..." I pause and Sam looks at me expectantly. "Oh. Because she kept the menorah? No, that can't be it. We had nothing to do with the insurance claim, and it was ours to start with, or Mom's.

"Unless when they asked her about it during the grand jury investigation she didn't tell the truth," Sam says.

"That would be perjury, not insurance fraud. And why would she do that? If she did."

Sam shrugs. "I don't know. You know your sister. There's always more to the story. So they arrested Lev and released him in the same two hour span that they threatened to — what? Arrest Lilly? She probably got it wrong. Won't be the first time."

True. Lilly does tend to overdramatize things. I text Lilly. *Who said they were considering arresting you? And for what?*

I see that the text is marked *read* but I don't get an answer. "Maybe she doesn't want to put anything in writing," I say, and rub Sam's head.

"Rule one, right? As if Lilly would ever hold back." He smiles. "Let's have lentil soup for lunch."

---

An hour later my phone chimes again. "Hi," Lilly says, all sunshine and bluebirds.

"So, recovered from this morning?" I ask.

"Oh yeah, it turns out that they're going to drop the charges against Lev."

"That was fast!"

"Well, it isn't official but his lawyer says that there's a high likelihood of a dismissal. Not sure why they went ahead and arrested him this morning. That was fucking traumatic."

Coffee with the agents notwithstanding. "I don't get it. That's not how things usually work."

"Maybe they don't have all the evidence they thought they had," Lilly says. I hear her smiling. My hands get clammy. I wait. "Maybe something is missing from their investigation file. Something critical."

"Lilly…" I've heard that smug voice before, and it never bodes well.

"Oh don't worry, I didn't destroy any evidence. I only took it to make a copy of it for my files."

"Are you kidding?" My heart is pounding. I take meds for that, it isn't supposed to happen unless I'm in real distress. I feel my throat narrowing. "Lilly, did you take something from the investigator's file?"

"Just a page. And not from their file. I borrowed it, and planned to give it back. But then the Pause prevented me. It's not my fault."

I get quiet.

"Don't judge, Zara. You always judge. You're so holy, aren't you?"

I close my eyes, I don't want an onslaught. "What page?" I whisper. I repeat myself. "What page?"

"Who cares!"

"Lilly, tell me what page you took." It's an order, in my court voice.

"The one, you know, the handwritten one from the Nazi looting records, the one that proved that the menorah was ours. I took it because I don't trust the FBI, I don't trust the government, and I sure as hell didn't trust them then. Remember? Or have you already forgotten?"

I remember. How could I not? I shouldn't be stunned but I am. "Do you still have it?" I croak.

"Somewhere, I'm sure."

At least now we have some idea what they'd be indicting her for.

"Did anyone mention this to you? I mean, who said you were even under investigation? When did this come up?" I'm babbling, and Lilly knows it.

"Relax. I only called you because I panicked this morning. I'm fine. Nothing's going to happen."

# Chapter Two

# The Grand Jury

"It's a detail, Lilly," I explain over FaceTime that evening. Lilly has a glass of wine in hand, clearly not her first of the evening, and it's not the first time I've explained it. "You knew that Lev had claimed the loss of the menorah on his insurance, and that he spent the money, and we both knew that the menorah had been recovered, and didn't tell the insurance company. None of that is criminal. Well, not our crime, anyway. It's the fact that you have the menorah, and when you were asked about it by the grand jury you said you didn't. That's the detail."

"And you told them we had it. That's the real detail," Lilly snaps. "You were the good little girl scout, *yes, sir, we are now in possession of the artifact, yes, my sister Lilliana has it in her hot little hands.*"

So no, I didn't lie to a grand jury. Lilly did. And they knew it because I told the truth. Since neither of us was allowed to attend the testimony of the other, and I didn't think to ask, I hadn't known that Lilly had lied. Or misspoken. Though it's hard to misspeak when the question, "Have you recovered any of the stolen artifacts?" is answered, "Yes." Or, of course, "No."

Lilly's relationship with the truth has always been a little strained. "And the reason you lied is..."

"It wasn't a lie! I didn't *recover any artifacts*, like that pompous pigeon lawyer asked. I got back our fucking menorah, and it was ours to start with, and Mother's, and not theirs, and besides," she takes another sip of wine, "they have no record of it."

"Right," I say, "because you stole a page from the precious, internationally valued and cherished record book that we got from Walter Rosen."

The record books are albums containing lists of items stolen by the Nazis, kept in their satanically meticulous way. The one in question showed the menorah as being taken from an unnamed *Juden* at a Warsaw address, in the building where our mother had lived. The record books are far, far more valuable than the little gold and blue menorah, whose sentimental worth I'm sure vastly exceeds any monetary value. But Lilly had torn a page out of the record book, and lied to the grand jury about the menorah. I feel sick.

"I took it, yeah, so what? I did what I had to do. That's what Mother would have done. Survival is everything, Zara. Your holier-than-shit attitude would have gotten you killed, you know. Little Miss Priss on her way to the gas chamber. Or not. Maybe you would have loved the rules so much you would have been the Nazis' little helper! Little Judas-Rat!"

I slam the phone on the table. Then I turn it over and click *end*. Lilly hasn't been the same since the assault, and when she drinks she's worse. I take a few deep breaths but they don't calm me. Nor does understanding. Everything seems to shimmer and glow, and I see black in the corners of my eyes.

I clench my fists, willing myself not to black out. It's coming. The visions I thought had abated, the ones where my mother is speaking in my head and I'm seeing her before me as a young woman, have started again.

---

# *Family Scrapbook: Aurora — Visions in black 1945*

*The screaming stops and I walk away. The screaming never stops and I walk away. In my dreams, it will never stop.*

*I arrived in New York clutching the telegram.*

My dearest Aurora. You are alive. I can't believe it. Please, please come. We will come for you next week. Your loving uncle Harry.

*I wait for him in the hot, smelly room I have above the Salvation Army headquarters. They've given me the room as part of my "pay" for translating: German, Polish, Russian, as the desperate immigrants arrive by the boat-load.*

*"Why are you living above a Christian service?" he asks, after a teary embrace.*

*I tell him I work for them, all I could find in the first week I'd been here. "They're good to me."*

*"You're so thin," he says, smiling. "You were a dumpling as a child." I shudder. That word is no longer pleasant to me. "Of course, we are all thin now. But you're alive, thank the good lord, blessed be he," he says in Yiddish.*

*I answer him in Polish. I don't speak Yiddish anymore. "I didn't eat for six years." While he sat comfortably in Philadelphia, USA. And didn't send for us.*

*Tears run down his face. "Were you in a camp?" he asks, whispering the word in German for prison camp, Gefangenenlager.*

*I shake my head, no, "I was in a town. I worked."*

*He looks at me. "You worked?"*

*I look away. When I look up again he's gone, and I never see him again.*

---

The *Judenrat* was the council of Jews charged with carrying out Nazi orders in the Jewish communities. Only those who were at once obedient, trustworthy, and terrified were part of that council, and they were reviled by both sides. Lilly is implying I would have been part of it. Hell, she's not implying it, she's saying it outright. And my rule-following, orderly mind will not dismiss it out of hand. Our biggest fears are those closest to the heart.

Aurora was accused by her own uncle of collaborating. He who sat safely in Philadelphia while a fifteen-year-old girl was raped and enslaved, called her a Judenrat. Because she did what she had to do to live.

And I am a rule-follower. I know that. And Lilly is a rule-breaker. Is one better, more moral than the other?

Sam finds me staring at the wall. "Don't talk to her. She's out of control."

I lean against his hand, working to bring his face into focus. Only his hair is grayer now, otherwise the pandemic hasn't taken much of a toll on his looks. Even his body looks great. He spent hours watching videos of weight-lifting, all while curling and pumping in the middle of the living room. When he could, he jogged three miles a day, and if it rained he rode the old exercise bike we had in the storage room for years. I, on the other hand…

"She called me a *juden-rat*."

"Like I said, she's out of control. Did you learn anything more about the big excitement this morning?"

"Besides Lev getting arrested? And released almost simultaneously? And someone telling Lilly she was next? I guess that's the lot of it. Oh, except for one block-busting revelation: she tore a page out of the

Nazi record book, the one with our menorah listed on it. She stole evidence from the FBI, and destroyed a world-important artifact, and lied to the grand jury. That's all."

Sam shakes his head. "Unbelievable. I mean, we knew about the lie, but really? She tore a page out? When?"

"Remember when we took the photo albums and records to the FBI and met Agent Skordall?" Sam smiles, because yes, she was gorgeous. Like an iceberg is gorgeous. "And we brought the one with the menorah to Lilly's? Then. I had no idea. What's amazing is that she didn't tell me for eighteen months. Incredible self-control for someone who blurts the first thing she thinks of."

"Impressive discretion."

"Is that all you can say? Is that all? She insults me a level that's so beyond offensive, she destroys an historical treasure, she puts herself and in a way me at risk for arrest and prosecution, and all you can say is *impressive discretion?*" I admit I'm howling.

Sam steps away from me. "Now you're out of control. And you haven't even been drinking."

He shuts the door to my pantry softly. *He's* not out of control. Oh no. Not him.

———— ·꞉꞊◆●◗◖●◗꞊꞉· ————

Angie and Meghan FaceTime me. Meghan would have started kindergarten this past August, if there had been one to start. Schools reopened, recessed, opened halfway, closed halfway, and ran online. But kindergarten in front of a computer is not kindergarten, so Angie's been pod-schooling her. That's the current term for gathering a few children from close-by households and taking turns teaching them. The pod meets in the North Beach neighborhood of San Francisco, where Angie lives, right in Washington Square park.

Most days, since we've had disastrously little rain in the past year, they meet outside. On the rare rainy day they meet in the basement of Saints Peter and Paul Cathedral, where in prior years Meghan went to Bosco Pre-school, named for the saint, not the syrup.

And once a week Angie takes her to the San Francisco Jewish Community Center, for a children's club. I was stunned, but Angie was serious. "After everything that happened in New York last year, I decided Meghan needs a bit of Jewish education. Since I had none."

Something else to feel guilty about.

But now Meghan wants to show me something. "Look, Grannie! A lettersaurus!" She holds up a piece of colored paper, and looking at it sideways I see MEGHAN spelled out in something that looks like brontosaurus letters.

"A lettersaurus!" I say. "And the lettersaurus says *Meghan!*"

"Yup!" she says. She gets the *yup* from her dad, Derek, whom I've never heard say *yes*.

"I've got news," Angie says as Meghan squiggles away from the phone. I steel myself. Derek used to never be home, but in the past year he was there, a lot. I hope she isn't pregnant, but I try to just look interested. "You look like you just bit into an unripe persimmon, Mom."

I adjust my face. "Sorry. I had something in my tooth," I lie.

Angie rolls her eyes, another new mannerism since the pandemic. "Derek is going to be home only one week a month now, instead of all the time, and my office is opening back up. So I'm going back to work two weeks a month. On site. Out. Of. The. House!"

"Hooray!" I say, and I'm happy for her. She's just managed not to go nuts, home all the time with Meghan and Derek. Before the plague, Derek was home perhaps three or four days a month, leaving Angie with sole care of their daughter, but also with complete autonomy. Just before everything stopped, Angie had started working for a software company south of San Francisco, two days a week, while Meghan attended the Bosco.

When the plague hit, Derek no longer flew to Australia and Saudi Arabia and wherever the hell else he went, and Angie's work just stopped. While she was out of work, she developed a program that moved unwanted furniture to homeless housing, and the press had run with the concept. Her internet fame didn't translate into a fortune, at least not yet, but as soon as the company she'd been hired by before the Lockdown got going again, she was able to command a significantly higher salary.

"All that in the way of saying that now that I'm going back, in person, I'll be returning as a superstar, not a re-entry mom."

"You always were a superstar, Angie. The rest of the world is only just finding out what I already knew. Congratulations, sweetie. So Derek with be home with Meghan, and do the pod-school one of the weeks?"

Angie glances sideways, and I realize that Derek is home. "Not exactly, Mom. That was one of the reasons I was calling. I was hoping that, well, that you would like to do it. You know, spend a lot more time with Meghan, meet other moms....'

"I'm a grandma, not a mom," I interrupt.

"Jeez, Mom. I thought you missed Meghan."

I close my eyes for a moment. "Let me think about it, okay? I've got a lot to deal with right now, but let me just give it some thought. When do you start?"

Another eye-roll. "Monday. In three days. Shabbat shalom, Mom. Call me tomorrow, okay?"

• ❙❙ ❧⊙❂⊙❧ ❙❙ •

Our beautiful Victorian, on the island of Alameda, is small, but it was completely sufficient for the two of us back when Sam traveled, taught, and had an office — *elsewhere*. I too had an office, across the

Bay in San Francisco, with a view of the underside of the Bay Bridge.

Much like Angie with Derek, I relished my alone-time, and my time with Sam was special.

Once we were confined to the house, the little space was completely filled by Sam. His presence daily, all day, every day, turned our sanctuary into a suffocating box. The tiny yard and the raised vegetable garden provided some escape but even then, when I ordered seeds online because the nurseries were closed, I ended up with weird tomato types and an overabundance of sage. One can only use so much sage.

Now that most of the Covid nightmare seems to have passed, a nightmare where I was awake but couldn't move, life is looking a whole lot more like "before." Just as Lilly was the one to get the virus, now she's the one wreaking havoc out in the world. She's at the forefront of every movement.

And so, after eighteen months of stasis, I'm looking at airline schedules. If Lilly's also been stealing evidence, maybe I need to go to New York.

## Chapter Three

# Our Father

Lilly texts early the next morning. *Sorry about the early call yesterday. All good. Lev is okay and I think they'll overlook my mistake about the menorah.*

I pick up the phone. "Don't text, okay? Don't put anything else in writing."

"You're paranoid, Zara," Lilly says. I take a breath. I really don't want another fight. But yesterday she called me a *judas-rat* and today I'm *paranoid*. "So, more silent treatment?" she says, before I've gotten ahold of myself enough to answer.

"If that's what you want," I say, and hang up.

*Don't hang up on me, you little bitch.*

I ignore the text, put the phone on vibrate, and go make myself a cup of coffee. I can hear the phone buzzing repeatedly on the counter, but I don't look at it. I know what it says. *Answer the phone.* Plus expletives. How did we end up like this?

When FedEx arrives the following day, there's a fat, padded, insured envelope for me from Lilly. I know that she's started going through the last of the boxes from Mom's house, boxes that had been sitting in her attic for four years, with all the down-time she had. But she'd been scanning and emailing whenever she came across something interesting, for the past year, and I didn't expect her to mail me anything. I tear it open.

"For crying out loud," I mutter. There's the page from the ledger. The purloined paper, the docked document.

And there are several other envelopes inside the main one. I open them gingerly. Inside are ancient, yellowing papers. My hands shake as I lift them one by one: a letter from our grandfather, my mother's father, to his brother, in Yiddish; a typewritten notice in Polish, with my sister's looping writing translating the notice paperclipped to it — it's from the Prisoners of War Family Search Committee; Mom's original passport; Mom's Naturalization Certificate; and our parents' original marriage license. And the telegram she'd told me about, from "Uncle Harry", which had appeared in my vision yesterday.

At least she insured the package.

I look at the translation of the letter that Lilly's provided, and her note: "*He had kidney disease. He wrote to his brother in America.*"

*My dearest brother. I am so sorry I haven't written to you in so long. The situation here is very dangerous. I'm worried about our brother Izhak, he's not able to find work anymore. They don't let us have our shops, and he is worse off than even before. And I, well I am still able to live, my factory is so important to them that I am still able to run it. Textiles will always be needed, by every army and every despot, no matter what country he's from. So I think we will be safe for now.*

*Chana is not helpful. She spends as if Izhak is still working, though where she spends is a mystery. Her family has meat, and she must be going to the black market to get it. She's never known how to be frugal and I worry for our brother and his children. This is a good time for me and my vegetarian ways.*

*My Leokadia is such a good homemaker. She never complains, and is so inventive with the dinners that she cooks herself, now that we have only one maid. She was so delicately raised, but she never shirks. Those funny dishes her people make are so savory now to me. She finds greens in the parks near our home, sorrel and dill, and uses honey that she can still get from the farmers when they come in to sell their produce.*

*I have two children, you know. We are hoping to send my boy to England to study. Bless him, I am so proud of him. He is not excellent at school, but he is very strong and athletic, even if he is shorter than he'd like. I am sending him away so he can make something of his life. My daughter Aurora is so tall she's bigger than my son, and a little round and plump. As long as we get butter and can make bread, our Aurora is happy! She can't keep her nose out of a book. And she's the prettiest girl in her class, and the top student, too.*

*So, my dear brother, it seems I must save the bad news for the end. My kidneys have failed, and I am thirsty all of the time. I had hoped to get to Switzerland for treatment, but that is looking less and less likely. Even with the restrictions and privations, there are still ways out, but not for an old man. If I can, I hope to gather enough for Aurora to come to you. Will you receive her? I know you will.*

*Write soon. Write in the old language, not in Polish. We have very little time left.*

*Your loving brother, Avram*

And Lilly's end note: "*He never got an answer.*"

The room wavers a bit but I assure myself this is not a hallucination. It's just a vision of my mother, of Aurora, on the screen of my mind. The visions aren't as strong as they used to be, when I couldn't tell reality from the horrors in my head. Now they just shimmer, and my mother's voice is so very clear.

## Scrapbook — Aurora: Honor your father: 1939-1942

*He never got an answer. And soon we were under far more duress than before. I was no longer in school, my brother was conscripted, we were gathered into small apartments, our treasures gone, and the factory completely taken over by the Nazis. And then, father was taken away. I was working in the factory by then, and my beautiful, delicate mother was forced to sew buttons on garments like a common seamstress. Her hands were swollen with arthritis, she was so thin from eating only herb soups. She was not at home with me when they came for him. When she returned, he was gone, and the neighbors told her before I could. He had collapsed, and when word got out, somehow, two German soldiers came and took him out. They carried him by his shoulders and feet, down the stairs, and he was barely conscious. He moaned, and called for Leokadia once, but the soldier said something and he was silent.*

*I was there when he was taken away and I play the scene in my head, over and over, until I no longer remember it. I never saw him again. I wasn't with him when he died. My mother wasn't with him when he died. I had fantasies that he was still alive, that he had somehow survived, not just the war but his illness. It was ludicrous, of course, but I was a child, still, in some ways. In some very few ways, and only for a very short time afterwards.*

The other documents are lying on the floor, and I pick them up one by one, in my ice-cold hands. I look at the least terrifying one: my parents' marriage license, issued in Philadelphia, Pennsylvania, in 1953. Its grotesque time-bound questions of race ("Color") aside, it's an artifact of history.

*Name*, my mother used her real name. I suppose she had to, but I know that when she left New York City for Philadelphia she'd abandoned her father's last name and taken on her mother's Sephardic surname. So much less identifiable as Jewish in America, the name had a vaguely Spanish sound despite its very Polish spelling. Coupled with her unusual first name, she sounded exotic and mysterious, not like one of the many refugee Jews who'd arrived, penniless and terrified, on America's shores in the past three years.

Our father had his own unusual name, as Hungarian Jews were less common than Germans, Russians or Poles, and *Persil* could be anything. He listed his occupation as "student" and she as "secretary." Though she was in fact the editor of a small magazine, that wasn't an acceptable occupation, especially for a foreigner, and certainly not for someone with no formal education beyond the equivalent of tenth grade, so *secretary* it was.

I turn the paper over. My reading stops on a new line: Our father had a "prior marriage" that ended in divorce? What the hell was that?

He was just twenty four at the time of the wedding, and had been in the army from ages eighteen to twenty, so when had he had time to get married? And divorced? And to whom? And the reason listed for divorce? *Physical indignities*. What the hell is that supposed to mean?

Suddenly Lilly's throwaway comment comes back to me. "We might have siblings." Or was it *cousins?* I can't remember. But more importantly, was she serious?

I reach for my phone to call Lilly, but stop. We're still fighting, and surely she saw this when she sent me the packet. After all, she translated the postcard.

My ally, my friend and confidante, my almost-twin. This has to stop.

Meanwhile, there are court records to dig up. And the purloined page to be dealt with.

———— ·‖═❖⬦◗❖═‖· ————

The Commonwealth of Pennsylvania keeps its records in ways that don't make it easy to find someone else's old divorce record, and I don't have the time to go down that rabbit hole today. Instead, I invite Angie and Meghan for dinner. Derek is traveling this week, although I can't imagine where since few countries are willing to have Americans, even now. Retribution, I guess, for all the prior nonsense that we did to them.

I pick the last of the tomatoes from my weird vines, and it's September so I still have jalapeños and basil. Angie isn't much of a meat-eater, and therefore at five years of age neither is Meghan, so a Caprese salad and chicken tostadas will make up our international fare tonight. Having grown up on the Texas-Mexico border, sometimes on one side, sometimes on the other, I love real Mexican food, and Tex-Mex, and Italian food too. Oddly enough, there were plenty of Germans in San Antonio, and a good wiener schnitzel is not to be sneezed at. Can we say *sneezed at* again? Or is it too soon? I start to re-think the menu, but realize that the line for the grocery store will be too long at this hour to get veal cutlets, and there's no way Meghan will eat "baby cow", so tostadas remain on the menu.

I steel myself for the issue of being Meghan's pod-teacher one week per month. I am ashamed to admit that I absolutely don't want to do that. I love her, I adore her, but I brought Angie up, and have no desire to bring anyone else up, and definitely I don't want to be the Grannie-teacher to a pod of precocious kindergarteners.

———— ·‖═❖⬦◗❖═‖· ————

The secret to good tostadas is the frying of the tortillas. I use the little ones that are for street tacos, and dip them in hot oil, quickly turning them on each side, until just golden. Once they're fried, I let them drain while I make some salsa with the tomatoes, the jalapeños, a little chopped onion, and some cilantro. I'll put it all together ten minutes before sitting down, when I'll put the fried tortillas on the cast-iron skillet to reheat, crisp up, and serve them *à la minute.*

I realize I'm obsessing on food to distract myself, much as I did on Election Night and beyond, during the counting and recounting that led to Biden's, and our gal Kamala's, victory over — I still can't say his name. Forty-five. That was the closest I've come to loving Lilly like I did before we fell apart.

Lilly is a true believer in the American Way, in all caps, and she works extraordinarily hard for the candidates she believes in. And that was a long, long four days while they counted the votes. I was so worried that I spent the entire time in the kitchen. I baked bread, made flautas — those delicious rolled up, fried tacos filled with chicken, spices, and peppers — I made chocolate meringue pie, chicken paprikàs, and even Cutlets Pojarski, a Polish take on the afore-mentioned wiener schnitzel. Only with sauce. I must have gained ten pounds in those four days.

Tonight I'm distracting myself from my worries about Angie. Or actually, my worries about me and Angie. Not only are my relations with Lilly strained, but now I'm hardly communicating with my own daughter.

I cook to avoid the obvious conclusion: the common denominator in this ugly stew is me.

<hr />

I take the deep dive into searching Pennsylvania divorce records the next day, after what proved to be a semi-disastrous dinner with Angie and Meghan. Sam saved the dinner by tabling the discussion, but not before I felt completely blindsided and betrayed by his lack of support. Notably, no one was asking *him* to be the new pod-kin-dergarten-teacher.

To get divorce records in Philadelphia, Pennsylvania, one must contact the Orphans Court clerk's office of Judicial Records, and request a Request Form. I busy myself with that process, not unmindful of the comparison between my internet search from the comfort of my pantry-office, with shelves lined with canned tomatoes and Sam's preferred chili brand, in a well-heated room with a view of the Oakland estuary, looking for evidence of my father's surprise prior marriage and subsequent divorce, and my mother's frantic search.

She wanted her father to be alive. I want my father to be single.

During the Covid restrictions, it appeared that Philadelphia had allowed itself to be dragged, kicking and screaming, into the twenty-first century, and one could, in fact, make the request — not for the records themselves but for the form for the request for the records — on line. I quickly fill out the form, copying the Orphans' Court case number — further irony of "Orphans' Court" not lost on me — into the system. The results of my request — if obtainable — would be mailed to me.

I reach for my phone to text Lilly with the ironic and yet annoying process, and remember that we're fighting.

I'm considering baking a Texas chocolate cake when my text goes off. It's Lilly herself, she must have felt my vibe, with a happy-happy text telling me she's been subpoenaed again. Auto-correct has changed it to *seasoned* but I know what it is. She doesn't fix it.

This is her second go-around with the grand jury, and we all know why. But her text is nonchalant: *Hi Zarita the dumb court seasoned me again. Looks like more fun and games, hopefully with that hot attorney general, instead of that pouter-pigeon from the FBI. Making hair appointment now. Manipedi too just in case I get lucky.*

I hesitate between sending a thumbs-up emoji and letting the text lie unacknowledged. I also have an intense desire to text her back and tell her to talk to Alan, the lawyer we have for the claim on the menorah, and get some advice before the date of her testimony. And when I realize I don't even know what that date is, I make my decision.

*Hey. What's the date? And can you talk to Alan about this? I think there's some real risk.*

*What risk? I didn't do anything wrong.*

Oh, but you did. A couple of things wrong. *Just please talk to him. We don't want to lose the claim to the menorah. And Lilly, I think you shouldn't text.*

*Then call me. I called you six times yesterday and you didn't pick up. If you don't want me to text then answer your phone.*

I can't. Not just yet. I know that any conversation will devolve into a shouting match.

*Can't right now. Later. TTY.*

*I found another letter. I'll translate it from Polish and send it to you.*

*From?* I can't resist.

*Mother's best friend from before. But the letter is after the war.*

For the longest time, my entire life, I had my mother divided into *before* and *after*. Since she wouldn't talk about her war years, we knew of her childhood, and we knew about her life from the first date with our dad onwards. But if the war was a blank we were beginning to fill in, the time between the end of the war and when she met our father, a stretch of four long years, was a black hole.

*Look forward to getting it.*

I think of my argument with Angie. Does she know all of my secrets? I sure as hell hope not. So why am I so intent on learning my parents' secrets? Let the sleeping dogs lie. Everyone else seems to.

*September 22.*

*???*

*My subpoena date. They have to wait til after Yom Kippur. Everything's shut down here.* No autocorrect this time.

*Talk to Alan.* I go back to my computer, and flip the search bar to JetBlue, still marked as a favorite.

I wake up to the sound of the goddamn phone text. Of course, of course it's Lilly. *We made the papers!* her text squeals. I squint the sleep from my eyes. It's actually late enough that I can't even carp about the time. Sam's side of the bed is empty, and cool to the touch. I've slept in.

As the meaning of her text sinks in I feel my throat tighten. I hate publicity of any sort, always thinking, thanks to Emily Dickinson, "How public, like a frog." So I type that into the phone, hit *send* and go take a shower.

When I emerge, there are seven texts waiting. One of them is in French. All are from Lilly. I make coffee and settle in. In essence, her county paper did a small story on recovered art, currently a hot topic, and picked up on our escapade of two years ago. Although the article focuses on the big, important pieces looted by the Third Reich, Lilly has provided a bit of local human interest. "Even the smallest of pieces carry deep sentimental value, and are the living proof of the era's deep and abiding scars," she's quoted as saying. Not bad.

The story came out this morning, and there's a small picture of Lilly holding the menorah. *We're famous!* she raves. *You're convicted,* I think. Two of the texts are screen shots of congratulatory texts she got from a couple of Jewish sites devoted to major art recovery. One, in French, is from Lev's father's step-sister-in-law if I'm translating right, basically saying she thinks Lev's father had one just like it. Awkward. We're going to have to face the music on that one. And one is an audio-copy link to a voicemail she seems to have gotten earlier today as well: *Good morning, Lilly. My name is [garbled — sounds like ragweed alar] I [garbled — sounds like screw your] father and... [garbled] and I know the story of the menorah. I'd love to meet you. You can text back to this number.* She doesn't repeat her name, the voice sounds younger than we are, but not a youth.

*Who's the phone message from?* I text. *Screw your father?*

*IDK* she answers. *And it's knew your, not screw your father you loony! Cool though, huh?*

I weigh the issue of the picture. But I know better than to text.

She picks up on the first ring. "I knew that would get you! Pretty cool, huh?"

"We need to talk, Lilly. Yeah, it's cool. But look at the situation we're in: you lied to the grand jury about having the menorah when everyone, I mean *every one*, knew you had it. I still can't figure out why you did that. Now there's a freaking picture of you in the freaking paper..." I feel myself going off the rails. "Hold on." I take another sip of coffee, and a few deep, calming breaths from tae kwon do. "You're going to have to see Alan, get his help to, um, clarify your testimony."

She laughs. "Way ahead of you, you Miss Legal Beagle. I already called him. He says it's no problem, people correct the transcripts of depositions all the time so there's no reason he can't call the lawyer who was asking me questions and just tell him I misunderstood. I could say it was because he was so gorgeous I lost my head!"

Last week he was a pompous pigeon. No, that was the FBI guy. I don't know why this irritates me more, but it does. "When did you call Alan?"

"Oh, after the article came out this morning."

After I told her to do it two days ago. No sense in mentioning that. "And Lev needs to talk to his aunt."

"I think Lev has bigger fish to fry right now than dealing with the old lady."

That's crass, but probably true. "Does Lev know about the article?"

"Lev, do you know about the article?" Lilly says. "Yeah, read it," I hear him answer in the background. So he's there with her. "He knows," she adds unnecessarily. "Here, let me put you on speaker."

"Hey, Lev," I say.

"Hi, Zara. Hey Lilly, can you put this on FaceTime?"

In addition to his other traits, Lev is deeply Hard of Hearing. He wears a cobalt-blue hearing aid to match his brilliant eyes, but that only goes so far. Speaker-phone calls are a nightmare for him, but he's an accomplished lip-reader.

The call switches over and he smiles his knock-out smile. "So you heard about my little adventure day before yesterday, huh? Damned FBI came and arrested me. I was so pissed. But luckily my lawyer got me out right away."

"What was the charge?"

"Conspiracy to commit international art theft. Of my own stuff! My lawyer says they'll drop the charges if I agree to testify about the scam truthfully. I mean, we're all supposed to be truthful anyway, right? But since I've got a record, it's a little...particular. Or something. Oh, I know. I'd be immune. Anyway, that's what Simon says." Lilly giggles. "She laughs every time I say that, but that's what's so cute about her. Simon says that's why they arrested me. To give me something to think about in considering whether to take the fifth on the theft scam or tell them all about it."

"So nice to be needed," I say. "And Lilly? What about her?"

"Beats me. She didn't do anything wrong. In fact, she's the biggest victim around. Bigger than I am, that's for sure!" They both laugh. Lev, though spectacularly handsome, with black hair with a streak of gray, and wicked blue eyes, barely clears five feet seven. Lilly towers over him. Of course, Lilly towers over almost everyone, and most of it is legs.

I don't mention the page she took from the Nazi album. Right now, I think that no one except Lilly and Sam and I know about that. It's the closest thing to proof we've got that the menorah belongs to us, that and my ring with the same unique pattern in turquoise enamel on it. There's no requirement that we turn over the page, and it may be useful, I admit. But the fact that she tore it out of an internationally coveted and significant historical artifact, a ledger of stolen art kept by the Nazis contemporaneously with their looting of Jewish homes, amounts to destroying a piece of the past. But is that a crime?

"You with us, Zara?" Lilly asks.

I bring myself back to the present. "Who was that lady who called?"

"No idea, like I said. Some friend of Dad's, probably some doctor or something. There's a part I can't really hear, but sounds like she's saying her name, it comes out like Ovaltine Waters. I couldn't make it out, it was like she was gargling when she said it. Anyway, she wants me to text her back, but what kind of person leaves a message and doesn't give her name at the beginning or the end? I'll call her sometime. Or I won't, and she'll call me."

I nod. That's what I would do.

"So Zara, would you consider coming out? I think, especially for my subpoena date, I'd like to have you here."

There's tenderness in her voice. It catches me off guard. "I haven't traveled in eighteen months. I haven't seen my friends in that long. I haven't had an in-person interview in an investigation. I'm not sure I'm ready to get on an airplane full of people I don't know, and I don't know where they've been or who they are."

"You're vaccinated."

"But there's the variant. I'm waiting for a booster shot."

"Sam travels. Angie's Derek travels. And you see them. It's like an STD. You're sleeping with everyone your lover's slept with. So come on. Do some sleeping around yourself!"

## Chapter Four

# The Law is a Jealous Mistress

I t's been said that the law is a jealous mistress, but that's because she saps all one's time, energy and sex-drive, leaving nothing for family and friends. It makes for good incomes, good television, good novels, and a lousy way of life. Now that, thanks to Lilly, I'm deep into the consumer side of the law, it also seems grotesquely unfair and cumbersome. Sort of what our clients have been saying for a long time. Walking a mile in their shoes is giving me blisters.

Sam and I are eating smoked salmon on bagels, with sour cream, capers and dill. It's Sunday morning, we have the New York Times and the Chronicle spread all over the table. The kitten Sam gave me when we were in New York City, whom we named Eastside, has now grown into a sleek grey cat, and is pacing between my feet, hoping I'm careless with my lox. I pinch off a piece and give it to him.

"Now he's going to expect it every time," Sam mutters, barely looking up.

"You give him spaghetti," I reply, my mouth full.

"Hey, look at this!" Sam says, pointing to the paper. He's got the New York Times city section open, and he reads it to me. "*The trial *of the alleged international art thief with ties to neo-Nazi groups in Europe suffered another delay Friday, when the defendant, Walter Rosen, tested positive for Covid-19. Rosen, 62, began exhibiting symptoms on Wednesday, and a positive test result was shared with the Southern District court on Friday afternoon. The trial, which was expected to begin a week from Monday, was postponed for two additional weeks in order for the defendant to be isolated for fourteen days, or longer if his illness progresses.*

*"The matter involves a complex scheme to remove Jewish artifacts of lesser worth or renown from museums across the nation, and transporting them back to cells of neo-Nazi sympathizers. Unlike the thefts of famous artworks, whose provenance can be proved, the artifacts were typically looted from homes across Eastern Europe during World War II, and sold in black markets post-war to American high-ranking soldiers and French collectors. 'The true ownership of these [artifacts] is much more difficult to trace,' said the current director of the Jewish Culture Museum, the scene of the most recent thefts. The Jewish Culture Museum is currently closed for renovations, taking advantage of the shutdowns that resulted from the Pause, and the inability to open the exhibits to sufficient museum-goers to warrant staffing."*

"Did you know that the trial was supposed to start next week?" Sam asks.

I shake my head. "I know that there were some state waivers of the speedy trial requirements and some stays due to the pandemic, so they didn't have to try him immediately. The Southern District is the Federal trial court in New York, though, and I had no idea that there was even a trial date. So maybe that's what Lilly's subpoenaed for. You'd think, as witnesses, that Lilly and I would know."

"Maybe they aren't going to call you. They don't need you, you know. Just Lilly."

"Except for the tiny little fact that she has the menorah."

"Except for the tiny little fact that she said she doesn't."

"I think one of Lev's lawyers, Simon Cree or Alan Seskin, says that she should, um, correct the record."

Sam smiles. "That's Lilly, always correcting the record."

"I hope he hangs." I realize that I've not told Sam about yesterday's mail. "And to top it all off, along with sending me these amazing letters and postcards that Mom had gotten right after the war, she also sent me the page she tore out. So now I have it. And I don't know what the hell to do with it."

Sam tears out the article for me. Something's fishy, and it's not the salmon.

⟶ •⸻⚜⸻• ⟵

"Did you know it was set for trial starting September 17?" I ask Lilly when she calls.

"No! That explains everything," she says. I wait. "You know that subpoena I got? I thought it was for the grand jury like the last time, but Alan said it wasn't. It was for the trial. And I was supposed to go on September 22, *and day after day until released.* So I bet that was my subpoena to testify at the trial. Thank goodness it's being postponed. Did you get the package?"

There's so much to unpack in that statement that I actually get a notepad. "Hang on, I need to make a list."

"Of what?"

"All the craziness you just laid on me." For once, she stops talking and lets me write. I list everything that the last five minutes have brought up, and then some.

"Okay," I say, "here goes. Listen all the way through. One: the trial was set to start on September 17, two weeks from yesterday, and I didn't know."

"Poor baby, they didn't tell the queen," she says.

"Just hear me out. Two: you were subpoenaed to testify. Three: Lev was arrested — or something — two days ago, and released within a couple of hours, for conspiracy to commit art theft. Simon thinks they'll drop the charges. You're worried they'll charge you. Four: you told the grand jury you didn't have the menorah. I told them we did."

"I told you, I might correct that. I misunderstood the question."

I let that go for now. "Five, or is it six? No, five: you sent me the fucking page from the ledger. I now have possession of it. That should get three or four lines of its own. So next, is what, seventeen? Or —"

"I thought it would be safer with you. You'll figure out how to manage that."

"Gee, thanks."

"I'm doing all the sorting of a million boxes of letters, and translating them, and sending them to you. You can figure out how to finesse one lousy page of the ledger."

"I'm flattered. I really can't fathom why you took it."

Lilly sighs. "Ok, you're right, and I know that. It wasn't the right thing to do, and I shouldn't have done it. And I should have told you I took it, but I didn't because, well, I guess deep down I knew you were going to disapprove, and I can't stand it. You disapprove of everything I do, and since the pandemic, you're so damned touchy."

I'm mollified a bit, but I still need to know. "I appreciate that, and yeah, I know that I'm still on edge, but really, why?"

"If you really need to know, quite frankly," my lie-radar goes off, courtesy of Mom, who believed that anyone who said *quite frankly* was lying, "here's what I thought. The museum's records showed that the menorah was stolen. It showed that it belonged to Lev. Lev made a claim on his insurance and on the museum's insurance, and they paid up. We got the menorah back, and Lev and I didn't want to return the money."

*Lev and I?* "You didn't get any of the money!" Lilly's silent. "Oh for f-, oh for crying out loud, Lilly. Did you guys split the money?" More silence. "Oh god."

I can hear that Lilly's crying now. "And so when you left the ledger with me, Lev and I figured that if we were going to keep the money, we should take the page out, so that there wouldn't ever be a question about the menorah. Which was stupid, I know, because obviously that's how we got involved, and how Rosen got caught. But at the time we were thinking about the money." She pauses to get a drink of water.

"Besides, I was afraid that since Lev's father has Alzheimer's, there would be no one to explain why he even had the menorah in the first place. So if the menorah was a war-looted item, and Lev's father was in possession of it, and the ledger proved it was looted, and that would look really bad, and the shame, even though the real way he got it..." Lilly's sobbing now.

I get it. It actually makes mixed up sense. I wait for her to get through the worst of it, and somehow, I don't feel that angry now. "I get it, Lilly. I really do. We'll fix this. And there's Lev's sister, who can help corroborate the legit way Lev's dad got the menorah."

Lilly gulps more water. "No, yes, I don't know."

"She knows that the menorah was stolen from the museum, now, doesn't she?"

"Yeah, but she doesn't know we got it back. Because if she found out, maybe she wouldn't let us keep it."

"Oh, I'd see that she did," I say.

"That's another problem," she says. "You'd go in with all your legal guns blazing, and attack Lev's family. His sister, who's doing all the heavy lifting when it comes to their father."

Point taken, I guess. "Well, at least the trial is postponed — Rosen's got Covid — and we have time to figure this all out. So, I guess, number eleventy-seven or whatever on my list, is Dad's divorce. I mean, who the hell knew? He was so obviously devoted to Mom that it's just old news, though it does feel weird that he never even mentioned it."

"Yeah, it's like he said about Mom. He didn't want to know anything except from the moment he met her forward," Lilly says.

I hate that he wanted to deny her her entire past, just to shield himself. But apparently he was also denying his own past. "I sent away for the records. I feel weird, though. I mean, do you want all your various sons to know all your secrets?" I ask.

Lilly laughs. "I don't have any secrets. They're all on my Facebook page!"

I smile at the phone. That's my old Lilly. "Did you ever figure out who called you?" I ask.

"Nah. If it's important they'll call back. A friend of Dad's."

"I'm also wondering about that other text you copied to me — from what looks like Lev's aunt, or great aunt or whatever. His father's step-something. She might not have known him in France, but she would have known his story, I'd guess. I think she must have some idea, and could vouch for the fact that it was Lev's father's menorah. Doesn't her letter say that she thought Lev's father had one just like the one you have in the news article?"

"True," Lilly says. "I don't know if that makes it better or worse."

"Neither do I."

After we hang up, I make another cup of coffee and consider the new information. If we approach it simply, I will let the FBI know that we mistakenly took the page out, thinking we needed it for verification, and not understanding that there were major implications to removing it. After all, we had recovered five photo albums and ledgers for them. And Lilly would tell them that she indeed had the menorah, and had misunderstood the question. I'd work with Lev's sister to sort out ownership, now that the ledger sheet could be used. And they'd have to give the insurance company back the money.

The insurance money. I grab my phone. *How much did the insurance company pay on the menorah??*

*Which one?* she answers.

Is she being stupid? *Our menorah of course.*

*No-which insurance company*

Holy mackerel.

*Um, both? Did the museum's insurance and Lev's insurance both pay? LOL yeah. Fifty grand a piece. Pretty sweet, huh?*

As happens to most others when dealing with Lilly, Sam is, for once, nonplussed. I've just told him the whole tale of Lilly's and Lev's insurance caper. I'd expected the insurance payout to be a pittance, something easily returned. But a hundred grand?

"At least I get why she did what she did. I had no idea. Follow the money, as usual. So I guess that means that the menorah was worth fifty grand?"

Sam nods absently. I could see his wheels turning. "How many pieces were stolen in the Museum theft?"

"Quite a few, I think. I remember making the whole list when I was pretending to be the insurance investigator, and there were about fifteen pieces, five of them from Lev's family collection." I pause and meet Sam's eyes. "Yeah. That's what I was thinking too. So there was a pretty big insurance payout. Only three pieces have been found, counting the menorah."

I'm putting away the dishes from the dishwasher when I have another thought. "Hey Sam, remember when Trump got Covid and got better in a week? And we were all saying he probably didn't have it, he was using that as a political ploy to say, *see, it's really no big deal?*"

"I remember, but what are you suggesting? That Rosen doesn't really have Covid? Or that it's being used as a ploy? It isn't like the Feds are on his side, you know."

I need to think about this. Something is off about this whole situation, but I can't put my finger on it.

In a sense we've been waiting two years for the other shoe to drop. The big mistake was thinking we knew who was wearing the other shoe.

Now that the trial, which I didn't even realize was happening, has been put off, I ponder with a bit of leeway what to do about what Lilly and I are calling *the purloined page*. We confer at length with both Simon, who's Lev's lawyer in the insurance case, and Alan Seskin, whom I retained to help us with the civil matter. New Jersey lowlifes are his specialty, he assures us. He went to school with Sam, so he should know.

Sam joins us in our Zoom meeting. I imagine there are folks making love over Zoom, marrying, and with the right technology, maybe even procreating. I spin that out for Sam, and we come up with a process that involves Zoom, the UPS delivery, a willing participant on each end, and a turkey baster.

And then we realize folks have been doing exactly that far longer than the pandemic. Nothing new under the sun.

Alan suggests that we just come clean, explain that Lilly had no idea that taking the page would harm anyone, and if they needed it on loan for evidence, we'd certainly produce it.

"Well, it's actually ours," Lilly asserts. "We got it from Rosen's desk."

Alan raises a thin eyebrow. The screen makes him look washed out. He's blond anyway, or was in his hey-day, and now he's more or less pink. He wears gold-rimmed round glasses that reflect the doughnut light that he's got shining on his face. But behind the owlish look are a pair of very sharp eyes. "We did?" he asks.

"Actually, Zara did," Lilly says, seeing that her first comment wasn't meeting with the approval she'd obviously expected.

If one could tell where people were looking on Zoom, Alan would be looking at me. As it is I can tell that he's got us all up in gallery view, and I'm somewhere on the right side of his screen. I wave.

"As I explained, Lev and I went to the museum, knowing that Rosen was AWOL, and asked his assistant for a list of what was stolen. She was under the impression that I was an insurance inves-tigator — " the eyebrow goes up again — "well, I *am* an investigator, just an employment investigator, but my card says *Investigations*, and that's not a lie."

Lilly smirks, clearly enjoying the sight of me defending my own prevarication. A message appears in the chat, to me only, saying *no one's perfect*. I feel my blood pressure rising. "I asked for a list, and Lev was with me, giving her the Tom Cruise smile, and Sheila, the little assistant, went into Rosen's office and came out with the album ledgers. I had no idea what they were until I got them back to my apartment. I was stunned. Sam and I called the FBI, and we turned over four of the five. One I left with Lilly. The rest is history."

"What's the big deal, anyway?" Lilly says. "It's not like the ledgers are gone, and they're only for historical reference, not for looking up anything except our menorah. And it's proof that it was ours. That's why I kept it."

"I know," Alan says patiently. "But that really impacts the value of the album. It's now incomplete."

"They don't know that. Whoever *they* is."

"Now that you've gotten your menorah back, why not turn over the page? It isn't like you could ever sell it." Alan doesn't see the connection yet.

I wait for Lilly to explain, but she doesn't. Her beautiful long hair shines in her screen light, and she tosses it like a girl a third her age, but doesn't give away the bottom line. Well, *no one's perfect*, right? "She and Lev split a hundred grand. The museum insurance and Lev's dad's homeowner's policy. After Simon Cree made the claim against the museum for Lev, um, Lev and Lilly made another claim against Henri Zimmerman's policy. Just in case the one against the museum failed for some reason.

"And both insurance companies paid. The museum's insurance company may want the money for the menorah back, and there are suggestions that Lev was in cahoots with Marie, Rosen's curator, who actually did the stealing for him."

Alan's eyebrow almost exits the screen. I do *not* type in *Nobody's perfect*.

"Why are we plowing old ground?" Sam finally chimes in. "We know who did what. The problem, Lilly, is that, one: you're withholding evidence that could help convict that SOB Rosen; and two, that you and Lev double-collected on the menorah that was stolen, when it's no longer stolen. I can tell you what you ought to do, but you already know."

Everyone takes a few deep breaths. Then I say, "And to top it all off, there was an article in the county paper about art theft, and there's a bit about Lilly and the damned menorah right there. So anyone who needs to know, or bothers to look, will know that you got it back. Or should I say, *we*, since you've had it for two Hanukkahs and it's my turn. And the insurance companies are going to want at least some of their money back. And the ledger page..."

"Is the only thing that ties us to that menorah, and I'm not going to give that up."

"The money?" Alan reminds us.

Lilly's silent. Then I hear the obnoxious sound of a cell-phone on loud. Lilly raises her hand to have us hold on, and mutes herself.

◦ ⊹ ═ ⦉⊙⊗⊙⊱ ═ ⊹ ◦

"She's probably spent the money," I say while we wait. But before Alan can reply, Lilly unmutes, gesturing.

She holds her phone away from her ear for a second and switches to speaker. There's a woman on the line.

"...was with your dad when he died."

*What?* No one was with him, except the hospice nurse. Mom had refused to go. Lilly points to the phone, mouthing something I can't make out. Lev, of course, lip reads, so Lilly's gotten used to speaking soundlessly and being understood. I gesture that I don't get it. "Jeanine, slow down," she says. "How could you and your mother have been with my dad? I mean, where? Are you a nurse?"

Lilly had been in Paris, I was here on the west coast, and no one told us that he'd had another heart attack and wasn't going to make it. It had always killed me that he'd died without family with him, but all Mom would say was that it was what he wanted. That's when her dementia had started to show, I thought.

"...not his nurse," this Jeanine is saying. "I told you, my mother was a friend of your dad's. Do I have to spell it out for you?"

"Oh, that kind of friend!" Lilly says, typing MUTE YOUR-SELVES in the chat box. We do, immediately. "Yeah, Lilly. *That* kind of friend. And then some. And you know what? I saw your picture in the paper a few days ago, and the penny dropped, you know?" Her accent, deep New York, is getting stronger. We're all riveted.

"It did?" I'm impressed, Lilly's got some investigator skills.

"Yeah, it did. So, maybe we can get together. What do you say, get a coffee somewhere, maybe near your dad's old apartment. You know, the one on thirty-first street." She chuckles, a little dirty sound.

"I don't socialize inside," Lilly says. It's a good thing I'm muted, my guffaw is so loud. "You know, I didn't catch your last name, Jeanine."

"Cuz I didn't give it. But fine, we can get a drink or something at an outdoor place. You pick it. Anywhere within eight blocks of the apartment is fine. I don't walk so good these days."

"Neither do I," Lilly says. She still limps from the horrible break in her leg, but only on very cold or wet days. It's a gorgeous September day in New York according to my phone, so she's playing along.

Lilly looks at me, I can tell, and I nod. I type in the chat, *go ahead*. "Okay, Jeanine. I'd love to meet you. How's next Thursday. I can't make it before then."

In the silence I can almost hear the wheels turning in Jeanine's mind. "All right. Thursday the tenth. Three?"

"No, just me," Lilly says.

"Very funny ha ha. Poppi Persil always said you had a stupid sense of humor. Meet me at the front of his apartment at three, we'll go from there." The phone clicks off.

*Poppi Persil?*

---

We stare into the screen at one another. Finally I break the silence. "Well, that's fucked up." Not being the most helpful comment, it doesn't get an answer right away. I realize I'm still muted. I unmute, and say it again. Now everyone's talking at once.

"Don't meet her." Alan.

"I'll go to New York and go with you." Me.

"Let me find out more about her." Sam.

"What will I wear?" Obviously, Lilly.

"Agreed," I say. "Sam, if you could investigate, figure out who she is, Lilly, can you give Sam the phone number she called from, Alan, we'll set up a pre-meeting strategy, and Lilly, I'm coming out."

"You are? That's awesome!" Lilly smiles, and turns her donut lamp at the screen, lighting up her face into a sunlike glare.

"Ow, don't do that!" more or less all of us say.

"No, I'm so happy! It's been so long. Oh," she cackles, "the real question will be *what will you wear!*"

"Let's talk this over," Sam says, and I can feel the weight of his calming hand on mine. I squeeze his hand back, but I know what he's thinking. *Not a good idea.*

"It's perfect," Lilly's still chirping. "This way you can go with me to meet this Jeanine person," she says while Alan repeats *Don't meet her*, and Sam says *We'll talk about this.* "And then, you can go with me when I have to testify at the trial, if they even have the trial. I can't wait to tell Lev! He'll be so excited!"

I am already having second thoughts, regrets, and realizations. "Okay," I say. "We'll go over the details and the game plan. Let's talk again tomorrow."

* * *

Tomorrow is Rosh Hashanah. I decide to bake sourdough bread instead of Challah, and work out my anxiety. Since the pandemic started, there are a lot of home bakers giving sourdough a try, but I've made it for, well, fifty years. I've had this particular starter for over three years, and it's mighty ripe. Maybe a bit over-fermented, but it gives a unique taste to the finished product.

I skip the bread machine, a pando-gift from a neighbor who, after a few uses, realized that machines took the fun out of the process for her, and go the hand-made route. I love the machine for brioche and challah, unbraided of course, because those doughs are so soft I never trust myself with them. And as part of my experimenting, I've used my starter for both of those, to great effect. The brioche, especially, gets a complexity that enhances the sweetness. I can hear the purists, both French and Jewish, howling already.

Sourdough, on the other hand, is deeply forgiving. It's also a lot of work, which is what I need right now. As we enter the eighteenth month since the first lockdown, pause, or whatever, flour and yeast are easily available in my grocery store of choice. At first, Angie's husband Derek went foraging for me, and bought me two bags of generic all-purpose flour from...somewhere...when there was none to be found anywhere. He also turned up with a case of toilet paper. For a guy in oil and gas, he's got some odd connections. Now, fortunately, our *new abnormal* doesn't include shortages.

I'm kneading the first dough, gathering the scraps and flour in, standing slightly on tiptoe to get some weight into my arms, when the darkness starts. *Bread...we have bread and they had none...* My eyes drift to the postcard, still sitting on the edge of desk, its weight in sorrow keeping it from falling to the ground.

*"We kindly inform you that we have no record."* Aurora was nineteen, she was in New York City all alone, having made her way from

Poland, to Germany, to survival, to France, to New York. She was trying to find out if her father was dead.

I hold fast to the edge of the kitchen table as the waking nightmare begins.

———————————⋏———————————

*Family Scrapbook — Aurora: Visions on paper: 1946*

*The mail comes twice a day but the letter is never there. Until today. It's a flimsy airmail postcard, and the postmark is Lodz, but there's also a stamp, in French, Correspondence de Prisioners de Guerre. It's the permit to allow the correspondence, and in typewritten Polish there are blanks filled in for the prisoner's name, the communications number, and a space for IS and IS NOT.*

*I turn the postcard over, my vision too blurred from fear to read it. It's addressed to me in my old name, the one I vow to lose forever if he's dead.*

*I look again, and it's unambiguously clear. IS NOT. He is not in our records. This prisoner of war has not been found.*

*Of course not. When he was taken from us, he was so weak he could no longer walk. "Get this piece of crap out of here," the soldier had said, dragging my father as he gasped for breath, his ragged pajama pulling down on his bony hip.*

*He'd had such beautifully tailored pants. His cravats had been silk. Always slender, he'd had a brilliant diamond stickpin to hold the silk to his linen shirt.*

*The soldier was only a year or two older than I was. I put my hand out to him, an offer in my eyes if he would be gentle with my father. He blushed, his fair skin reddening from some deeply buried shame, but he turned away, taking my poor, dying father with him. I heard him hitting each stair as they went down.*

*I put the postcard in a drawer, and never look at it again.*

*I catch myself in the mirror. I am dark-eyed, chestnut-haired, and beautiful. I am alive, and I am in New York City. I am alone, and no one will ever again see me as I once was. I put on lipstick. I change my name.*

———— Y ————

I've over-kneaded the bread and need to let it rest longer than usual so it doesn't become tough. I put it in the refrigerator to slow the rise a bit, let the glutens relax.

The visions are more like memories now. They don't take me over, body and soul, like they used to. I hear my mother's voice, I see what she's saying, but I know that I'm simply channeling her spirit, not hallucinating. I know the source of the story. And I know why this particular one came to me now.

"Sam, I think I should go to New York."

He comes all the way into the kitchen. His face is a little ruddy from the wind that's picked up over the water, as it does so many afternoons. He's been out on the beach and he smells like ocean. He also tracks sand onto the kitchen floor.

"You ready to fly?"

The rest of the country has been flying for about six months, cautiously returning to travel. I haven't. "I guess so. I think it's safe," I say, the tentativeness weighting the *think*. "After all, you fly, Derek flies…"

"I agree. It's probably as safe as going to the store. But I'm talking about you. How you feel. How comfortable you'd be."

"You were encouraging me to get out more," I say. I've always tended to hunker inside when I feel the world — or my world — spin out of control. This time, I wasn't considered crazy, just cautious.

"Maybe it's time," I add. "Truthfully, I don't want to go, I don't want to fly, I'm still deep-down angry at Lilly. I also realize I need to let my anger go if I want to have a normal relationship with the person I've been closest to all my life. It's the High Holidays. We have to reconcile at some point. And I'm going to grow roots in this house!"

"Nice enough place to grow roots," Sam said.

I look out the window at the diamonds of sun glinting off the estuary. We'd bought this little Victorian on the island of Alameda years before, when prices were lower and the place needed enough work to take it out of the running for average buyers. We were living on the Peninsula, south of San Francisco, prices there were astronomical, and the whole tenor of Silicon Valley was getting beyond its elite tradition to downright suffocating.

Angie had moved to the city and she and Derek had just started dating. We weren't ready to move yet, so we stayed put, fixed up this house, and rented it out. When we returned from Sam's New York sabbatical, we knew it was time.

There could not have been a better home to shelter-in-place. Little shops were open soon after the first closures, there was the beach along the Oakland estuary, there were breezes and clean air even in the summer of the fires, and soon the Alameda-San Francisco Ferry was running again. I went on the ferry on the Monday after Biden won the election, just to celebrate. It was delicious to be out on the water once again.

The kitchen is the star-piece of the house. It's got a huge window over the sink with the view of the estuary in the distance. In the living room the windows give even better access, and though we're a block from the actual shore the position of the house on a little mound gives it more light and great sight-lines. My cozy pantry-turned office has no view, only a circular port-hole window far above my head, but the ceilings are high throughout, and the air is sweet.

Why would I go to New York?

"Because I wasn't there when my dad died. And neither were my mother or Lilly. And this lady, Jeanine, says she was. I need to do this. Plus," I add, "I want to attend the trial, if I can. And if I can't,

I want to be on the spot for Lilly. Even though I'm still furious at her. Plus-plus, I have the album's page, and I need to put it back with the rest of the historic ledger. And that's going to be an issue..."

"It certainly is," Sam says. "And the hundred thousand dollars is going to be an even bigger issue."

"Yeah, I know. I just don't get it. We both got plenty when Mom died, what does she need to grift on insurance money?"

"For you, thrifty little soul, it was a lot of money. For Lilly, not-so-thrifty, it was a pittance. It's long-gone, and you know it."

I nod. All my inheritance is still in the bank, earning interest, and hasn't been touched in the nearly five years since Mom passed away. Except for some really amazing cookware...but other than that, I haven't spent a dime. "Well, I can afford to buy a last-minute ticket," I say.

"If you're set on going, I'll do a little checking on that Jeanine person. It's better if Lilly doesn't go alone, if she's going to that meeting, and I'm not sure Lev is the one to accompany her. They both are more than indiscreet, and speak more than they listen."

I kiss Sam. He's been a bit bored since Biden's election. His Coalition did a fine job underground, helping out in Pennsylvania and Nevada, bringing around certain groups, getting information on others, while more above-the-radar folks like me sent donations to the ACLU and Stacey Abrams. But with that mission accomplished, his university lectures have been online, his Coalition is quiet, and he could use the task.

"I'll get my flight." I'm giddy with the idea.

I get the dough out of the refrigerator, and let it rise.

Chapter Five

# Even He Has Secrets

The mail finally comes. Couldn't the Orphans Court have just sent it by email? I take my coffee out onto our little deck. The sun is sparkling on the water, and the steam from my cup warms my face. The weather has turned cold overnight, dropping from mid-eighties to mid-fifties. I have a flannel top over my long-sleeved T-shirt, for the first time in six months.

I tear open the envelope from the Orphans Court, and I stare at the divorce document, breathless and shaking. *Daniel Persil and Gertrude Andrade Persil, married November 15, 1950, granted divorce on May 3, 1952, on the grounds of Indignities to the Person. Gertrude Andrade Persil to revert to her maiden name, effective May 3, 1952. There being no children of the marriage, and no property, there is no alimony awarded to Mrs. Persil.*

I pick up my phone, snap a picture of the decree, and text to both Sam and Lilly. To Lilly I add, *Gertrude???*

"*Great name, right? I guess it was popular back then. Gerty, Ruddie, Trudy. Wait. Trudy—who took care of Mom, what was her last name?*"

"*Semple.*"

But Dad left her ten grand, *a gesture of appreciation,* his will had said.

A bell is going off in my head. *Hold on,* I text. *I need to check dads will, but didn't she have a middle name?*

I dash into my pantry-office. I slam open my computer, and with a mountain of typos from my cold and shaking fingers I type in the search icon for my dad's will. I scroll down to the "bequests" section. Sure enough.

"*He left ten K to Gertrude Andrade Semple. ANDRADE!*"

*He was married to Trudy ?* OMFG Lilly replies, and then my phone rings immediately.

"That's unreal," I say. "Trudy? Trudy who took care of Mom? That's beyond fucked up."

I'm reeling with deep shock. When Mom first got sick, before Dad died, he hired a caregiver to help him with Mom's needs. She could still manage herself quite well, but he felt she shouldn't be alone in the house when he was out, so he — "He said he found her in the Pennysaver. What a fucking liar!" Lilly is raging. And for once I don't blame her.

Trudy came to the house, and he made a room available for her to stay overnight. Mom didn't know. She called for Trudy when she remembered her name, but otherwise didn't even look at her. Trudy fixed unpalatable lunches for Mom, who had been such a fine cook, and Mom ate them. Trudy sat and read her Bible while Mom listened to Bach, Shostakovich, Mozart and Tchaikovsky on the radio. Until she couldn't anymore, Mom read Polish novels, English poetry, German magazines, and Trudy sat, with her mouth a bit open, reading scripture. Trudy stayed overnight, and fried eggs with Tabasco Sauce. But Trudy was oddly pretty: trim, fair-haired, great cheekbones, huge eyes. Trudy called my dad Poppi, like Angie did.

I want to throw up.

By then, Dad had gotten an apartment in the City, since he was still active at the hospital where he was the Fellow at the clinic, so he could stay over when he had early cases or lectures to give. Occasionally, Mom had gone in and stayed over with him, especially when there was an exhibit of her work, or there was a play they wanted to see.

In his last year, he started staying there more and more. Soon Trudy started complaining about the commute to Dad's suburban house, and then quit. She was replaced by a much younger, energetic Jamaican woman named Pally, who slept in, and Trudy only came on Saturdays when Pally was off. Finally, she stopped coming in at all.

I thought back to what I knew about Dad's final week. "Dad had been staying at the apartment, right? When he collapsed?"

"Yeah, and after he had the heart attack he was able to return to the apartment for what turned out to be his final days," Lilly says. "He said he was recovering but it was too hard for him to go back to the house. Nothing like, *the end is near*, and we knew there was supposed to be a nurse with him."

Mom knew, or had been told, that he was ill, but she couldn't go into the City, and didn't seem to remember from one day to the next that he'd had a heart attack. In fact, there was no indication whatsoever that she even cared.

"All I knew was that the nurse called the insane funeral director, instead of me, or Mom, or you." That itself was another story. I had to stop that lunatic mortician before she could have Mass said for him. *He was Jewish*, I'd screamed into the phone. It took three weeks to get the ashes from her.

"Remember how that funeral lady said she had instructions? And they weren't from Mom, or anything. She said they were from Dad."

"Right. Now I bet it was that Trudy."

But Jeanine, whoever she is, said she and her mother had been with Dad when he died.

This is all moving too fast, it all makes no sense. Unless…

# Family Scrapbook Photo #2: 2014

It comes in a manila envelope with a Long Island city's postmark a week after Dad died. Inside is a black and white photo, glossy, sized eight by ten. A man is lying in a wooden coffin, with only a paper lining, no cushioning. Clearly he's very tall, as the coffin extends slightly past the end of the table at the foot end. There's a seam about ten inches before the end of the coffin where an additional piece has been nailed in.

He's covered by a sheet of paper, but his hands are folded spiritually across his chest. His long face, once difficult and lively, is still. His lips, always full, are slightly pursed, and I can see that there's a skinny band under his chin, like plastic wrap, keeping his jaw from dropping open.

Clipped to the photo is a letter from the funeral director. "I thought you and your family would like to see a photo of your beloved father, at his final rest. He looks so peaceful, doesn't he? Though he left instructions that nobody was to be told of his death until his ashes were interred, I wanted you to have this anyway.

"He also left instructions that you would pay the final bill, please find attached. Blessings in Christ."

I look at the photo again. His strong hooked nose is drooping a bit, but the deep dimple in his chin is clean-shaven, and his silver hair is brushed.

Above him is a crucifix. He does not look at peace.

---

"What the hell does Indignities to the Person mean? And who was doing the indignities?" I say to Sam when he emerges from his office a few minutes later. "And what the goddamn hell was Trudy doing, taking care of Mom? This is sick — outrageous and sick."

"It gets worse," Sam says gently. I wait, and he hands me a printout. "What does all this mean?" I ask, unable to read it through my fury.

"Just what it says. It's a birth certificate. Jeanine is Gertrude Andrade Semple's daughter. No father listed on the birth certificate. *Father unknown.* Born in San Antonio, Texas, in 1967."

"What? Are you saying that Jeanine is Gertrude's daughter, and they both were with Dad when he died?"

Sam walks to the French doors leading to the deck. His back is to me but from the set of his shoulders I see he's tense. Finally he turns back and his face is in silhouette against the light of the sun setting into the hills behind the bay.

"What years did you live in San Antonio?" Sam asks, though he knows.

"That can't be true," I say, reading his mind. My own mind screams back at me, *yes it can.*

He reaches out a hand. "It probably is. Why else would Trudy be in San Antonio giving birth? She was from Philly, and based on what we know she was probably at least eighteen in 1950, so that would make her in her late thirties in 1967. San Antonio was not exactly a Mecca for northerners at the time, was it?"

"On the other hand, 1967 was not a good time to be a single mother anywhere. Maybe Trudy got pregnant in Philadelphia, and since my dad was in San Antonio, and was a doctor, and an old flame — to say nothing of an ex-husband — she went down there, where she'd be away from family and prying eyes, and had her baby. It doesn't necessarily, or even credibly, have to be his baby."

If I sound desperate it's because I am.

Sam nods. "That's true," he says. I can see that he's unconvinced. "And he could help her get into a hospital without being grilled for being unmarried. Not an easy time at all."

I need him to be wrong.

"And if her family was in Pennsylvania, they could very well have rejected her for getting pregnant, and even though she'd be in her thirties she would possibly need to go away, to hide it all from them. Can you find a marriage record for her to whoever Semple was?"

Sam goes back into his office. He's got a network that can get behind practically any firewall. Meanwhile, I go back outside. The breeze is picking up with the dusk and I'm sure that's what makes me shiver. I sit at the glass table, eyeing my phone.

I don't think it's advisable to tell Lilly anything just yet. She's liable to fly off the handle, call Jeanine, post a screed on Facebook about her.

That gives me an idea, though, and it doesn't take long to find Jeanine Semple of New York City on Facebook. Her privacy setting is clearly Friends-only, since her personal page, beyond her picture and her hometown, is inaccessible to me. But it indicates two mutual friends. She and I are both friends with my father's colleague, a retired doctor with twenty-eight friends. I remember him vaguely, though Lilly will probably recall more, and he and Dad thought the whole Facebook thing was obscene, pandering to voyeurs and liars. Turns out they were right. The other mutual friend, of course, is my dad.

Dad's page is still up. I had tried to have it taken down, but Lilly felt that it should stay up so those who wanted to could still see him. I thought that was ghoulish so as a halfway measure we just had it archived. It's creepy to look at the little that was on there: his picture, taken now ten years ago, and birthday wishes from year to year from his few internet friends, and from my cousins. A posting by Lilly when he died, and some beautiful condolence posts as comments to the that. I feel the tears as I read them.

And there's a comment from Jeanine Semple Cruz. So she was married at some point. It's the same Jeanine Semple I found earlier, so at least I'm on the right track. I read her comment: *Poppi, you are always in our hearts. We love you* followed by a broken heart emoticon.

Not a good sign.

As soon as I text Lilly my flights she calls.

"Thank god you're coming!" she gushes. I feel my shoulders stiffen. "I couldn't do this without you."

She can't see me nod, so I force myself to answer audibly. "I can work as easily there as here. Okay if I stay with you?"

Now it's her turn to be silent. Then, "Of course, Zara. For chrissakes, don't you think this has gone on long enough?"

"Yes. But if you call someone a Judas-rat it takes a while to get over it."

"Then why are you coming? I mean if you're so pissed at me..."

"I am. I need to go because, well, there are some things I discovered." I take a deep breath and instead of breaking the Jeanine-news, I say something I've been thinking for a while. "Look, maybe we need to go to a joint therapist or something. This is not getting better."

I can tell that she's having a little war inside, just as I am. And for once, she doesn't say the first thing that comes to her mind. How do I know this? Lilly's been my sister all my life. She's sixty, I'm almost sixty, and we are who we are. If there's a more profound way to say that, I don't know what it is. And notably, I'm not saying this to Lilly.

"Yeah," she says finally. "It really isn't getting better."

And that is exactly *not* the answer I'm hoping for. I want her to say *Yes it is! Just suggesting joint therapy is a huge step forward!* When she doesn't, I feel crushed, but I've made my reservations and I'm going to go anyway, so maybe I just need to stay in a hotel.

"Never mind, you're right. It isn't getting better and it probably isn't going to. I just thought it might help to talk things out with a trained professional. But it probably wouldn't help. Unless the therapist took your side, you'd think that she was biased, and maybe, I don't know, maybe I'd think the same. It happens all the time in my investigations."

"'This isn't one of your investigations, Zara."

I hang up.

The phone rings almost immediately. "God, Zara. Be an adult for once." I wait. "So, at least you haven't hung up on me again. Just the silent treatment, eh?"

"I'm thinking, Lilly. And I don't talk when I'm thinking." I don't say *unlike you* but I've said it so many times before that I don't need to. Lilly hears it loud and clear. "Look, I said I'm coming out. I asked if I could stay. I suggested therapy together. And what do I get? Nothing!"

"No, you get an enthusiastic hostess, happy you're coming, and I get a cold, *I can work just as easily there as here.* Not *I can't wait to see you too.* No *I've missed you.* All of a sudden I'm a business decision for you."

I can't find words, so I sit.

"I know, you're thinking. Little Miss Cerebral. Show an emotion."

Anger is an emotion. Hanging up is showing anger. Still, I don't say anything, because anything I did say would definitely be retaliatory.

We sit in silence for a while, then I hear a long exhalation. "Zara, I'm sorry." I swallow. I want to answer but I can't. After a moment she goes on. "I should never have called you a collaborator, a turncoat, or anything else that being in the *Judenrat* implies. That was shit of me, and I shouldn't have done it. And I don't even think it."

Tears start in my eyes. I want to reach out, but my heart is hardened. I do the next best thing. "Hey," I whisper. That's as far as I can go.

I guess I've been Lilly's sister for as long as she's been mine. She understands that *Hey* and lets it breathe a bit between us.

"It's the judgment, Zara. The same judgment Mother felt from her uncle and the people she met. They rejected her because she'd done what she needed to do to survive. And just like them, you judge and reject me."

I have a choice here. I can express the outrage that I feel that she dares equate herself with Mom, or I can take up the underlying issue. While I'm pondering my choice, Lilly beats me to the punch.

"I know, it isn't the same. I know you're ready to explode with fury on me, because I've compared myself to Mother. No suffering is good enough, remember?" I nod though she can't see me. But she sure *knows* me. "But you judge what you call my promiscuity. You judge what you call my dishonesty. You judge me for having three husbands, for never having enough money, for . . . for everything. And you look down on me. That gets old, Zara. It really does."

So maybe we don't need a joint therapy session. She's figured it all out.

"You're probably right," I finally say. My voice is steady even though my heart is running like a hamster. "I do judge you. And you judge me. But I'm tired of this. Tired of fighting with you, of not being able to call you when I want to because you'll launch into a story about yourself before I get a full sentence out of my mouth. Tired of your constant need for approval from me, now that Dad and Mom are gone. And tired of not being appreciated for biting back every other word so I don't set you off."

A therapist would have a field day with all of this.

"I appreciate you, Zara. And I do try to let you talk, I really do. Remember how I let you explain the entire bit about historical American antisemitism? You went on for at least twenty minutes, and I didn't interrupt once."

"Wait. You were timing it? You called me and asked me to explain something you'd read right after the election, and you were timing my response?" It takes all of my self-control not to hit *END*.

"No, I happened to have a meeting that day and I realized I was going to be late, so that's how I remember. And it was a great explanation. But don't say you never get to talk."

*One time. One goddam time.*

"Okay, okay. But at least let's try to be kinder to each other, okay? Because otherwise we're no better than the Facebook catfights, each side making points, and…"

"And trying, and failing, to stop ourselves from hurting the other," she finishes for me. Oh, if she only knew.

"Exactly," I say. "We have to try."

Lilly's crying. "I love you, Zarita," she sobs.

*Oh for chrissakes.* "I love you too, Lilliana."

She laughs, and I close my eyes. I guess I really do.

---

I have to call Lilly back after she's composed herself. I still haven't told her about Jeanine. I wait until it's after dinner in New York, which might be a mistake depending on the number of glasses of wine she's had, but when she answers the phone I hear unusual sounds that tell me she's not at home. Jazz in the background, for one. And horns honking. In Katonah, her suburb, no one honks their horn on her little street. And jazz?

"Hey sweetie, I'm with Lev at a thing. Can I call you tomorrow?"

"Of course," I say. *A thing?*

---

The next day dawns clear and sunny. I sit on my deck, a shawl over my shoulders to temper the slight morning freshness of the salt air coming off the bay. I've got my laptop open on our glass outdoor table, and I'm finishing up a short investigation report — *he did it, and he should pay.* I'm a genius at compartmentalizing. After the emotional rollercoaster of the past forty-eight hours, work helps me regain my beloved self-control. I'm typing in the company's email when I get my daily Lilly text.

*Had a blast last night. First live music in eighteen months. Bars reopen officially tonight but Lev's friend jumped the gun.*

Lucky Lilly. I can't even imagine. I call her.

"Hey, well listen to what I found. How old's Lev, by the way?"

"There you go again," Lilly says.

"No! This isn't about how much younger he is than you. It's important."

"If you say so. Fifty-three."

"His mother must have had him late."

"Yeah, his sister's our age. Sixty, I think." *Your* age, I don't say.

"Ok. Here's what I found out. Hold on to your socks. So, Mom was born in 1927, as was Dad. They got married in 1953, you were born in fifty-nine, I was born in nineteen sixty. Joseph, Joey, was born in sixty-two, and poor soul died in sixty-five."

"Zara, I know all this."

"Wait. Just putting it in context for you. Trudy Semple was born Gertrude Andrade, in 1932, so she was about five years, six, younger than Dad. She married him in 1950, they divorced in fifty-two so a year and change after they got married, and about seven months before Dad married Mom. So all that about proposing on the first, second and third dates, until Mom said yes, had to have been while he was going through his divorce."

"And he claimed he didn't want to know anything about Mom's past, or so he said. Probably he didn't want to tell *her* anything about *his* past so he waved a magic wand, oh so romantic, and disappeared both their pasts. *Canaille*," Lilly adds in French. Loosely translated as SOB.

"Right, but she goes along with it. And now I see why, sort of. Her only living relative, as far as she knows, rejects her when she finally throws herself into his allegedly loving welcome." I feel a little awkward, but push on. "She desperately tries to find out if her father is alive, only to get the terrible reply from the Prisoner-of-War agency. She's lived through almost a decade of horrors, and has left Europe. She's a damaged, tragic figure, and Dad is there to catch her."

Lilly sighs. "It has all the makings of a movie."

"It does. Meanwhile, as we know, Mom's falling into a deep depression, repression or whatever, we're living in Texas and Nuevo Laredo, shuttling back and forth between Mexico and the US, trying to be American and resisting at the same time, and everyone is slowly going crazy." I take a big breath, close my eyes and say, "And now for the clincher. Gertrude goes to San Antonio, probably in the early-mid sixties —"

"How do you know *that?*"

"Sam and I have been researching. He can get into systems the rest of us can't. But wait. Here's the insane part — like the rest isn't bad enough. In 1964, in San Antonio, Texas, two years after our brother's born, at the same hospital where Dad's working, Trudy has a baby girl. And guess who she is?"

I can hear Lilly's breathing, hard and fast.

"Indeed," I say. "Jeanine Andrade is born to Gertrude Andrade Semple in September, 1964."

"Oh my god. So Jeanine is the same person I'm meeting? That's Trudy's daughter? Which is why she was with Dad when he died."

I prepare to drop the bomb.

"Yeah. And even though Trudy is Trudy Semple at this point, Jeanine's birth certificate is listed as *Father Unknown*. Which can't have been easy in 1964. I wonder why she didn't list this Semple, whoever he was, as the father, even if she didn't think he was?"

"Who knows. But who — oh my fucking heart! Do you think it was Dad?"

"I don't know, Lilly. But it looks like we're going to find out soon enough."

"Thank god you're coming out, Zara. This is unreal. And I can't believe that Dad was married to old frumpy-dumpy Trudy and her Bible and her half-open mouth. And what a liar, saying he found her in the Pennysaver in the want-ads for caregivers. Shit," she adds, "what if she's like, a half-sister? But he was already married to Mother.

He wouldn't… I don't know."

She's babbling. I wait it out. After all, I was right there yesterday. I've had a whole day to absorb the insanity. Absorbing insanity is something Lilly and I have Olympic gold medals in.

"I know it's creepy to do, Lilly, but check out Dad's old Facebook page. You know how we archived it so folks who knew him could still see his old pictures and all those nice things folks said on his birthdays and when he died? Check out his birthday wishes from when he turned 86. And the condolences."

"I don't even want to know. I mean, I'll do it, but I don't want to know." And after a longish pause, "Do you think Mother knew?"

"And Joey died the following year."

There's really no bottom to the well of grief.

# PART TWO

---

# NEW YORK, NEW YORK

# Chapter Six

# On the Road, in the Sky

It's been eighteen months since I've flown. I used to go back and forth, and Sam and I thought nothing of jumping on a plane for a trip somewhere. In fact, my last flight before everything shut down was a "last fling of my fifties" trip to Honolulu, a gift from Sam, for four days. It was odd, that trip, for a number of reasons, but the prices were right. There was a virus in China that stopped Chinese tourists from traveling, Honolulu was half empty, and rooms were available at great prices on a moment's notice. We took advantage, found cheap-ish flights, and found ourselves in smaller-than-usual crowds of tourists from Japan wearing masks.

I will confess: we laughed. Masks didn't prevent people from getting diseases. We all knew that, right? But they wore them, and we just ignored them.

That was then.

Two months later, "now" started. Eighteen months after that, it's still "now."

I adjust my KN95 around my nose as my glasses fog up. My glasses have been fogging up for eighteen months. Lilly's technique of washing the lenses with dish soap, and only giving them a light rinse, does help, if only for a while. I did that before I left. Before my vaccination I wore my patterned cloth masks when indoors, saving the KN95s for serious encounters. Even now, a trip to the airport, boarding an airplane, is the most serious encounter I can imagine.

Sam, of course, has been flying for months, as has Angie's Derek. Sam assures me that it's as safe as going to the grocery store, but even now I'm skittish and nervous.

Oakland Airport is a delight, with two terminals an easy walking distance from one another, and with my PreCheck, security is a piece of cake. When the agent asks me to lower my mask for identification, I smile at her. A human!

I flash my vax card and proceed.

In the waiting area most people are keeping a decent, if not six-foot distance, and everyone is wearing a mask. We board in very small groups, and my blood pressure skyrockets when I enter the plane. Suddenly I'm in close proximity to almost a hundred people, in a metal tube, breathing their air as they breathe everyone's they've been around for the past two weeks. Maybe they're vaccinated, maybe they're tested, maybe they're carrying a variant, maybe I'm having a full-on panic attack.

I take my window seat, and, having paid for the more expensive exit row seats, I hope that the price has kept anyone from grabbing the other spots.

The pilot tells the flight attendants to prepare the aircraft for takeoff, and I'm still all alone in my little row. I breathe a sigh, coffee-scented, of relief. Not great for the airlines, but a truly welcome emptiness for me.

We fly over Lake Tahoe, a more southern flight pattern than I expect, and over the salt flats of Utah. Flying east, we are losing the sun rapidly, and by what would be five in the afternoon at home, we're flying into darkness.

It's deep night when I catch a glimpse of the urban glow that is the New York metropolitan area. I feel the old excitement that I used to feel as a younger woman, when traveling meant adventure, something new and different, something I'd never seen or experienced. Is that what late middle-age is? A feeling of *been there, done that,* for every event? Sure, there are lots of places I've never been. Scandinavia, Asia, Africa, the Middle East, India. In fact, in that context I've been very few places. But a trip to New York had long ago stopped being special. Until we couldn't go anymore.

We touch down and we're reminded that now we deplane by row, not a mob of folks all standing at once, faces pressed into each other's bodies, grabbing bags and rushing to get out. Even so, a few people stand up, even while we're taxiing, and are reprimanded over the speaker by the flight attendants. Even in these days some folks just don't get it.

JFK is eerily empty. I've landed there a hundred times, in all sorts of weather, hours, economies and political regimes and I have never seen it like this before. I walk through the familiar terminal, everything looks the same, but it's completely empty. Stores are shuttered. The food court is open but there are no lines anywhere. Even Starbucks only has three people waiting. I text Lilly as I ride down the escalator, *I'm here. Go outside,* she answers. The scary self-propelling revolving doors — they've always freaked me out for some reason — move me gently to the outside area, and the humid, warm air, so not-like-home, so everything-about-New-York, embraces me. I feel my hair, lightly wavy in California, frizz right into a ball. Lilly's going to have a field day.

For the first time in two decades, Lilly has decided to pick me up at JFK. It's a haul from Katonah, and it's late by now, nine at night in New York, but when I go out to the curb, there's her big white SUV. She leaps out of the car, dark hair flying behind her, and in two long strides has wrapped her arms around me, pulling me into her chest. I turn my face to the side and rest it on her shoulder as she kisses the top of my head. I drop my bag and one-arm hug her back.

What fools we are to fight.

---

Once out of JFK there's much less traffic than usual. We go over the Whitestone bridge because Lilly likes it, and I see what used to be Shea Stadium on my left. "Remember how Dad used to say, *one wrong turn here and we'll end up in California!*"

I see Lilly smile in the darkness. "We're taking the Hutch," she says, as if I remember the difference. "There's construction on the Saw Mill." New Yorkers like to talk like that, and Dad was the most traffic-oriented person I knew. I look at the city lights and can see the Empire State Building, lit up in its magnificent, garish way. It's good to be back.

"Everything's open," she says as she merges in what has to be the shortest merge lane in the country. I clutch the armrest. "Relax, Zara, I've done this a million times. Everything's open, but it's going to be slow getting people out."

"Same at home," I say. "Not quite everything, but a lot's open. It's just after three false re-starts, I think we're all a little paranoid. For good reason. You know the old saying, just because you're paranoid doesn't mean there isn't someone out to get you."

"How was your flight?"

"Good, it was hardly half full but — "

"Yeah, I've read that. When my friend Lisle flew from Germany home to New Jersey last month she said the same thing."

I don't know who Lisle is. I was about to tell Lilly about how those few people still stood up when they should have waited, but she's on to a new topic. "So, wait to you see my new kitchen. I have new cabinets and I finally replaced the old dishwasher. It was crazy. We're having an interim election next month as you know, because the county supervisor died, and the replacement is temporary, so I was talking to the installer and asked him if he was registered to vote yet..." I close my eyes and drift off, tired from the flight though it's barely dinnertime back home. When I wake up, she's registered the dishwasher installer to vote, and is asking me if I'm hungry.

Fortunately I haven't missed much, and before I can answer she's detailed what she has in her refrigerator for me to snack on when we get there. "Since the boys haven't been here much, what with stay-home orders and travel and — oh, I bought the fizzy water that you like! Well, there wasn't the flavor you like, the grapefruit, so I got passion fruit, but we have it, just for you!"

"Thanks," I say. That's Lilly.

"And tomorrow..." and on she goes.

This is a parody of her former self, I think. Or maybe I'm just not used to her monologues anymore. I know she's lonely. Desperately, deeply lonely. Even Francis Xavier, her youngest son and the most attentive of her boys, has been living with his father in Chicago ever since the first Pause was lifted almost a year ago. She hasn't really had any personal contact, no one to talk to besides Lev. No wonder she talks my ear off.

Her little house is always perfectly maintained, again thanks to an abundance of sons, step-sons and sons' friends, who shovel her snow, rake the leaves, clean the gutters. She's always been meticulous as a housekeeper, and even with her limp, which is more noticeable now than in the brief greeting at the airport, she manages to clean the house to a high-buffed shine. And the new cabinets are, actually, quite nice.

When Mom died, we each got a small inheritance of cash, the rest of Dad's old IRA, and the house. It took two years to clean out the darned place, with Lilly doing most of the work, and then, once we were ready to put it on the market, the first shut-down happened. It wasn't until the first lifting of restrictions that we were able to sell it, and even then, it sold for less than half of what a place like that would have sold for in California.

New York closings are a nightmare, and I had to do it over Zoom. I snap back to Lilly and her house. "Everything looks fantastic," I say. I put my bag down and take the album sheet from where it's been burning a hole in my carry-on. "Here. I don't know why you sent this to me. Put it somewhere safe.

She looks sad as she takes it from me. "If you say so," she says, and ducks into her room with it.

"I'll take some of that cold chicken, and a bagel and a tomato," I say when she emerges. Suddenly I'm hungry, and there is nothing on earth like an East Coast tomato in the early fall. "Do you have salt?" I ask.

"I don't use salt much," she says. I side-eye her. "Have some *sazón*." I shake my head, declining the packet of seasoning, and go to her cabinets. On the top shelf, high above my head, there's salt.

After I've had my delicious sandwich, Lilly's ready to crash. "I'm still a teacher at heart. Even though I don't have to get up at six, I still am ready to climb into bed at nine. And it's almost eleven. The guest room is ready for you. See you in the morning." She kisses me.

"Good night, sweetie," I say. "See you not too early. It's three hours earlier for me, remember."

"Well, you'll just have to get on New York time," she says. I shake my head, smiling. Same old Lilly.

I close the door to the guest room.

In contrast to the jet noise, the airports' incessant announcements, the ride back with Lilly, the guest room is like a vault. Maybe I will be able to order my thoughts once more.

On the airplane I'd pondered in endless swirls what the motive for the meeting could be. *Jeanine says she knew Dad, I'm betting that she's Trudy's daughter — though she hasn't divulged that yet... In fact, she never even gave Lilly her last name... that she was with him when*

*he died, and so she knew that neither Lilly nor I were there. Or Mom.*
*I don't even know if she's aware that I exist. Unless of course Dad men-*
*tioned me. But she says she learned about Lilly through the article on the*
*menorah. Or maybe just that she learned about the menorah that way.*

It all seems preposterous. Meeting outside my father's old apartment, in mid-town Manhattan, seven years after he's died, is just
plain weird. And I'm guessing it's only going to get weirder.

I pick up my phone to call Sam. Tomorrow is Wednesday, and
we have a day before we need to meet Jeanine. I have to make sure
Lilly's ready for this.

———— ✦ ———————

Wednesday dawns with one of those clear early fall days in New
York, warm, scented with fading summer, a tickle of decay. The
sky is so blue it hurts, and the grass on Lilly's front lawn shimmers
emerald with dew. Lilly's waiting for me on her little cement patio,
two cups of hot coffee at the ready.

She's wearing a terry caftan with little red stars on a black
background. I can see that she's put on a bit of weight, the long
convalescence after her broken leg having melded into the even longer
lockdown. She's got her hair braided, and it hangs heavily over one
shoulder. "Wanna see the scar?" she greets me.

"If you feel up to it," I say. I don't say, *not before breakfast*, because
it's her pain, her scar, and she can share it any time she wants.

She unzips the caftan, and there, between her two generously-en-
dowed boobs, is a scar, thin lined and about five inches in length,
pinkish against her olive skin, of what appears to be a childishly
scrawled 4. The last leg of the swastika didn't "take", nor did three
of the end pieces of the symbol, so instead of the ominous, hated
icon, Lilly's scar looks like a first-grader's writing.

Still, we know what it is.

"It isn't very deep," she says. "Dr. Maylee says she can't completely get rid of it, but she can make it almost invisible, as soon as it's totally subsided. Meanwhile, I have a gel I rub in twice a day."

All my anger at Lilly melts away at this sight. For me, the entire episode was a psychological mountain made out of my mother's memories and my own inherited trauma and guilt. For Lilly, it was all of that, along with an affair with Walter Rosen — art thief, killer, breast-fetishist, Nazi. It left her with a compound fracture of her leg, which at sixty took a long time to heal and resulted in a limp, and most of a swastika carved into her body. How could I not see the damage?

And the plastic surgeon could only make it *almost invisible*. Nothing could make the scars go away completely.

"I'm glad you've got a good surgeon," I say, not trusting myself to make any other comment.

She nods. "And Dr. Maylee says she'll testify at Rosen's assault trial, whenever that is, and at my civil action for damages from Rosen. Problematic as that will be."

Yes, given the lusty intimate relationship between the two, and the fact that he's definitely going to jail for art theft, if not for murder, as it is, a civil suit will be problematic. "If you're upfront about the relationship it will be less so," I say.

"So says Alan."

"It could come up in the criminal trial too," I add. "It's unfair, that you suffered so much and yet you're a pawn in their trial game." I sigh. I wish that on top of that she hadn't taken the ledger sheet from the album, or the money from the insurance company. But if I want my witnesses pure, I need to be in a different line of work, and this isn't even my case. I repeat that to myself, *this is not my case*.

"Life isn't fair," she says jollily. "Hey, I just thought of something." Which to me means that she's been thinking of a way to bring something up. "What if, just an idea, if we sneak the ledger sheet back into the album. Then, it's there. No more problem!"

"Really, Lilly? What, knock on the US Attorney's office door and say, *hey, dude, can we just borrow some of the evidence against Rosen for a few minutes? Quiet contemplation, you know?* And then, while we have the ledger, just sort of slip the page back in, scotch tape it, maybe? Then, they'll never know, right?"

"Yeah, okay, bad idea."

"And besides, if the page is back and they ask about the menorah, the whole insurance thing is back. If the ledger sheet is returned, then it's easier to prove it's our menorah. If we have the menorah, the insurance companies may want their money back."

The more I think about it, though, Lilly's idea has mild potential, in a more forthright way. "What if we just say, hey, here it is, maybe they'll just put it back for us. And on the insurance issue, Lev made claims where he needed to, and the fact that both companies paid up doesn't mean he's a bad guy. *He* doesn't have the menorah, we do. And as to what it's actually worth, who's to say it isn't worth twice what the museum's carrier paid. So the companies paid half the reimbursement value each, you have the item, and the Feds have the ledger. Who could complain? Except, you know, the museum, and they wouldn't dare."

Lilly's face lights up. "Let's do that. We'll just turn in the ledger page like we just found it — "

"*You* just found it."

"All right, *I* just found it, but we'll get someone to say — wait, I used to date a guy at Sotheby's, maybe he can give me a valuation! After all, it's our mother's, and now we can show that we have the ledger to prove it. I know that companies like Sotheby's are really into getting Jewish art back to the original owners. And as long as the valuation is fifty grand or more, we're in the clear. Let me see if Andres still works there."

"A hundred."

"What?"

"It has to be worth over a hundred thousand dollars."

"But each company only paid fifty thousand each."

"Right. But they both did."

I can see that the point is lost on Lilly, but that she's willing to go with it. She's looking at Facebook, to see if she can find out where Andres works now. "How long ago did you date him?" I ask.

"Depends on what you call dating," she answers, distracted. "Either twenty years ago or about three."

<hr />

While Lilly's on Facebook looking up Andres, I check the court's website to see how much in-person work they're doing. We know who's assigned to Rosen's case, but given that I haven't been notified of the trial and Lilly's only been subpoenaed for an indefinite date, ten days from now, I'm wondering what the status really is.

I find the email for the Assistant US Attorney, and compose a note: *My sister, Lilliana Persil, has been subpoenaed for the trial of Walter Rosen, set, I think, for September 20. Do you think this will go forward? And do you think it's possible for us to meet with you? I have traveled to New York in anticipation of this trial. As you well know we were victims of Mr. Rosen's many crimes, from the theft of artifacts while in the care of the Jewish Studies Museum to the physical assault of Lilliana. Since we are important witnesses for the prosecution as well as victims of the crime being prosecuted, I'm surprised that we have not been kept more in the loop. Can we meet?*

I wait for Lilly before hitting send, and also compose one to Agent Skordall, the FBI agent who took possession of the albums with their Nazi-created ledgers.

*Agent Skordall, do you know where the Nazi photo albums with ledgers enumerating the items stolen from individual Jewish households*

*in WWII, that we turned in to you two years ago, are? We would like
to see them one more time. Thank you.*

Lilly looks up from her iPad. "I'm looking at Dad's old page.
I don't see what you were saying about Jeanine."

I take her tablet from her and scroll to Dad's eighty-sixth
birthday posts. "It's in a comment to a comment. Start with Dr.
Lovinsky's birthday wishes. Who knows why he posted, except
that he was treating Dad during that time but had known him
from before. So, there's his, then a "reply" by her. It's the *Poppi* that
makes me want to barf."

Lilly looks. "Oh for crap's sake. There's her *forever in our hearts*
comment, and then that broken heart emoticon. That's gross. What
do you think she wants?"

"We'll find out," I say. "But given the timeline, it's possible that
she's, oh god, related to us. I mean, she could be a half-sister."

"I can't believe it. I won't."

"A DNA test would prove it. But here's what I've been worrying
about. Dad's will. It all went to Mom, of course, thank god he died
first —"

"In more ways than one," Lilly interrupts.

"I know, I know," I say. Lilly had a really problematic relationship
with Dad. "So even if she was going to try to make some sort of claim,
well, Trudy got ten grand, so it's not like he forgot her. You and I got
nothing, then, either. And any claim would be time-barred since he
died seven years ago, and on top of that, I'm pretty sure everything
in his will went to Mom, and thence to us."

"*Thence*. Cool, Zara. Say *thence* again!"

I laugh. "I can say *whence* too. And *heretofore*, if you'd like."

"It sounds so lawyerly. No normal person uses those words!"

I ignore that last part. "Anyway, so she's SOL on the SOL."

Lilly frowns.

"More legal terms: she's shit out of luck on the statute of limitations. But also, on the succession. You know, inheritance, since Dad

left everything in trust to Mom. As I recall, all his assets were in the trust, and they went to her. And then, from Mom to us, when not much was left."

"Jeez, Zara. Your mind really works differently from mine. So what do you think she wants?"

"I have no idea. But her call wasn't exactly warm and friendly, not giving her last name, alluding to Dad's final days in that gloating way. So it's got to be something. Maybe there's something Dad had that she wants, and she thinks now that she's found you she can try to get it. But you've been here in New York for over forty years. It's not like you've been hiding."

"Well, Trudy wasn't the sharpest tool in the shed. Even if Dad is her father, oh my god that sucks, maybe she got her mom's brains. I can't believe he brought his ex-wife in to care for Mom. That's beyond sick."

"It is. It's disgusting. And we'll know soon enough what Jeanine wants. Do you know if Trudy's still alive?"

"I don't have a clue. Can we look it up?"

We search the internet and don't find anything. "I'll ask Sam to take a look."

"Secret Agent Man."

I grin. "Yeah, cute. I wonder," I add. "She stopped taking care of Mom when Mom needed diapering. I fucking hate Alzheimer's. At least Mom probably had no clue who Trudy was. That would be the worst."

"For Trudy too. I mean, what possesses a woman to come take care of the new wife? Unless she was either saintly — her constant Bible reading, for example — or guilty. But she was the first wife, not the second, so it wouldn't be like Trudy stole Dad from Mom."

"Unless she did, over the course of the marriage."

"Unreal. You hungry for lunch? Lev's coming over in about a half hour. He texted this morning, he says he's found something cool for you to look at."

"I'm terrified of whatever Lev thinks is cool," I say.

"Don't be mean."

"I'm not. I'm more like, *just kidding*. He's come up with some doozies."

"True that," Lilly says. "You want another bagel? I bought tuna salad at the deli."

"Who buys tuna salad? You open a can, chop a hardboiled egg, some celery, some parsley in, you add a little mayo and salt and pepper and you're done."

"You have celery and parsley in your fridge?" Lilly says. I stare at her. "Well, I don't keep exotic herbs around like you do. You want some or not?"

<hr />

Lev lets himself in, and Lilly's new dog, a white Maltese that has to fill the big shoes of dear departed Lucy-the-hound, bounds up to meet him. "Hey, Sherlocke," he says, scratching the tiny dog's ears. She drools. It's not like he's a burglar. Sherlocke's a *she*, and like any other female, she's smitten with Lev. And why not? His black hair, with that streak of white up front, hangs thickly on his brow. His cheeks are perfectly ruddy, and below there's a two-day growth of beard he keeps trimmed to exactly that length. And in between are the bluest eyes on the planet.

He smiles, a flash of perfect white teeth, and I can't help but smile back. He takes off his jacket, throwing it over the back of the sofa, and the long-sleeved gray T-shirt caresses his broad shoulders. Lilly always jokes that it's a good thing he's only five seven or so, otherwise he'd be insufferably perfect. Oh, and he's three-quarters deaf, but only those who know him know it. He lipreads, and has a hearing aid not-so-discreetly behind his good ear, in bright blue.

He opens his arms to me. I hadn't planned on a big hug, I was going in for a handshake, but he's so welcoming. I let him wrap his arms around me.

Once he releases me, he goes to kiss Lilly. She, of course, is much taller, but he doesn't seem to mind. Nor, evidently, does she. "Hey, gorgeous," he says to her, in almost the same tone as he greeted Sherlocke.

"Woof!" she says.

I realize that his hearing must have deteriorated further, and the intonations are getting tough for him. Lilly winks at me. "Want tuna salad?" she asks Lev.

"What kind of salad?" he asks.

"Tuna," she answers.

He shakes his head. "No, I ate. Let me make myself and Zara some coffee. I remember that about you, Zara. Bottomless cup of coffee for you." He wiggles his eyebrows and goes to the coffee maker.

Over the roar of the single-cup maker, I whisper to Lilly, "His hearing's gotten worse?"

"Yeah, but my lipreading hasn't," Lev answers from the kitchen.

"My bad," I say.

"No worries. Yeah, I need to get this thing tuned up. With Covid, I kind of let that get away from me." He brings me a cup, black. "No sugar, no milk, right?"

Once he's sitting on the couch with Sherlocke's head in his lap, he turns his head to me, reminding me to address his good side. "I've got something for you." He reaches into the pocket of his jacket. He pulls out a little leather book. "You're going to go nuts for this. I told Lilly, Marcia-that's my sister, remember? — Marcia found this going through my Dad's stuff. It looks like a diary, from before he came to the States. When he was still in France, even before he'd married Chantal. When she died, based on the dates entered, he started keeping the financial pages. Mostly it looks like an inventory. But there are some lengthier writings, from well before then. It stopped when he married my mother."

He hands me the old book, its cover smooth and worn, and stained black on the edges. "Why are you showing me this?" I ask.

"I want you to take a look. You and Lilly might understand. Others won't."

"Have you seen this?" I ask Lilly. It's strange that he'd give me this to read, if he hadn't given it first to his lover. And she hadn't mentioned it.

Lilly shakes her head *no*. "Lev showed me some photos of it his sister took. Even though I can read French and German, I can't read this, and neither can Lev, and it's also a lot of numbers."

Lilly's allergic to numbers. I open it, and I can see what Lev and Lilly mean. There are entries that look like inventory, and dates, but the words aren't in German or French. The language looks like Latin, but isn't. I know most romance languages, and it isn't Italian, Spanish or Portuguese either. And the paragraphs are in strange writing that I don't recognize at all.

"Wow," I say. "Fascinating. I'd love to spend some time with it, but I don't recognize the language either. So, he was from Alsace, and that would be French or German, or some mix of the two. And this isn't in any of those."

"No," Lev says, "but numbers are universal."

Lev has an accounting background, though he can't get his CPA license due to some legal issues that go back a ways.

"Do they tell you anything?" I ask.

"Not yet. I need to study them some more. Marcia thinks it's a list of the pieces of art he worked to rescue from Germans after the war. Some occasional words stand out in Polish, transliterated Hebrew," he winks at Lilly, "Lilly taught me that word. And some French. But not enough to be consistent."

"Are the paragraphs in Cyrillic?" I ask Lilly.

"No, not even Cyrillic script."

Lev is squinting at the letters. I watch his face shut down. He shakes his head, puts the book down, pushes it away.

"Can we make some copies?" I ask. "I'd hate to see something like that get lost again."

"Marcia's been doing what Lilly's been doing, finally going through the boxes. They kept everything, didn't they?"

Lilly nods. "Yeah, because they lost everything."

"Let's get this duplicated," I say again. "Or triplicated, so we each have one. I wonder if it's in some kind of code. You know, like the Voynich Manuscript!" That gets me excited. Lilly knows that, and I can see her smile a little. She knew about this surprise. Amazing that she didn't spill the beans beforehand. "I think between the three of us we can figure this out. Meanwhile, you've heard about Jeanine, right?"

"Yeah," Lev says. "Our parents were really up to a lot, weren't they?"

"It kills me that they lied to us so much," Lilly says.

"Hey. They got to have their secrets. We don't tell our kids everything," I repeat.

"What are you keeping from Angie?" Lilly asks. "I tell Francis Xavier everything. Or did, until he moved out."

"Isn't he just living with his dad for a bit?" I ask.

She looks sideways at Lev. "No. He's actually moved to Chicago. He lived with his dad during the second big shut-down, but he moved out of that place as soon as he could."

"No fun with dad?"

"I don't know. But according to him, it's no fun with either of us. Or something along those lines."

"Well, he is twenty-one. Not a bad time to move out." She hadn't told me that either. Not in all this time. It was always, *Francis X is still in Chicago. It's so hard to get back to New York.*

Lilly shrugs. "We were so close. I don't know what happened."

Lev puts his arm around her. "Not now, Lilly. Let's not start."

# Chapter Seven

# Take a Bite Out of the Big Apple

We're on the train from Katonah to Grand Central Station. I'm anxious, but Lilly is cool about riding the train. It's only half full; the tickets, always bought ahead of time, now specify which train you can ride. The seats are taped off, but we can share them anyway. After all, we're a pod. I get the window seat.

The green of northern Westchester fades into the old brick of the southern suburbs, and Lilly and I sit close together. We're worried. Lev has agreed to chaperone at a distance, like a *duenna* monitoring a Spanish virgin in the Seventeenth Century. He'll hang out in front of Dad's old apartment building, and just kind of keep an eye out. We're pretty sure Jeanine won't know him, though he does attract lots of Tom Cruise fans.

Not that we're afraid of Jeanine Semple, whoever she turns out to be. After all, Trudy wasn't exactly the most fearsome person on earth. Had Aurora been of sound mind towards the end, she would have made mince-meat of the woman.

"From her profile picture, Jeanine is sort of blondish, like Trudy was. But it's hard to get a good look at her because the way the photo is taken the flowers are in focus, not her." I'm looking at my phone, and trying to get a read on the person we're meeting.

Lilly looks over my shoulder. "Yeah, I can see Trudy in her, sort of. And those white lilies? Totally funereal. I wonder..."

"Hmmm?" I'm not really paying attention to Lilly, I'm distracted by the little we can see of Jeanine's profile. "The kind of woman who posts a profile picture where the flowers are in better focus than her face."

---

## *Family Scrapbook Photo #3: 1952*

*A blonde woman is standing next to a car. I'm no judge of automobile-flesh but I can tell it's expensive: from the logo on the front it's a Pontiac Silver Streak. The woman is wearing a hat that looks like the bottom round of a layer cake and her dress is pure forties. The skirt is flared and comes just below her knees, and the matching jacket, in windowpane plaid, flirts, bolero-style, above her waist.*

*Her light, shoulder-length hair curls under in a stylish page-boy, and in one picture she's standing with her hand on the car's door handle, looking up at a brick building to her left. In the other, she's turned back to the car and she's leaning towards the driver's window. She must be no taller than I am, maybe even smaller.*

*They seem like candid photos, and I wonder if they're of Trudy from back then. She's very pretty, and even in the old photos she's brittle, and her mouth is slightly open.*

---

I look at the photo that Lilly extracted from Mom's endless baskets of papers. "What do you think? Photos of Gertrude Andrade when she was Gertrude Persil?"

"Gertrude Persil," I say. "That sounds creepy. Also, I didn't even do a search under that name. It didn't click in my mind that she would have been Gertrude Andrade, then Gertrude Persil, then Gertrude Semple."

"The other Mrs. Persil."

"Exactly." We gaze at the photos and back at Facebook. "For divorces, they used to have to have a reason, like cruelty, or infidelity. Usually the man did the gentlemanly thing, admitted to infidelity, and that was that. But Dad and Trudy divorced for Indignities to the Person."

"I wondered what the hell that meant," Lilly says. "Thank god for no-fault!"

I had looked that up. "In Pennsylvania, it's still a grounds for divorce, if only one party wants to divorce and the other doesn't. It means verbal or mental abuse that's so extreme that it renders the other party's life burdensome or unbearable. Kind of old-fashioned. Cruelties and barbarous treatment is how they call physical abuse. And the divorcing party has to be *innocent and injured*. So, not an angel, maybe, but free of fault. That's now. I'll bet it was even stricter in 1952."

"I wonder who was the inflictor, and who was the innocent," Lilly says.

"I don't."

"Don't what?"

"Wonder. We know, don't we? Dad was something special."

"I'm going to start having flashbacks like you do about Mother," Lilly says. Dad was particularly harsh with Lilly.

I have no words of comfort just now. Instead, I try to redirect. "Take a look at Jeanine's picture," I say. "Besides the blondish hair, I mean, anyone can have blonde hair, do you see any resemblance to Trudy? The mouth-breathing?"

"Yeah," she smiles, "though Trudy's lips were thin, and Jeanine's look fuller. In these pictures the woman — maybe she's Trudy — is pretty. Really pretty."

Of course she would be. Daniel Persil had exquisite taste. "And blonde. And with the last name Andrade, I don't think she was Jewish. Of course, you never know, but if she wasn't, that must have gone over like lead. The pictures look candid, as in not posed. I'll bet they were by a private detective trying to show infidelity or something for the divorce. Looks like Dad was setting a pattern for future marriages. Fidelity wasn't his strong suit, and maybe hers wasn't either."

"I'm not judging," Lilly says. "But Dad sure did."

We're starting to pass high-rise apartment buildings, and they're getting closer together, so that means we're in the Bronx, and we're almost in Manhattan. Time to get serious.

"Game plan?" I ask.

"Well, it's what we discussed. Lev hangs out at the cafe across from the apartment. We meet Jeanine, go to the cafe, and see what she wants. What's to game?"

"I don't know. I think we should try not to talk about the menorah, or Rosen or anything like that. Try to understand what happened with Dad at the end. See who she is, see what she wants. But not blab ourselves."

"Worrying that I'll say something that embarrasses you?" Lilly says.

"What the fuck? Where did that come from?"

"You're already trying to tell me what to say, what not to say, the usual."

I know she's nervous, but if I point that out I'll be condescending. If I let it go, I'll be hurt. If I don't make sure she gets that we need to listen more than talk, she's likely to yap away, giving and not getting.

"I'm sorry," she says, while I'm still weighing options. "I know that you think I talk too much. I promise you I won't."

I'm still blinking away the surprise attack, but I rally. "I know. We're all about finding out, not giving out."

"Of course," she says, and I wonder what she would have blurted if I hadn't said anything.

We definitely aren't the loving pair we were two years ago.

* ⊷≡⟨●⟩⊶≡⊷ *

It's a fifteen block walk from Grand Central Terminal to 31st street, where Dad's apartment was. Grand Central itself is busy, busier than anywhere else I've been in a while, though not to pre-pandemic levels. I feel myself constrict behind my mask. Masks are becoming less evident everywhere, even in valiant New York City, with the slow victory of the vaccine, but I sure don't trust the world yet. And of course, there's the variant, and I haven't been qualified for my booster yet. The problem with being fifty-nine, not sixty.

I still look up at the ceiling and feel my deep connection with the stars in the constellations painted in on the dome, in gold against the light blue sky. It's a sight that always stills my fears.

"Watch your purse, Zara," Lilly says. "Moon eyes."

I smile. *Moon eyes.* Someone whose eyes fill with drops of moonlight. The *Jaime Sabines* poem. I squeeze Lilly's arm.

We emerge onto the street, and the sky is bright September blue. It's warm, but not as humid as it was yesterday, and there's an excitement of imminent Fall. People walk briskly, some in bright-colored tank tops, though the weather hardly warrants it, and others with autumn-hued dresses. "I guess black is only required after October first," I say, recalling the monochrome of the City uniform from my last visit.

"Oh, it's the style this year. Colors are the new black."

I process that one for a moment. I'm wearing a black silk T-shirt with a white, soft-fabric skirt, and black ballet-flat sandals. I thought

I'd be right on the money. I realize that Lilly's long top is gold, with a red zebra pattern, over black yoga-style pants. And her shoes are gold too. How did I miss that shift?

"You look fine," she says. "Not everyone has to be stylish."

"The Lord giveth with one hand, and taketh away with the other," I reply. She rolls her eyes, but not in an unfriendly way.

In the windows of the shops, it's all Fall. Summer is in the rearview mirror here, but with the good weather outdoor cafes are still serving and we won't have to go inside. Since I won't.

"Okay, we're almost there," I say. "Should you text Lev?"

"Nah, he's pretty punctual," Lilly says, and I get the feeling he may or may not show. He was always on time when he was meeting me, when I was here two years earlier, but I'm not his girlfriend. Folks get casual with lovers.

Which brings me back to Jeanine. "Here we are."

The building has a semi-circular driveway, and a little parklet of its own, as well as a doorman, a lobby, and indoor, underground parking. It was phenomenally expensive to rent, and I remember having a long discussion with Dad about the merits before he went ahead. Of course, he was totally compos, unlike Mom, so he got to do what he wanted with his money, and I didn't take part in the leasing process. This was his deal, and he only talked it over with me because he liked the sounding board.

I had visited him several times while he had the place, and had even stayed in it early on, during one of my trips back East, when he was up in the suburbs with Mom. It was his *pied a terre*, a phrase he'd learned from Mom, since he didn't speak a word of French. Mom spoke seven languages, but I doubt she spent more than seven nights in the place. After a while, she couldn't manage trips into the City. It was Dad's refuge, his last living place.

That was seven years ago, I remind myself, trying not to feel queasy as we approach the building. We're about ten minutes early, so I suggest we sit on one of the parklet benches and wait. Lilly is jiggling her leg with nerves. I put my hand on it. "Uncle PeePee," I say, trying to break the tension. Mom used to say that when Lilly jiggled her leg as a teen.

Lilly chuckles and stops bouncing. "You look left, I'll look right," she says. "Let's see who spots her first."

I'm practically face-blind, and Lilly knows it. Having only seen the one slightly out-of-focus picture on Facebook, there's no way I'll recognize Jeanine unless she's got a sign around her neck with her name. Lilly, on the other hand, will know her in an instant.

What we don't expect is that a blonde woman emerges from the building itself, and walks towards us. I guess she was waiting inside. She approaches us without hesitation.

Lilly looks up, obviously surprised, and stands quickly. I follow suit. The woman is as tall as Lilly. She's fair-haired, and while her hair may be dyed to keep the color as she ages, she's definitely an original blonde, and light-complexioned. Her hair is cut in a stylish short bob, with a longer side, and it curls softly on the longer side. She looks to be in her mid-fifties, which makes sense.

"Lilly?" she says. "I'm Jeanine." She's got a strong New York accent, the kind you don't hear that much anymore, television having washed out so much of regional speech.

Lilly offers her hand. "Lilly Persil, and this is Zara." I take Jeanine's hand, and the handshake is limp and a little moist.

"Nice to meet you," I say, and that's my first handshake in eighteen months. I barely resist reaching for the hand-sanitizer in my purse.

We stand there a moment. "Well, shall we go across the street to the cafe, and get acquainted?" Lilly says, as if this whole thing were her idea.

Jeanine nods and we troop off to the corner to cross the street, Lilly and Jeanine striding along, trying to outdo each other's long-legged gait, me following like a baby duckling in their wake. My shorter legs put me at a disadvantage, and I usually find myself taking three steps for every two of Lilly's, but here I'm willing to lag a bit, to observe the interaction. I'm amused to see the competitiveness of their steps.

Like Lilly, Jeanine is narrow-hipped and slope-shouldered, but although she's as tall she isn't as graceful, and she stumbles a bit when Lilly stops to turn and wait for me. I give Lilly a quick grin.

The entire front of the cafe is open, and there are tables on the sidewalk and in the front, marked off with a low iron fence. When we enter the gate of the cafe I take a quick look around for Lev. I spot him inside, at the coffee bar, perched on a stool, with a foamy coffee drink in front of him. Our eyes meet but we don't react to one another. It's a little Spy vs. Spy, and I try not to laugh.

Lilly grabs a table in his sight-lines, already having taken over the hostess duties for the event. Jeanine has no choice but to fall into line, as I do, when Lilly's in charge.

As soon as we're seated, a waitress with a mask comes over. I realize that Jeanine is maskless, something that in my nervousness I'd overlooked. We take menus, and I sit somewhat paralyzed, unsure if I'm willing to share the table with an unmasked individual whose habits, vax status and care I don't know.

"Don't worry," Jeanine says. "I had it, I've got antibodies."

"Same," Lilly says.

"My mom died from it," Jeanine says, and we're off to the races.

———— ❖ ————

Lilly sits back, temporarily nettled. Jeanine has won the Covid one-upmanship. But we've also learned something very important: Trudy is dead.

"I'm so sorry," I say. "Your mom was such a help to my mother. When did she die?" I'm going for notes of ingenuous sympathy.

"Last year, in the second wave. That's when I got it too. At least it wasn't in the first wave, and she didn't suffer horribly. Just enough to kill her."

"How old was she?" I ask, though I know.

"Eighty-two, but if you remember, she wasn't in such great health to begin with."

I nod, thinking back to the fact that we hadn't seen her in eight years. "I'm sorry," I say again, but I don't say, *may her memory be for a blessing.* I'm pretty sure Trudy and Jeanine aren't — or weren't — Jewish.

Jeanine's fair skin has pinked up from the exchange and I genuinely feel for her at the moment. Losing a mother is a wrenching thing, and she was obviously close to hers. My soft heart is promptly hardened, though.

"I heard your mother finally died in 2017. Took her long enough."

"What a nasty thing to say!" I exclaim.

"Well, Alzheimer's is a pretty nasty disease," she replies. "Most caring children can't wait for their parents to die if they have that. Besides, that holds up the whole inheritance, and runs right through the money. I'll bet you didn't have a lot left."

I'm trying to keep my mouth from dropping open, but Lilly picks up the slack. "Not wanting someone you love to suffer is different from wanting them to die. But I guess you're glad your mom's gone, huh? All that big-money inheritance, right in your lap! Or not!"

Jeanine goes pale, and I see that her eyes, a honey-brown that works well with her hair and skin, are rimmed in pink. I hadn't noticed at first, distracted as I was by the glittering gold eye-shadow in a shade that I hadn't seen in a few decades. She isn't as pretty when she blanches. I wonder what nerve Lilly's struck.

"Well, we're going to see about that. You can't disinherit your own flesh and blood without saying so," she says after a sip of water.

"Well, Zara's a lawyer, so she'll be able to tell us," Lilly says, putting me on the spot. I'm about two steps behind these two.

"Jeanine, it's nice to meet you, but what's this all about, really?" I say, both because I'm buying some time and because I really would love to know.

"Yeah, your dad always said you were the practical one," Jeanine says, "and the straight shooter. Unlike Lilly..."

I smile. "I'm also protective as hell, so why don't you just tell us what's on your agenda, and we can get on with things. Oh, and I'm vindictive, too, just so you're aware."

"You're definitely the family bitch," she says, almost amiably. "So let's get down to business, shall we? Your dad, or should I say, *our* dad, seems to have run out of money on his co-op maintenance, and I'm about to be evicted. So, ladies, unless you want an eviction on dear old dad's record, and an ugly estate lawsuit on your hands, you'll pony up the dough, or hand over Poppi's co-op to me. Your choice, girls."

Lilly and I look at each other, bewildered. I, for one, have absolutely no idea what Jeanine is talking about. And I should know. I handled Dad's estate issues, all of his assets were in a trust, and everything went to Mom. There were a couple of charities in his will, a bequest or two of pieces of grandpa's jewelry to me and Lilly, the ten grand to Trudy, and that was that. It did say, of course, that if Mom predeceased him, the estate would go to me and Lilly, equally. No matter what he said to Lilly, he got that part right.

There was no mention of other property, or a mortgage, or a co-op, or maintenance payments.

I decide split-second to act innocent, mostly because I am, and Jeanine will probably figure I'm faking it anyway. "I actually have no idea what you're talking about."

"Bull-dinky, Zara. I know you know, because Poppi said you would take care of us. In fact, at first he promised to just give the co-op to my mom, but then I'm pretty sure he said setting up the life estate for her instead was your brilliant fucking idea. Nobody bothered to tell me what a remainder was, or how this was getting paid for."

I glance at Lilly to see if she's getting any of this, but she's got her *I don't do numbers* face on. I'm getting an inkling, and I don't like it one bit. I grab on to the legal phrase Jeanine's just dropped. "Well, sure," I temporize, and Lilly turns away so Jeanine can't see her face, "I get it about the life estate, though I can tell you I was dead set against it. But he didn't go through with it." I really have no idea what I'm talking about.

"Oh, but he did! Too bad you were out of the loop, Zara. I guess he didn't trust you as much as you thought he did."

I want to punch her but I'm cool. "Guess not. Your loss, then."

She realizes she's trapped herself. "Well, I'm not leaving quietly, so unless you play ball you've got a fight on your hands. Unless there's something else you'd like to give me, you know, a going-away present…"

Lilly starts in her seat and we both look at her. She visibly forces herself to settle down, but Jeanine has seen it. "Yes indeed, I know all about that prize you won in the Jewish artifacts lottery: that menorah of yours will do nicely. Give me that, and I'll leave the co-op. Of course, the bank and the board may have something to say to you about the payments, but that's not my problem, is it?"

Lilly may not be processing the real estate issue like I am, but she's hearing the threat loud and clear. And to my relief, she does me proud. I'd forgotten how deft she is with liars, cheats and scumbags. "Well, the menorah's evidence right now, we have to keep it locked in the safe deposit box," she starts. We haven't had safe deposit boxes in years, I don't know if banks even do those anymore. But no-one contradicts her, so she goes on. "And there's competition for that little item, too. You're not the only one who wants it."

Jeanine smiles, and she has the feral canines that Dad, and alas, I have. "I know. I saw the article in the paper. And that guy, the museum guy who stole it, has Covid and isn't going to live to see his own trial, I bet. But it's your choice. The menorah, the co-op, or enough money to get me a new place. Think about it."

The stakes, at least, are now clear.

"Now, all this talk's made me hungry." She turns to look for the waitress. "I can't go too long without a nibble. Just like Poppi."

"You must have a real sweet tooth," Lilly says, looking her over.

"No, you idiot," Jeanine snarls, sounding genuine for once, "I'm diabetic." And with a return of her crafty look, she adds, "And so was our dad."

"No he wasn't," Lilly and I say in tandem. "Trudy was."

Jeanine turns scarlet, and I suddenly see it. I glance at Lilly. She's seen it too. It's almost as if Dad, in profile, had become blonde and female. There's the honey-brown eyes, the sharp ridge above them, the full lips. Lucky for her, there's no big bump in the nose. *Dad*, Lilly mouths at me. I nod, I hope discreetly.

Jeanine looks away, then turns her back on us. "Oh my god," she squeals. "There's Tom Cruise!"

Shit. Lev's been spotted. "Well, act cool, for heaven's sake," I say. "You don't want to come off as a deranged fan. I'll bet he's got bodyguards all over the cafe."

Jeanine looks around the half-empty restaurant. After the nasty things she's just said, I wouldn't mind if some movie star's security detail tackled her to the ground. Maybe even broke something in the process. But I know it's just Lev she's seen, even if she doesn't.

I shrug. "Maybe it's not him, it's his doppelgänger," I say. "He wouldn't be hanging out at a coffee-bar in midtown all by himself."

"I'm going to go get his autograph," Jeanine says, jumping up from the table and clutching her handbag.

"Knock yourself out," I say, and Lilly raises one perfect black brow. "Literally," I mutter, but Jeanine is already halfway to the bar.

"She's definitely Dad's," Lilly says quickly.

"Yep. Or Trudy had a preferred type, and that was Dad."

"I didn't think of that. Is it true that you can't disinherit your own kid? 'Cause Dad threatened to disinherit me all the time. It would have been nice to know if he couldn't, even though it all went to Mother anyway. But he used to hold that over my head, knowing I was always broke between divorces."

"We've got bigger fish to fry than that right now. But if he knew she was his daughter," I almost choke, "he should have mentioned her in his will. Even if it was just to say he was disinheriting her. But I've got to get to the bottom of this co-op business, and quick."

Lilly nods. "Let's leave. No reason to sit here and be insulted." She throws a couple of twenties on the table, more than enough to cover our coffees, my croissant, and a tip. I'm reaching for my bag when Jeanine comes back to the table, waving her menu.

"I got it!" she's grinning, and for a moment she really is pretty. I look at the menu. Lev has signed it *Pablo Escobar*.

I smile back at Jeanine. "We'll be in touch."

⁘

I'm tempted to walk across the street to the apartment building and demand to see the manager, the leasing agent, the president of the co-operative corporation, someone who can help me find out what's going on. But I see Jeanine settling up with the waitress and there's nothing more powerful than my urge to get away from her.

We hustle towards Grand Central, Lilly's limp returning as we hurry. It's mid-afternoon, the air is soft and scented with exhaust and pizza, and the city is beautiful. "Want to grab a cab uptown? We can go to the museum…"

"It's still closed. After they closed it when Rosen was arrested, they stayed closed for Covid, and now they're only open two days a week. Wednesdays aren't one of them. I think only Thursdays and Fridays. Budget cuts, with the Pause and all."

Everything has struggled since the virus started. Over a half a million Americans have died, the economy has collapsed, restarted, regrouped, and reformed, and we're all in limbo. After the election we were all filled with hope, and the vaccine's arrival gave us joy, but with reality of variants and fools, the weight of the pandemic continues to crush us.

Just as we're turning up Park, Lev catches up to us. "Damn, that lady's persistent. She demanded that I give her the *right* autograph," he says, making finger-quotes. "I told her that I don't give those away. I said, *I think a Pablo Escobar autograph is even better, definitely rarer than a Tom Cruise one. So she says, Name something he was in.*"

"I hope you said, *jail in Colombia!*" I add.

"She finally left me alone," Lev says, grinning. "I watched her. She went back across the street to the building where you say your dad had his apartment."

"I think she's still living in it," Lilly says. "I don't know how, after seven years. The rent was astronomical, not surprising given its location."

"I think maybe it was a life-estate. Maybe Dad owned it, and left a life-estate to Trudy. It sure sounds that way, but I never knew about it. I thought he rented. If he bought it, there must have been payments, because that would have been hella expensive, and he didn't have that kind of money separate from the accounts that he left to Mom. But it's a co-op. They work differently. I don't know. Can you even leave a co-op in a life-estate? This is all very disturbing."

We keep walking, and soon the entrance to the terminal looms. "Maybe he had another account," I continue. "But that would have come up in probate, I think. And when he died, maybe the payments kept coming out of the account. But..."

I keep trying to sort the whole thing out, walking behind Lilly and Lev as they chatter on. I need some peace and quiet, I need a computer, and I need to talk to Sam.

Because if Dad left the co-op apartment to Trudy in a life-estate, and I didn't know it, and left a full bank account to pay for it, and I didn't know it, I screwed up. And I'm going to be very unhappy. Further, if it was a life-estate, the co-op board would have to approve it. I need to know who was the remainder-person. Mom? Me and Lilly? Clearly not Jeanine. And that's making *her* very unhappy indeed.

"Ok, so what's a life-estate?" Lilly says as soon as we're seated in the train.

I realize I've been muttering to myself since we left Lev at the doors to the station. "It's when you leave someone some property for as long as they're alive. Once they die, the property, called the remainder, goes to someone else."

"So do you think that Dad left the apartment to Trudy as a life-estate?"

"If it was a condo, yes, it'd be simple. You own a condo, like you own your house. You leave it to one person for life, and when they die, it goes to someone you've named.

"If there was a mortgage, even a condo can get dicey because sometimes banks won't take payments from anyone but the borrower. If it's a co-op, though — and I'm pretty sure this is one — it's way more complicated and restrictive. But bottom line, it seems that if Dad owned it, he somehow left it in a life-estate to Trudy, and now Jeanine is living there. And she doesn't have enough money for the monthly payments."

I'm really upset, and I'm as upset that I didn't know about it as I am about what he did. Injured pride. "I helped him through every single legal thing he ever did. I helped him when he slipped on the sidewalk, I helped him when he banged his head on the door jamb at Brooks Brothers, I helped him with his will, I managed all those goddamn payments after he died — and he never ever told me about this!"

And from the mouth of sixty-year-old babes, "Maybe he didn't want you to know."

"Or maybe *he* didn't know," I say. "We need to see the date on that conveyance. We need to actually see the documents. And how was it being paid?"

"Fuck the property!" Lilly says. "I can't believe he had a whole secret family!"

"That too. If Jeanine is actually Dad's daughter, how long was — oh hell. So Trudy comes to take care of Mom in, like, 2011, and stops in 2013. So they had to have reconnected in 2011." I do the arithmetic. "Dad was about eighty-four then. Hubba hubba."

"Unless they never unconnected."

"I can't see Dad being faithful to his ex-wife-turned-mistress for fifty-some years. He sure wasn't faithful to Mom."

I text Sam with the latest, but the train is in the tunnel and it doesn't go through. I swear again, knowing I'm swearing about the situation, not the text. I can send that later.

"I've never been faithful to anyone," Lilly says softly.

"But you had the decency to get divorced," I answer.

"After the fact. Maybe I inherited the adultery gene. Have you been faithful to Sam this whole time?"

That's a hell of a personal question, I think. The answer is *yes*, but there have been plenty of temptations. Temptations, flirtations, but no actual adultery. Somehow I don't want to tell Lilly that. Something else she'll hold against me. *Little Miss Perfect.* And if I tell her of all the near-misses, will she bring those up at some inopportune time?

"Remember when I was here two years ago and you thought Sam was fooling around?" I say instead. "Turns out he wasn't."

"It sure seemed like it, and I should know!"

I had said as much at the time and we'd had an actual not-speaking fight for a whole day. Back then, it was a shocker for us to argue like that. Now, it's the norm. We walk on eggshells with one another, until we don't. Or, of course, in my opinion, when *she* doesn't. It's hard to see oneself in the wrong.

The text goes through as we come out of the long tunnel into the Upper West Side and Harlem. In the late afternoon sun the streets are full of people, shopping, walking, holding children of all colors by the hand. We go by fast.

"So Trudy died of Covid," I say. "That sucks. But still, Jeanine didn't seem too broken up about it."

"Well it did happen over a year ago," Lilly says. "And what's she supposed to do, cry into her latte?"

"You know, she should have at least tried. The way she said it, it was more for one-upmanship than grief. Like it's a competition."

"It is," says Lilly. "Who had it, how bad, especially if you had it early, before we really knew how to avoid getting it, so it's not your fault. Otherwise, you're treated like you've got an STD. Though I was too, back when I had it. It was, *you slut, what were you doing outside your house?* It was too late to stay home, by the time I got it everyone who'd been to that funeral had it. But still, now folks understand that it was sort of inevitable at the beginning, here in New York. But to have someone in your family die from it, that's real status."

She looks like she's near tears. It must have been terrible. Not just the illness — I know how bad that was — but the social opprobrium. "Hey, it's all in the past. You're good now. And I'm glad we don't have anyone who's died from it."

Of course, it infuriates me that Angie is going back into the office now, and Derek is flying all over the place in god-forsaken countries and seeing who-knows-who, but they say it's safe with the precautions and the fact that all thinking adults have gotten the vaccine. But with Meghan being only five years old, I still worry. And since she's in pod-kindergarten, it can't be all that safe.

"Did I tell you about pod-kindergarten?" I ask Lilly, mostly to change the subject in a reasonably related and non-obvious way. "Angie wants me to volunteer to be a pod-kindergarten — I don't know — monitor, teacher, so she can go back to work two weeks a month."

"Oh, that sounds like so much fun!" Lilly says. "When do you start?"

I look out the window. "I'm not going to do it."

"Why not? It would be hilarious!"

She's a born, and now-retired, teacher, who fills in for long absences like maternity leaves and quarantines. In her district they've gone from staggered groups to all-back, but they're a little ahead of us.

"I'm not a teacher, and I don't want to commute into San Francisco to do this. All the parents take double turns, and there are six kids in the pod, so Angie needs me to do her turn one week of the month. She can do the other one. Of course, Derek is not on the list. Just Grannie."

"She'll figure it out. She's resourceful," Lilly says, "but you should still consider it."

"Meanwhile, we need to figure out what this life-estate means to us," I say, trying once again to get on comfortable, if unsettling, ground. "And we've forgotten all about it, but Rosen's trial is supposed to start Monday!"

# Chapter Eight

# Monster's Return

On the phone that night, Sam and I talk through all the steps we have to take to address all the issues. Typical lawyers, we sort the issues, concoct theories, and then set up the to-dos.

We need to get the purloined page from the Nazi album back into its place before we land in more hot water. Neither the FBI agent nor the US Attorney have answered my emails. We need to get Lilly ready in case she has to testify. Lilly is reaching out to her friend, or former lover, or whatever he is, at Sotheby's, for a valuation of the menorah. We need to look into the mysterious bank account, the title of the apartment, and figure out what the hell is going on there. This list exhausts me.

I tell Sam that Lev is laying low, and though he can't leave the metropolitan area — a condition of his prompt release from custody — he's plotting a way to disappear as soon as the trial starts. He's talked over a plea with his attorney on the insurance fraud claim that will get him out of a jam, while hopefully not incriminating Lilly, but that's a wrinkle that stubbornly refuses to smooth out.

I've told Lev to wait for the valuation, but he's a practical sort, and figures that a deal in hand is better than no deal at all.

I send Angie a picture of all the green trees, a radical contrast to the tawny brown of California September. I get a smiley face back, but no conversation. Not even a picture of Meghan doing something cute. Sleep evades me, and I blame myself. At last, it's morning.

Lilly and I treat each other kindly, and she buys me New York style bagels fresh each day. "I don't eat that much starch," she says. I glance at her thickened waistline but don't say a word. Still, she sees it. "That's from wine."

"Fair enough. To each her own vice."

I want to order a title report, but first I have to look up the actual address of the apartment. It's been that long. "Why don't you just call the building manager?" Lilly says.

I can think of a hundred reasons why they won't talk to me, but I was, at one point, the one who handled the lease—so maybe someone there remembers me from seven years before. Or actually, ten. I sigh.

"What? It's not that stupid an idea!" Lilly says.

"No, I was sighing about how unlikely it is that they'll remember me, about how long ago this was, about how effing complicated Dad made everything. Calling is a good idea. And emailing might be better." I don't want to call.

I send an email to last person I dealt with at the building, reminding them of Dad's tenure there. *Can you let me know what the status of the apartment is? Is anyone living in it now?* I'm hedging. "There's a chance this is all bullshit, you know," I say. "She could be making it all up and just trying to get something, money I guess, out of us. Dad may not have ever bought the co-op, he may never have done a life-estate in Trudy's name, it's even possible that Jeanine isn't really living in it."

"After Dad died, what did you do? Did you contact the apartment complex to end his lease?"

"That's the rub," I say. "I did. I emailed them and said that Dad had died, and we needed to terminate the lease early. And they said that his lawyer had already taken care of everything, so I let that go. I remember thinking, *Thank god, because at that rent it will be a nightmare.* That fancy firm he used to set up the trust made sure that the trust assets went to Mom, and I saw to it that everything that went to her was in order. But I didn't even know about this. God, that pisses me off more than anything."

"You're weird, Zara, you know that?"

I nod. I do know that. I don't even mention the possibility that if the apartment was an asset of the estate outside of the trust, a probate might have been necessary. That level of complexity is best ignored. But it gnaws at me.

We start to cook dinner. "I'll cook," I say to Lilly. "This way you can relax."

"You mean, you can relax because you're a better cook and dinner will be better. Well I'm pretty good too. I'm making swordfish. I just grill it, and we can have broccoli rabe and pasta with cheese. It's simple but it's good."

I don't like swordfish, especially when Lilly grills it, it's too dry. And cheese doesn't always sit well with me. What a nudge I've become. "Ok, sounds good," I lie. "Tell you what. I'll make a sauce for the fish."

"It doesn't need sauce. I'll put extra cheese in the pasta and that will make a sauce if you want it."

"Oh, let me help. I'm not big on cheese, as you know."

"That right! I forgot! Well, a little won't hurt you. Take those pills with it, you'll be fine."

"Deal, but I make a sauce. This way I can compensate for the cheese."

I make a chimichurri sauce. I slice a bit of red onion and put it in ice water while I chop the parsley I bought at the little market next to Lilly's go-to wine shop, when we stopped for her semi-nightly bottle. "Do you have any peppers?" I ask.

"I can't eat peppers, so no. But I've got some pepper flakes."

They'll have to do. I add a chopped tomato, the parsley ("You're really chopping that up, Zara!") to the onion I've drained and minced, to some red wine vinegar. The hot pepper flakes, some salt, and, "Where's the sugar?" I ask.

"I don't use sugar. How about sweet-n-low?"

I shake my head. I've never added honey to a chimichurri sauce, but in it goes, just a touch to balance the hot. A splash of olive oil, a bit more salt and it's ready.

"Oh my god, Zara, this is amazing on the swordfish," Lilly says. "You'll have to show me how to make it." She pours herself another glass of wine. "You sure you don't want some? It's been a long day."

It has, but wine is the last thing I want, and it's too late for coffee. "Got any cookies?" I ask.

"I don't eat... oh hell. Yes. Top shelf above the stove. I'll get them down for you."

<hr />

On Saturday morning I wake up with what I think is a solution to the whole mess. "Lilly, where's the album ledger sheet?"

She gives me a side-eye, but reaches into her lingerie drawer and pulls out the yellowed, fading sheet. She's left it in the plastic zip-bag I'd put it in, so it's not been damaged. She hands back it to me reverently.

My eyes are drawn immediately to the line listing our menorah. Or what is presumably ours. "I wonder what happened to the rest of this stuff. Some other items from the same address, from our grand-parents' home, plates and such, are surely gone, but look here: a silver, jeweled cup, a — what's this word, is it a fork? — and spoon set," I say, having learned perforce to read the strange German writing.

"Good job, Zara. Yes, fork. And all these other beautiful things that were taken from other apartments, neighbors surely, all crying or screaming, or silent and despairing."

Two years ago, after Rosen was arrested, Lilly and I went back to the woods of Vermont, where Rosen had kidnapped her, slashed her, and buried some of the items stolen from the Museum. We only found the menorah and two other pieces, of the many he'd taken. Those two items were not on this list, at least as far as Lilly could translate, and the menorah was clearly the prize.

Now the menorah sits in pride-of-place in Lilly's china cabinet, while outside her little house there's a war on for its possession. It really should be in someplace more secure.

Lilly has it but the intent was for us to share it, going back and forth yearly, so that each one of us had it for alternating Hanukkahs. Francis Xavier has even made a replica, an artistic-license substitute, using the old Cost Plus gold-colored menorah, and gluing painted ceramic medallions of deep turquoise with tiny stars and planets, just like my ring. This way his mom would have a keepsake when it was my turn to have the real deal. Which turn has yet to come.

No one expected the pandemic.

The ledger sheet is the lynchpin to our ownership, it connects the theft to Rosen, and it provides provenance for valuation. In a sense, Lilly is right to have kept it, but on the other hand, divorced from the rest of the album it not only loses some of its credibility but it strongly diminishes the integrity of the Nazi albums themselves.

"You have a scanner?" I ask.

"I use the app on my phone." I hand her the sheet, and she dutifully scans the pages.

"Now email them to me."

"You have a copy," she says.

"We made a copy before we turned that volume over to the FBI, but I didn't notice that the page was missing."

Amazingly, no one has called this to our attention. Maybe it's because the ledgers themselves are thirty or more pages, and they alone qualify as heritage artifacts that should not have been in Rosen's possession, with or without our page. And the other items stolen from the Jewish Heritage Museum are documented as well by the museum.

"Of the Lev Zimmerman collection, what else was on loan?" I ask Lilly.

"There were five items loaned, two were not taken. Three of Lev's pieces were among the items stolen. There was the menorah, two silver plates that stayed and were returned by the museum, and two small goblets or chalices made of leaded glass, engraved with flowers, a crown and what looked like medallions. Those haven't been recovered."

"Were you able to see the glasses on the page?" The looters were meticulous, carefully annotating the pages with the addresses of the finds, the descriptions, and specifically numbering the items. What they didn't do, necessarily, is record the name of the family they took the artifacts from. Some were indicated, but others, unimportant to the Nazis, were just identified as *Juden*. Jews. So who cares who they were?

"No, they weren't on this page, so they weren't from this address."

That reminds me of the book Lev showed us. In all the excitement of the past few days I hadn't thought of it. "Do you have Lev's book, or did he take it with him?"

"I have it," Lilly says. "He left it for us to see if we could figure out the language." She takes it out of a drawer in her credenza. "I still can't make heads or tails of it. It looks like Hebrew written script, which I can't read, but even if I can sound things out they don't sound Jewish. Yiddish is written this way, I think, but this doesn't look like anything I've ever seen."

There are a few words in Polish, and some in French and a few in German, but nothing that makes any sense or gives us any clues to the meanings.

"Here, it says Saint-Avold, clear as day," I say. "That's in Alsace, isn't it?"

"How do you know that?" Lilly asks.

"I read a mystery series that takes place in Aix, in Provence. Got me through about two months of the pandemic, with nine books in the series. Anyway, one of the policemen in the series is from Alsace, and even though he's not a main character he talks about his homeland, and how he misses the orderliness and clean streets, but loves the sun of Provence. So, the name rings a bell."

I look on the map on my phone, and see that it's near the Lorraine American Cemetery and Memorial, which would have been a significant place in World War II. It's also between two huge national parks, the Lorraine and the Vosges du Nord.

"That's around where Lev's father was from, wasn't it?" I ask Lilly. "And his uncle. I remember that Lev said his father survived the war by living in the woods in Alsace. So that makes sense."

Lilly nods, still looking at the book. "Here, it says something about *pojemnik na przyprawy*. That's Polish, I'm pretty sure. Something about spices."

I Google-translate it. "Spice container," I say. "Probably something used for *Havdalah*."

"What's that?"

"At the end of Shabbat, there's this transitional moment, and observant Jews take this time to reenter the world. They light a candle, drink a little wine, and smell spices like cinnamon or cardamom, and that eases the transition to active time again. Best part — they extinguish the candle in the wine!"

"Waste of good wine," Lilly says.

"It's beautiful. I attended that a few times, and it's a pretty nice way to end the quiet of the sabbath. It used to be a definite part of Shabbat, but now I think most of us just sort of get on with it, if we even stop at all."

We run a search on the Polish Unrecovered Art website, where our menorah never showed up, and look at various spice containers. Some are obviously silver, deeply wrought. Others are less elaborate. One catches my eye: it's gold, a lightbulb-shaped container on a stem of vines and leaves, with a bird perched on top, and what look like rubies embedded in the sides. It must have been stunning, and definitely belonged to someone wealthy.

And it was never recovered.

There's something about that particular design, in addition to its beauty, that rivets me. "Look at this," I say to Lilly. "Gorgeous, isn't it?"

She catches her breath. "We've seen that, Zara. It was in the museum. But it says here that it was never recovered, and someone has it listed there."

"How can you know we saw it? It was three years ago."

"You remembered the menorah from thirty-five years earlier."

"Because of Mom. And my ring, and the pattern matching. And because I was being possessed."

Lilly smiles. "I'm not possessed, but I have a pretty damned good visual memory. Which you don't have. And besides, that little bird really spoke to me."

We both laugh. "Wait, what? The bird spoke to you?"

"Tweeted right at me! No, really, for some reason it moved me. It somehow resonated with me. But obviously we had other things on our minds that day, and afterwards. Seeing it here in the picture brings it back. I wonder if it was stolen by our friend Rosen." She shudders slightly. It never leaves her.

"Can you see anything about a spice container in the ledger page?" I ask. It's a long-shot, and she doesn't find anything. "Still, it's gorgeous. I wonder whom we can ask if this was one of the stolen items."

"Would the prosecutor know?"

"Maybe. I bet Sheila McConnaugh, you know, Rosen's little secretary with the T-shirts, she would know. I wonder if she's still working at the museum, or was she laid off or quit while it was closed."

"I don't know if she'd even speak to us," Lilly says. "We brought down the Feds on them."

"We helped them solve a terrible crime against the museum, and just because they had a viper in their midst, and it gave their reputation a black eye, that wasn't our fault."

"You sound like someone from the wild west!"

"It's Sam's influence," I say. "But I know who Sheila would talk to. Lev!"

"I don't think so, Zara. Let it rest."

I nod, but I file that thought away. I'll get to it after this all blows over.

———— ·꞉꞊꞊◦◗◉◖◦꞊꞊꞉· ————

On Sunday morning I wake up to a shaking roar. I dive out of bed and under the desk in Lilly's guest room, scraping my arm as I go. The windows rattle and there's a spattering sound, as I imagine the windows upstairs breaking. I wait a few minutes for aftershocks, then creep out onto the rug. I look up at the window, and shake my head. It's not the earthquake it would be back home. Just thunder, an autumn storm, as the clouds come in and the blue sky turns a threatening gray.

Rain comes down in sheets now, and outside, terrible lights flash. I cower a bit, then cover my ears as the thunder booms. I crawl to my door, and open it to the whining little white Maltese, Sherlocke, who bounds into my arms. Together, we shiver on the floor as the next round of lightening-count the seconds-thunder goes through, and Sherlocke licks the scrape on my forearm.

"We're a pair of brave ones, aren't we, Sherlocke?" I say. She nuzzles me under my chin. "You're like a cat, aren't you? You're not really a dog!"

"Hey," Lilly says from the door. "Don't insult my watch dog!" Sherlocke scuttles over to Lilly and yips to be picked up. "What happened to your arm?"

"Earthquake injury," I say. I haven't seen lightning and thunder in two years, at least, and it hasn't rained at home since late April. And that was an improvement over the prior year, when it rained three times total after the initial lock-down.

Lilly raises her black brow. "Come on upstairs, there's breakfast. And good coffee. And an email from the US Attorney."

"On a Sunday? The guy's a dedicated civil servant," I say. "What's he say?"

"You're copied on it," she says, halfway up the stairs. "Do you want cream cheese on your bagel or will that upset your stomach?"

"I'll fix my own. I'll be up in ten minutes."

"Don't say I didn't offer," she says, and I hear Sherlocke whining for my food.

I scroll past the twenty spam emails that have come in since midnight that have eluded the filter, and finally come upon the Department of Justice US Attorney's email. It's not in response to mine, and it's directed to me and Lilly, and it's only slightly more personal than a form. *Ms. Persil, and Ms. Persil-Pendelton, As you know, our office is severely impacted by the budget cuts, and we have limited resources to allocate to each case we process. Regrettably, we will be continuing the trial of Walter Rosen, in which you have an interest as an injured party and material witness, to a date uncertain. Any subpoenas outstanding are cancelled, and we will be in touch once the court has given us a new date certain. Meanwhile, if you have any questions, do not hesitate to contact the undersigned.*

"What the freaking fuck?!" I say, running up the stairs to the kitchen. "This can't be possible."

"Is it bad?" Lilly asks. "I could see this going either way."

"It's bad," I say. "And totally off the mark. Something is deeply, deeply fishy."

"Salmon?" Lilly says, passing me the plate.

"Dead, old salmon."

———— ·•·•━━•❦❖❦•━━•·•· ————

First of all, why is the US Attorney sending us an update? A simple cancellation of the subpoena would be enough. And why is he sending it to me? I'm not even subpoenaed. I did send him that email asking if we could see him, but he hasn't responded to me on that. Why this?

And why on a Sunday? Although I imagine he'd be busily preparing through the weekend for a trial that's set to begin the following week in Federal Court, in a case with substantial public interest, it's just odd.

Next, to blame it on *limited resources* is plain idiotic. The resources have obviously been allocated for this trial, since it's ready to start in less than five days, and the pre-trial work that a case like this takes has been, in huge part, done. If the court itself continued the date, that would be different, but that notice would be sent on Monday.

Lastly, I've never heard a lawyer use the term *date uncertain*.

"Hey Zara, is *continued* the same as *delayed*?" Lilly calls from the living room.

"Yeah," I answer back. "It's weird, though."

I enumerate my objections to her, and join her on the couch. The rain beats against the picture-window, and every now and then a gust of air rattles the pane, but the lighting and thunder seem to have passed. Nevertheless, Sherlocke remains snuggled against Lilly's thigh, and she trembles with each gust and rattle. "I think your dog is not a New Yorker," I say.

"She's a scared New Yorker," Lilly replies.

"More like a cat."

"Hush, don't let that nasty Californian insult you," she coos to the dog.

It's a homey scene, and despite the rain it's warm and muggy in the house. I take off my sweater, donned when I saw it was raining. "It's never warm when it rains back home," I say.

"How would you know? From what I've heard you haven't had rain in six months."

I don't belabor the rainy season/dry-fire-season dichotomy. We're just passing the time, being together, not fighting, and that's a good thing.

"Well, whatever the reason for this new development is, it can be a good thing, I guess, though I'd like to see Rosen tried, finally." I stretch out on the couch. "They won't do his assault trial until they're done with this Federal one, and I want him convicted. Especially since I don't think he'll ever be tried for poor Marie's murder. They don't have enough evidence, apparently. At least not now. There's no statute of limitations on murder, so if they find something, they'll get him for it. And if he's doing time for assaulting you, and he's doing time for international art theft crimes, they can get him into court any time."

"So why is it a good thing, then?" Lilly asks.

"For one thing, we have time to get the menorah appraised. For another, we can sort out the insurance problem, and get the ledger page back where it belongs, before anyone really notices or gets upset. And for another, you don't have to testify this week, or anytime soon, which helps, again, with sorting out the insurance problem for both you and Lev."

"Speaking of appraisers, I heard back from Andres. Still fanning myself!"

I try unsuccessfully not to roll my eyes. "Ok, what's he say?"

"Here, let me show you." Instead of showing me an email she goes on Facebook, and hands me her phone.

"Okay, truly hot," I say, looking at the man smiling back from the screen. Warm smile, deep-set brown eyes, curly gray hair. "What's his marital status?"

Lilly actually guffaws. "Oh, Zara, what a pain in the patootie you are. What's mine? What's anyone's?"

"I'm married."

"So was Dad. Look where that led."

"Mom knew he was unfaithful, I'm pretty sure, thinking back on her comments sometimes. She just didn't care that much, and neither did I. It was parent stuff, and they had their life, I had mine. Which is how it should be."

"Mother had her own flings, you know."

"We have no way of knowing that," I say. I sound pious even to myself.

"You always said people wanted her to be the perfect Holocaust victim: humble, broken, or heroic. But you wanted her to be the perfect mother. And she wasn't any of those things."

"Look, I know that. But how do you know about Mom? I mean, besides inferences and innuendo?"

"Um, letters?" Lilly says. "She had letters from men who'd been her lovers. Remember, she kept everything. I mean *everything*."

"Have you seen the letters? Or is it just Dad calling her a whore when he was raging? Sorry to mention it, but he called you one too, remember? It was one of his go-to insults."

"Oh, I know."

---

## Family Scrapbook: A picture-perfect Thanksgiving 2007

*I'm getting ready to serve Thanksgiving dinner at Mom and Dad's. The table is set for us all, the red and gold tablecloth, the gourds as centerpiece, the metal owl sculptured candle-holder that Angie and I found at a yard-sale, and all the beautiful hand-painted plates are set out. We're using the harlequin-set silverware, a mis-matched, themed grouping of real silver, in floral patterns.*

*There are seven places at the table. Me, Sam, Angie, Lilly, and a space for Mom's wheelchair. Dad's chair is at the head of the table, and there's an unmatched chair for Lilly's boy, Francis Xavier, since the set only has five remaining chairs. The sixth broke at a similar dinner, ten years earlier, and was never replaced.*

*I cook for everyone because Mom can't walk anymore, and Lilly just has no talent. I do get Francis Xavier to mash the potatoes. He wheels Mom in, here you are, grandma, his ten-year-old face just starting, barely, to change from child to man. She smiles at him, it will be a few years before she won't know who anyone is, but for now, it's only her legs that won't respond.*

*Sam is getting ready to carry the turkey in for me, and Angie is fiddling with her hair. I send her the look, and teenager that she is, she rolls her eyes, but stops. I can hear Lilly on the phone, she sounds like she's arguing with someone, probably Francis X's dad. They've separated, and he's moved to Chicago, but they haven't divorced yet. Francis X covers his ears, and Angie, kindly, pours him a glass of cider.*

*I go into the little alcove where Lilly's on the phone, and I see that her eyes are red-rimmed. Holidays are tough when a family's falling apart. I blow her a kiss and mouth that dinner's ready. She nods, and turns her back. I gotta go, she says, and clicks off.*

*We're all there, at the table, except Dad. Daniel! Mom hollers. I can see that his home-office door is still shut. I go down and knock on it. I can hear his voice. I open the door, He too is on the phone, and he too is arguing. He stands up. He's over a foot taller than I am, and still lean and strong. I back up. Get out! he says, menacingly. I repeat that dinner's ready, and slam his door shut.*

*In the dining room, Sam carves the turkey. Mom yells for Dad again, but there's no answer. The plates are served, I help Mom cut up her meat, and Lilly raises a glass. To Family! she says. We join her, though that's not the toast I would have chosen. Mom gives me a quick wink. Lilly always wants the family to be together, but she can barely get through a holiday. She's doomed to disappointment.* Go ahead, Mom says. No sense in waiting for your father.

*Francis X dives in, Angie goes for the vegetables, on her new vegetarian kick that will last six months, and Sam drinks his entire glass of wine before he starts on the turkey. He remarks on the wine's quality, somewhat self-congratulatory since he chose and packed two bottles of Sonoma County Zinfandel for our visit.*

*I glance at Mom, who's stalwartly eating her turkey.* I had to compete with them for food, *she says, as she does every Thanksgiving as she relishes her meat. Every year she avenges her starvation.*

*I hear Dad's bouncy tread as he comes up to the dining room from his office.* I see you started without me, *he says.* No one answers him. Well, since you're a rude bunch, no need for ceremony. *He sits down and takes a forkful of turkey.* It's cold, *he says.* I'll go heat it up for you, I *say, not wanting more unpleasantness.*

Sit, Mom *says to me,* he can heat it up himself.

*There's an electric silence at the table.* Really? Dad *says.* I can heat it up myself? Is that how you feel?

Since you're so busy on the phone, getting "tender loving care" from whoever was on the line with you, yes, you can, Mom *says, and puts another forkful in her mouth.*

Since when are you so virtuous? *Dad sneers, his voice becoming soft.*

Stop it, Dad, *Lilly says.*

Another whore heard from, *he answers.* A table of whores.

Daniel, let's go outside, *Sam says,* let's have a glass of wine on the porch.

He doesn't need a glass of wine, *Mom says*. He needs his girlfriend.

Stop it, I say. You're not talking like this around my family.

You're not my family, *he says, and picks up his plate*.

Go eat in your office, *Mom says*. Call her back.

Shut up, whore! You've got no right to say anything, not since you're screwing Henderson! *He takes his plate of food and throws it at the wall. The plate shatters and food drips down the wall. He storms out and I hear his office door slam. Angie runs out of the room, crying, clearly horrified. This isn't the norm at home. Francis X keeps his head down, and takes another bite.*

*Mom takes another forkful of turkey. Another holiday in paradise.*

*Sam catches my eye.* Henderson? *he whispers.* The baseball player??

Of course not, *I whisper back.* The poet.

———————————

"You with us, Zara?" Lilly touches my arm.

I shake my head to clear it. The visions used to be through Mom's eyes. Now sometimes they're just my own, and so they're far less terrifying, since nothing in my life will ever approach the suppressed memories of a Holocaust survivor.

A cup of coffee and some cookies should set me right.

"Remember the last Thanksgiving we had with Dad and Mom?"

"Oh, the one where Dad threw his plate? Or the one where he broke the chair? Or the one where he slapped me in front of Connor?" Connor was the husband that followed Francis X's dad. He was a brief moment in our family life. I can kind of see why.

"I think the chair was before the plate. And I wasn't at the Connor one, so the last one for me was the plate. That's when Dad accused Mom of sleeping with that weird poet, something or other Henderson. We went to a reading once. No way would she be sleeping with him. She had better taste than that. He wasn't handsome at all."

"She may have been. The letters I have are from long before, and they're from that famous director she worked with in the Village in the early eighties. But she liked their intellect. She said she married Dad because he was interesting. Even though he was poor."

"Now we know she was miserable, lonely, frightened. He was tall, handsome, and Jewish. Not that he could say that word, but he was, whether he liked it or not. And he was mad about her."

"Especially as he was getting ready to divorce Gertrude — unless he divorced her to get Mom."

"I think those photos are because he was trying to catch her — Trudy — in a compromising situation, so he could divorce her."

"I guess I got the infidelity gene from both sides," Lilly says, stretching.

"You know, Dad was the child of war survivors too. Immigrants who left Hungary and everything they knew, with nothing. I wonder if that colored his world, like Mom colored ours."

Lilly looks out the window, where the rain is coming down like a waterfall. "Who knows. He acted like the All-American-Boy from Philadelphia. I never thought about that."

"Me neither." I smile to myself. Dad abhorred that expression, *me neither. Either,* he'd correct. I, the family pedant, had inherited his grammar obsession, along with the correct-others gene. Making friends everywhere we went.

"Back to Andres, where we started. Is he still with Sotheby's?"

"No, he's indie now. He does appraisals and what he calls *provenance verification* for artwork and artifacts."

"Sounds just right. When can we get together with him? Especially since we have more time now, with the trial continuance. Which reminds me, I want to call the DOJ lawyer tomorrow. Make sure this is, I don't know, real?"

"Could it be fake?" Lilly asks.

"At this point, I think anything could be. You mean the continuance, right? Not the menorah."

"Of course. You call the lawyer, I'll set up an appointment with Andres. Maybe just me? Depending on where he lives."

"You don't know where he lives? I mean, where did you...you know...did you always come here?" *Unlike with Rosen, whom you took to my apartment.*

"Oh, definitely not here! His office, Central Park once, the back of a Gristedes supermarket..."

"Oh my!" I snort. "So what's your relationship with Lev? Isn't it exclusive?"

"As we were saying..."

Oh god.

# Chapter Nine

# Monday Morning Coming Down

The rain has washed the sky a sweet blue, with puffy car-toon-clouds floating around for decoration. I check my phone for weather, and it's a little cooler than before, a nice sweater-and-jeans kind of day. I have a melon-colored long top with grey trim. I'll wear it over the skinny jeans that I wear with pride, even after eighteen months of semi-quarantine. Adding cordovan ankle boots, I'm feeling Autumn-in-New-York-stylish.

I come up and see Lilly still in her bathrobe, her long dark hair wet and gleaming with product. "Look at you!" she says, and in a moment of regression I preen with her approval. "Putting the bar high for my outfit today, Zara." She smiles at me, her dark eyes alight. "But how'd you guess?"

I didn't. "What?"

"We're going to see Andres today. Lunch, noon, here in a cute spot in Katonah. He's living not far from here, in Chappaqua, you know, where the Clintons live, and he's happy to meet us. I mean, he doesn't know yet that you're coming, but you are."

"I am," I say. "My sartorial instinct told me that we were going to do something today."

She hands me a cup of coffee. "It's almost nine. I'm going to do a few things, answer a couple of emails, and then get ready. Should we bring the menorah?"

I think for a moment. "Yeah. I think so, but tough call. I don't really want to take it out in public, but on the other hand, he does need to have it to evaluate it."

"I was originally thinking he could come here to take a look." I smile at her, a quick wink. "No, not what you think. Or, maybe what you think!"

"Let's bring it. Put it in a Costco bag or something so it's inconspicuous."

While Lilly's doing her thing, I outline what I'm going to say to the Justice Department lawyer, assuming I reach him. At nine sharp I call. Using the direct number on his email, which I take the precaution of checking against prior emails, I reach him on the first try.

"US Attorney's office, Caravaggio speaking."

I resist the desire to ask how the art's going. Though it is ironic, a lawyer named Phil Caravaggio handling art theft cases. Or maybe he's a descendant. I must be nervous; these flights of fancy usually signal that I'm afraid of the present situation. I snap into professional mode. "Zara Persil-Pendleton, Phil, calling on the Rosen matter."

"Ms. Persil-Pendleton, what a strange coincidence." He sounds mystified, rather than sarcastic.

I raise an eyebrow he can't see. "Please, call me Zara. I'm calling because I got a strange email over the weekend and I want to verify it. About the Rosen trial being continued."

"*You* got an email?"

I feel chilly. "Yes. From you. Allegedly. So did my sister. Lilly Persil."

"I know who your sister is, trust me. But that's so strange."

I can see that he doesn't want to elaborate, which tells me that the DOJ emails have been hacked somehow. "I take it you didn't send me anything." He doesn't answer. "I got an email yesterday, and so did Lilly, in fact mine is a cc on hers, telling us that the trial's been continued and the subpoena is cancelled. It didn't make any sense to me, I was suspicious of it, and that's why I'm calling."

"I'm going to send it on to the IT guys, I mean, guys and women, um, persons, and—"

"Don't worry about the genders," I say. "Here, I'll forward you the email we got. This is creepy. But is the trial actually still on?"

Caravaggio clears his throat. "Uh, no. The court clerk sent an email *granting* my request for a continuance. But I didn't ask for one. I sent an email to the clerk asking for a three day delay in the start because Rosen is still hospitalized, though that's another thing...but they said they'd give me a new date in three months. Rosen apparently waived any speedy trial claim, so I figured, since I'd copied his lawyer on the request, it was actually his initial idea, and ok I'm babbling here, but wow. I just got your forward. *Budget issues?* And *date uncertain?*"

"Yeah, I thought that was a little over the top. It was a tip-off to me that there was something fishy. Kind of amateur playing at civil servant. So do you think that Rosen's attorney made the continuance request, then?"

"He didn't copy me on it, if he did, and that would be a breach of procedures. As you know. But someone did. And the court agreed to it, I checked the PACER docket, and yes, we're off calendar."

PACER is the electronic filing system for federal courts. I should have thought of that.

"So my sister's subpoena is vacated?"

"Yes. But since you're on the line, to answer your earlier question, you weren't called as a witness because you're in California. Budgets *are* a little tight, and we don't fly unnecessary witnesses out."

*I'm unnecessary?*

"And since you're here, I mean, since you've come out here, if there were a trial this coming week, I suppose I might subpoena you, but I don't know that you can add much to your sister's testimony. She's a good witness. As long as she sticks with the questions, she's an excellent one."

"I'll tell her you said so," I say. "She'll be more motivated to stick with answering what you ask. She's very anxious, as you know, to see Rosen convicted. He really hurt her."

"I know," he says. "That's one of the things that motivates me in this case. I rarely see the human effects of these thefts, since they're almost all from museums and extremely wealthy private collectors. This one rattled me. I would love to meet her in person."

*Get in line,* I thought.

"Look, I've got something to add."

"Yes..." he says, in good investigatory open-voice.

I hesitate. I want to tell him about the ledger sheet, but I hesitate. There is something else, though. "Rosen is a master computer manipulator," I say instead. "He can get into systems like no one else I have ever heard of. He may personally be the one who faked the emails from you, unless he's actually on his deathbed from the Covid. It doesn't mean he's hacked into your system. What he does is fake the sender, kind of like the phishing that crooks do pretending to be banks. And there's always a signature, or identifiers, like a misspelled word or weird Russian grammar in the bank ones. Rosen's real skill is erasures. Erasing tracks. But there's some special signature, and I don't know what it is."

Caravaggio pauses a bit, not answering right away. "Ok," he says, and he sounds distracted, "I'll tell IT. I've got to go," he says.

"Stay in touch," I say to an empty phone line.

---

I look at my emails as I chomp down on a breakfast Oreo. "Jesus, Mary and Joseph!" I say.

"What? What?" Lilly jumps up to come around to see what I'm looking at. She knows that when I swear like a Catholic there's something seriously up.

"Rosen's gone from the hospital! Phil, the US attorney, he just emailed me. Look!"

She reads over my shoulder. "He was in the hospital, under guard, as a Covid patient. And now he's gone! Son of a bitch." She pauses. "My god, that's a scary thought."

I nod and put my hand on her arm. Rosen loose again is terrifying. I read on. "It's worse! The attorney says that suddenly there's no record of his ever having been there!"

"That's nuts! But we know he can do that. Remember the way he erased all mention in the papers about Marie's murder, and her Facebook page? I mean, to erase a Facebook page you have to be a computer genius."

"I know. Look what we had to do just to archive Dad's." The Facebook talk is distracting Lilly from her shock, giving her time to pull herself together.

She moves away from the computer, and waves her hand in front of her face — her symbolic way of clearing her mind. "We need to leave in about forty-five minutes. Why are you eating Oreos? We're going out to lunch."

"Breakfast of champions," I say. "Coffee and Oreos. But we are eating outside, right? I'll borrow a sweater from you if need be."

"Stop being such a weirdo. Everything inside is well-spaced, they've got the windows all open, there's no need to freeze outside. Besides, any of my sweaters will look stupid on you."

"It's not my date," I say. "Let's see how it looks at this place we're going. But back to Rosen. If he's the one who phonied-up the email to the court, and got his trial delayed, and he's escaped from the hospital, we've got a real problem. We've got a felon on the loose. This is really serious."

Lilly musters a smile. "He'll stay as far from us as he can," she says. "The last thing he'd want is to return to the scene of the crime, or if not the scene, the people."

She has a point. "Before we go see this Andres of yours, I need to talk to Sam. I want him to look back at the stuff Rosen did and see if there's a computer signature that the DOJ can use to track these fake emails. I know they've got world class IT people but we've got the advantage of having looked at this before. No sense in reinventing the wheel."

Lilly looks at her watch and I see that it's a beautiful, delicate jewel of a timepiece. I've always had a thing for watches, especially men's watches, but women's too. "Where'd you get that gorgeous watch?"

"It was Mother's," she says.

I pause. I hadn't seen it when we split up the jewelry. "Oh. Fantastic piece," I say. "I didn't know you were into watches. In fact, I thought you didn't wear one, that your phone gave you all the precision and none of the tan line!" It was her usual joke.

She doesn't answer. It's almost like she didn't hear me. I decide not to press it.

Sam isn't picking up, so I leave a voicemail about the emails, and forward everything to him, including the most recent one from Caravaggio about Rosen's evaporation from the hospital and its records.

"Want some lip gloss?" Lilly asks me as we get ready to leave.

"My lips are too thin for gloss," I answer. I never wear lip gloss, lipstick or anything on my lips other than Chapstick.

"I haven't left the house without lipstick in fifty years," she says. "I got lipstick on every mask, I had to wash the fabric ones constantly."

"I'm that way about mascara," I say. "Luckily it doesn't get on the masks. Only my glasses steam up, and then I rub my eyes, and get it all over my face. Charming."

"Hey. I'll get you some good waterproof stuff. Really high quality." Makeup talk to ease the jitters. I can only hope Lilly's friend is the expert she says he is.

We pull into the parking lot of a nice little cafe. "I've been here before," I say.

Lilly rolls her eyes, something she seems to do a lot these days. "Yes indeed. About ten times, I'd guess. Come on. Oh!" she stops. "There he is."

I follow her gaze. Oh my. Gray hair, thick and wavy, combed back from a square, high forehead, strong jaw, lean build, and clearly lanky from the way his feet rest easily on the floor and first rung of the high cafe chair. If Lev looks like Tom Cruise, Andres looks like a thinner, slightly older George Clooney.

"Not bad, huh?" Lilly whispers.

Not bad at all.

---

"So, what's in the bag?" Andres asks as soon as we've picked up our sandwiches. The cafe has indoor and outdoor seating, and we compromise on an isolated indoor table by the open window. Andres is mask-less too.

I let Lilly do the talking and bite into a really luscious corned beef on rye, the way they make it only in New York and at Wise Sons at the Contemporary Jewish Museum in San Francisco. Which is now open, though I haven't gotten my nerve up to go. Even the pickle with my sandwich in this suburban cafe is nonpareil. I miss the first few words.

"...the turquoise enameling is."

"What?" I say, looking up from my sandwich bliss.

Andres winks. "Enjoying that, are you?" He has a faint accent, and I remember that Lilly told me he's Swiss-Italian.

"It's beyond wonderful," I say. "But you were talking about the enameling."

"Indeed I was." He's peering into the bag as if it contains something alive, holding it slightly away from himself. "That process is not used anymore. It was popular in the late eighteen hundreds, and spilled over into the early twentieth century, which makes it likely that the menorah is between a hundred and a hundred and thirty years old. In antiquity terms it's not that old, in other words. Anything after about 1850 is fairly common. And Judaica, while it has quite a lot of historical value, and emotional value of course, is quite common."

I feel a wave of disappointment. I want it to be priceless.

"Of course, to you and your sister," Andres continues, addressing me, "there's no dollar amount that can be placed on recovering a piece of your family's lost history."

His recital sounds rehearsed and much used to let heirloom-clutching families down gently.

"So you're saying it isn't worth much?" Lilly chimes in. I realize that Andres has been addressing me exclusively.

He turns to Lilly. "I can't say yet. I have to see the metal with my loupe, and weigh it. If the cone," he taps the base of the menorah, "is filled with sand or something, or the arms are steel, then of course even if the rest is gold it will only be plate. That is one of the measures of value: its actual content worth. And I need to research further on the provenance."

"We have the provenance!" Lilly exclaims. She tells him the story of the ledger sheet from the Nazi album that shows the looted items, Lev's father acquiring it from the Germans in his quest to recoup the losses of his people, and very, very vaguely, the theft from the museum and our recapture of it.

Andres looks concerned, but turns his gaze, his deep brown eyes, back to me. "So, have you actually seen this item in the ledger? It must be in an archive someplace. I have heard of the ledgers, and seen them on the internet, but not in person. Do you have a website where I can look?"

I flash Lilly a warning glance. "I can get that for you," I say. "Does that change its valuation?"

He nods. "A bit. It gives it history. It gives it depth. It won't turn a trinket into a tiara, of course."

I smile. That must be another one of his lines. "Of course."

"I will give you a preliminary estimate, as soon as I see the website with the ledger," he adds. "Are you hoping to sell?"

It sounds like the beginning of a sales pitch. "I thought you weren't with Sotheby's anymore," Lilly says.

"No, I'm independent now. After Covid," he trails off.

"I had it," Lilly says.

"Alas, so did I," he replies. He turns back to me. "I am very glad to see that you wore your mask into the cafe. I was one of the brave fools to volunteer for the vaccine trials. They needed, how shall we say, healthy older men. Unfortunately, I was in the placebo group, and one of the subjects who became gravely ill. All in the name of science and progress, but I had deeply hoped to be in the group that received the actual vaccine."

"That's horrible," I say. "You could have died."

He nods, looking soulful. "Yes, I could have. I had to sign something at the very beginning that said I understood that. It was a huge risk, but I took it. I have no one, you see. I am not married, my only child is grown and lives in Argentina with his very lovely wife, Anita, and their four children, but I am not an integral part of their lives. I wanted to do something valuable."

"That's a lot to live for," I say. "Four grandchildren..." I think of Meghan. One is a lot to live for.

"Yes, but I am of no use to them, and this would be a sacrifice for the world good. Of course, being a man, I felt that I was invincible, and would not get the disease even if I was in the control group."

"That's why they draft eighteen-year-olds," I say with a smile, "because they think they're invincible. By the time you're fifty or so, you should have outgrown that!"

He smiles back. "My dear, a man never outgrows his foolish pride. And you see, I recovered. Part of the deal was that we would get first crack at the vaccines, and immediate treatment with the newest medicines if we became ill, so I was the guinea pig for a second drug, and it worked magnificently. The same they gave to Trump when he got it. So, in that way we are a lot alike."

"I hope that in that way only," I say.

"I do so promise you that!"

"She's married," Lilly interrupts.

Andres and I both laugh. "So were you," he says. So we were laughing for different reasons.

"I certainly am," I say quickly. I hold up my left hand, with my wedding ring. He takes it, turning it over in his.

"Ah. You certainly are. And here is the ring with the pattern on it." He switches to professional mode, turning it around on my finger. I quickly take the ring off so he can examine it without touching me. Though his hands are warm and his fingers are long…

"I should have brought my loupe," he says.

"So you now work for yourself," Lilly says. "Do you have an office in the City anymore? Or just from home?"

"From home. I was too tired after my illness, the company gave me very generous severance, and they still retain me as a consultant, so I have my home office and I travel to sites to see the artworks and take them to my house if necessary. I would like to take this, and if you would, Zara, your ring. I will take excellent care of them, I promise."

I hate to take off my ring, but it's for a good cause. If Andres can risk his life for humanity, I can lend a ring for a few days to help with an appraisal. Illogical, faulty, but that's what I think.

"I should have an answer for you soon. Send me the link to the ledger," he says.

He kisses Lilly on both cheeks, and takes my hand. "I will refrain," he says, but lifts my hand to his lips.

---

At the car, Lilly says, "My god, Zara, Andres was all over you."

"Yeah, I wonder what he wants."

"Don't be so cynical. He was hot for you."

"Right. It was almost a cartoon of *hot for me*. I wonder."

I can see that Lilly's put out by the whole thing, and she's gearing up to be angry with me, even if I didn't do anything to encourage him. "Thanks for not telling him we have the ledger page," I say.

"Right, like I'm an idiot," she answers.

Yup, she's gearing up. "And he must still want to be with you," I add.

"Why do you say that?" Lilly acts nonchalant, starting the car, looking over her shoulder for traffic, but I can see that she's completely tuned into my answer.

"Because he went to such lengths to make you jealous. I mean, he knows about Lev, right?" She nods as she merges onto the Saw Mill Parkway. "So here's his chance to make you see what you're missing. I'm surprised that you didn't realize that was what he was doing."

"I'm always Leah to your Rachel."

"Right," I say. "Another patriarchal legend, courtesy of the Torah. Always pitched dividing the sisters. Don't you think they worked out what was going to happen? *You go first, I'll follow, and we'll always be together.*"

"You think?"

"Definitely. So we'll always be together."

She takes her eyes off the road for a second, and I blow her a kiss. "So you don't think he was interested in you?"

"Lilly, if you're his type, then I'm not. We may be sisters, we may sound alike on the phone, but we couldn't be more different than, what's that expression, chalk and cheese."

Lilly smiles, reassured. She was never this insecure before. The past two years have been cruel.

---

While Lilly's unlocking the door I'm distracted by the idea that Lilly is jealous of me, as a woman. I know about the financial envy, and I know how lucky I am to have a good career that lets me control my hours, make good money, and have intellectual stimulation. Not that teachers don't have intellectual stimulation, but their clients are twelve-year-olds.

And I have Sam, whose university teaching is only the icing on the cake and the provider of health insurance. His Coalition not only changes the outcome of bad things in this country, but provides a very substantial income. Lilly has had three husbands, plenty of lovers, but no financial security.

The last thing I ever expected, though, is that she'd feel that a man was interested in me rather than her. I'm not unattractive, I admit, with my neat little figure, my fly-away fair hair, my big brown eyes, my bigger crooked smile. But my charm has always been in my brain.

Long legged, long haired, smooth-complexioned, huge cow-eyed Lilly, with her bountiful bosom, has never had to compete with me in the beauty field. I'm not even *in* the field. I admit, it's a rush.

"Holy shit!" she says as she stands in the doorway.

That's taking it too far, I think, it was only a weird flirtation. Though I've always been a big George Clooney fan...

"Look at this!" she adds.

I snap out of my fantasy. Her living room is an upside-down mess. "Did Sherlocke do that?" I ask.

"Don't be ridiculous. We've been burglarized."

I peer around her, and it's true. The place has the look of a ransacked house on TV. Books have been pulled off shelves, little tchotchkes have been knocked off, some shattered on the floor, and cabinets are open.

"Don't touch anything," I say.

"Why? Do you think the cops are going to dust for prints or something?" She shakes her head. "What a mess."

I feel my hands go chill when I spot the drops of blood on the floor. "Lilly," I whisper. "There's blood."

She looks where I'm pointing. "Where's Sherlocke?" she cries.

A yipping from the bedroom answers her. Lilly opens the door, and there's Sherlocke, tiny tail wagging, her little coal-drop nose quivering. She definitely seems unhurt. She bolts from the room, and starts to run around the living room, sniffing and yipping.

"Careful, she's going to cut her paws on those broken shards," I say, and head to the kitchen for a dustpan and whisk. There the chaos is complete, with spices knocked down, flour on the floor, and packets of sweetener scattered about. It's a good thing they didn't find Lilly's secret stash of sugar, my mind spins irrelevantly. It would be so hard to clean up.

"Whoever did this just made a huge mess," Lilly says. "I don't see anything missing."

Somehow it hasn't occurred to us that there could be someone still in the house until this moment, but we check, and there is no one. And no real horrors, like the ones I've read about: no one has urinated or defecated on the floor, or written horrible things on the mirrors. Just trashed the place.

"I guess we should call the police," I say. Lilly nods. "No sense in calling 911, it's not like there's anyone here."

Lilly calls the local number, and in about twenty minutes two officers show up.

"And we're back," says the female officer. It takes me a moment for me to guess she must have been one of the responding cops when Lilly called the local police the day Lev was being arrested.

"Nice to see you again," Lilly says, unperturbed.

They look around, shake their heads, and take a report. "Can you tell what's missing?" the male officer asks.

We can't. There doesn't seem to be anything obvious. Lilly's ancient Mac is open but still there. There's a silver tea set she got from Mom, and that's sitting in plain sight. Lilly goes into her bedroom and I hear drawers opening and closing.

"My minimal jewelry is still there. Even my mother's ring. I don't see anything missing." She slides her eyes at me, and I know that she's found something. Something she's going to keep back.

The cops nod. "Maybe your pup scared them away," the male says, smiling down at Sherlocke. "She looks very serious to me."

They'll increase patrols for the next couple of days, they say. It's a small enough suburb that maybe they will.

"How'd they get in?" I ask.

The female officer, a woman with a tight blonde bun and a hard look, gives me the eye. "Uh, the window?" I turn and realize the kitchen window is wide open. She suddenly looks very interested. "Bruno, come look."

Little drops of blood are smeared on the sill. "And there are some on the floor," I say, pointing out the ones near the bedroom door.

"Your burglar probably cut himself making this mess," she says, pointing with her chin at the ceramics on the floor. "That's worth taking a sample of."

The male cop, Bruno by all accounts, takes out an evidence kit and scrapes up a drop. "Unless it's the pooch's," he says.

"We checked her, she seems fine. And with that white fur, it would show up," Lilly says.

"Or yours," the officer says, her penciled-in eyebrow slightly raised. She looks pointedly at my arm.

"What? No! I cut my arm yesterday on the desk downstairs in the guest room!" I say.

"She was hiding under it," Lilly says helpfully.

"It was the thunder," I say.

"She's from California..." Lilly chimes in.

"Ohhhkayyy," says the female officer. "Bruno?" The police give us their cards and leave, and we start to clean up in earnest. I'm putting books back on the shelf when it occurs to me. "Have you seen Lev's book?"

Lilly and I hunt through the piles of stuff, and can't find it. "That ices it. This is all part of the fucking bad-luck menorah," Lilly says.

I have to agree. "We'd better tell the cops. And the DOJ lawyer, Caravaggio — about the break-in, not the book. Someone must know about it. That's creepier than a stranger." And with Rosen vanished from the hospital, we know what the source of this is. "I don't think Rosen would come up and burglarize the place himself," I say.

"No. And he would never mess it up like this. It would be as orderly as when he arrived. And I'm a good housekeeper."

"Unless he was trying to send us a message..."

I sweep a pile of broken ceramic into the dustpan, and head to the trashcan. I'll tackle the kitchen next. It feels to me like terrorism. As in *the goal of this is to scare the shit out of you.*

Lilly shakes her head. "No. I can tell you. He would be a lot crisper, and a lot more direct." She puts an unbroken figurine back in the china cabinet. I hear a piece of something hit the floor and shatter. I turn and Lilly is standing in front of the china cabinet with her mouth half-open. "Oh, shit."

"What?"

"The Cost Plus menorah? The one Francis Xavier decorated when we first got the real one? That's what they took."

Boy will they be surprised.

---

"They're not going to like that," I say about the fake menorah. "If they're pissed, who knows what they'll do next." It was by now obvious that this was a targeted action, with Lev's book and the fake menorah gone.

"They didn't even take your computer," I add. I remember her side-eye. "And what didn't you tell the cops?"

"Oh, that. They didn't find the ledger sheet. It was under my bras."

I don't believe that was what she was thinking, but I play along. "Then it wasn't Rosen, for sure," I say. He's a fetishist. "Sherlocke was in your room. I wonder if she got put in there because she was barking? Maybe she even bit the burglar."

"Probably," Lilly says. "Good girl, Sherlocke. Good puppy." She opens her computer to send the cops an email about the menorah being missing, and lets out a low whistle. I go over to look, and there on the screen is a photo.

In the picture, Dad is sitting up in what looks like a hospital bed, but from the window I can see that he's in the New York apartment. He's holding a pillow with a big red heart on it, the kind they give patients after a by-pass operation to hold against their chests for relief, and if he's not smiling, he's certainly got a pleasant look on his face. He doesn't look like he's at death's door.

Standing next to him is a woman in her seventies, still pretty, with blonde-gray hair. She's wearing jeans and a long-sleeved purple T-shirt with what looks like a paisley design down the front, and her hand is resting on Dad's shoulder. She's grinning like a cat with cream. It's Trudy, looking more lovely than she ever did when she helped with Mom. And very self-satisfied.

Down by her hand is a piece of paper. "Enlarge this part," I say to Lilly. She's mesmerized by the photo, and I have to repeat my request.

"That's one of Mother's blouses," she says, instead of doing what I ask. "She got it at Bergdorf with me. What the hell is Trudy doing with Mother's blouse?"

I don't answer, the question is rhetorical. Unwilling to focus on that additional outrage, I go where I'm comfortable. I look closely at the paper she's holding. New York deeds don't look like California deeds, so I can't tell whether or not that's what it is, but it sure looks like an official document.

"What are you looking at?"

"I'm trying to see what's in her hand. That's the apartment, isn't it?"

"Definitely. How did this picture get on my screen?"

"Obviously, the burglar put it there. Are you password-protected?"

She shakes her head. "Not really. I mean, the computer comes on fully when I open it, unless I shut it down. I don't need to log in. And you can go right to my email."

"Check your email," I say. She opens it and there's an email, already read, from an unfamiliar address. "Do you know anyone with the email *texasmytortas?*"

"No. There was a Food Network program called Texas Cake House, but that was just some delicious stuff that was out of Austin. This is different." She opens the email, and I'm expecting some awful pop-up dragon or diabolical laugh, like the old computer viruses used to have. There's no text. "That's where the picture comes from," she adds. "It's an attachment."

"Don't open it," I say. "I think we need to save it, but you don't want it to infect your whole computer. Though come to think of it, it's already been opened and downloaded, so if it is a virus it's probably already given it to you. Do you have a color printer?"

She nods. "I'll print the picture, then shut this down. I don't want it to get any worse."

"Especially since Rosen can do crazy computer stuff. Want me to call Sam? He may know what to do. And I want him to see this picture."

"Yeah, Walter is a real computer whiz." It amazes me that she still refers to him as Walter. "Use my scanner, and we can send it that way."

———— ·❦·❦·❦·❦·❦· ————

"You know what I just thought of?" I say, licking the icing off my spatula. The email address of our burglar makes me hungry for Texas Sheet Cake, and I make Lilly get the whole bag of sugar down from above the stove for me. Luckily, that high-up cabinet was overlooked. She also has a half a box of confectioner's sugar hidden in her pantry, and even though it looks like it hasn't been opened in about a year, or at least since Francis X left for Chicago, it's still powdered sugar.

Texas Sheet Cake is basically a chocolate cake made in a jelly roll pan, and a high-sided baking sheet will do, frosted with chocolate and pecans. I substitute yogurt thinned with regular milk to the right consistency for the buttermilk, and use walnuts for the pecans. The key is to frost the cake while it's still hot, which, of course, is never done otherwise, so the sides on the pan are important.

"What?" Lilly says. She lacks my sweet tooth but she's intrigued by the amount of sugar I'm using. "You're going to put us in a diabetic coma," she adds.

"It's not diet food," I agree. "What I just remembered is that you know how I did Dad's banking after he died? I mean, I had access to his accounts, he put me on them when Mom wasn't able to think straight anymore, in case something happened and I needed to pay the bills, which I did, eventually... The one account I didn't have to access, that stayed open, was the Citi account. Because it didn't have any money in it, and my name wasn't on it, I didn't have to transfer anything to Mom. I just put it on the list for the lawyer to close. But I could go online and see it. I bet, well, it's worth looking at it, because it was the one account that I didn't have access to, or wasn't on with him."

I'm wandering, partly because the frosting is ready to go on the cake, and partly because I'm trying to think of how I can access it. But I know I can. It will just take some effort, and maybe some help from Sam. And I'm betting the estate lawyer didn't close it.

"You do that," Lilly says. "I'm so creeped out that I'm going to take a two-hour shower or something. I mean, it was bad enough..."

She's getting a flash-back from the horrors with Rosen at the end, I can tell. I put down the spatula, and wrap my arms around her. "It's ok. I'm here. Nothing is going to happen. And Lev will be here tonight. We'll be okay. I promise."

She nods, and heads off first to the pantry and then the bathroom. I hear the shower go on. We both favor hydrotherapy, and she likes hers with a little glass of wine on the side.

Dad was a practical man in some fundamental ways, and a wildly impulsive man in others. A child of the depression, a son of immigrants, he was beset by financial contradictions. Lilly and I had split the traits.

When he was in the mood to be practical, he'd call me. About a year before he died, we had a long conversation about the future as he saw it.

There was no inkling, at least none that he expressed, that he would have a big, nasty heart attack the following year. He'd had one before, and had had an angioplasty. In fact, he and Mom had come out to California and done the procedure here. He'd laughed at the California way of patient care, which eventually became the model for the rest of the country. He'd been a surgeon for forty years, and had never asked a patient who would be their support person for the procedure, had never invited that support person to accompany the patient up to the moment of the first anesthesia, nor had he counseled the family on the best ways to help with recovery, both physically and emotionally. In California, he encountered the holistic approach for the first time.

"I'm supposed to be his support person?" Mom had asked, astonished. "What am I expected to do? Hold the bedpan?" She was a bit short on empathy.

"Your mother has no intention of going to the threshold of the operating room," Dad said to me. "Nor do I want her to. She'd be sketching the interns."

"I hate hospitals and I pass out at the sight of blood," I reminded him.

"We'll have to fly Lilly out. She's the only one who'll be any good at this. Of course she'll demand that I pay her way."

"As well you should, Dad. She shouldn't even have to ask." I knew she'd be willing, and was definitely the best suited to the task. And yet he couldn't allow himself to be gracious. Well, I would see to it that he was.

"Arrange it for me, then," he said. And that was how I first became his financial assistant.

Our big conversation took place five years later, well before the second heart attack overcame the benefits of the earlier surgery. "What do we do if you're incapacitated?" I'd asked.

"I've made sure my affairs are in order," he'd answered. "If I die, you're the executor."

"Not that. I mean, let's say, something temporarily makes you unable to pay bills. Mom can't do it anymore. What arrangements do you have?"

He'd never thought of that, despite having had that one big scare. "If I put Lilly on the accounts she'll steal my money."

"No, she won't," I replied, though only because I quibbled with the word *stealing*. *Using without permission in an emergency* would be more accurate. Like when Francis X broke his arm in three places when he was doing school service in Honduras, and the insurance said it didn't cover events outside the US, even though Lilly thought she bought the rider for the policy. And Lilly had an account with Mom, and used the money for the surgery. Dad had hit the roof, but I paid him back, and Lilly, to her credit, paid me back most of it. It *was* an emergency.

"I trust you, though, Zara. You're always on the level. And you're sharp. Nothing gets by you. And you're never impulsive, I know that. That's why you're the lawyer. Though you probably are missing out on some great moments in life, you know." There had to be a little dig in there, but I did warm to the compliments. After all, it's what I pride myself in. "You're my one certainty in life. Even if you did major in Golden Age poetry of Spain."

I smile. "My one indulgence. Anyway, you don't need to put Lilly on the accounts. She's there for you in other ways." And so he had, and when the time came, I was able to take care of Mom's bills, from

California, with the money from Dad.

Now, of course, seven years after he'd died, all the accounts have long been closed. But it's worth a try, because if Trudy had been accessing his funds, at least one account would still be open. And if she'd notified the bank that he'd died, they would have required letters testamentary—such as the will—as I so well knew, having done the accounts for both Mom and Dad.

I log in and go directly to Citi, but I have a different computer now than I did all those years ago, and while it seems to recognize the log-in, the password doesn't work. I smile. I do know someone who can get around that.

But before I can call Sam, I see something new in my inbox. It's the preliminary title report. I feel my heart pound as I open it. The address is right, and the apartment, sure enough, is a co-op listed under Persil... And it shows a loan and maintenance payments in his name..., and it's phenomenally expensive, but about right for this part of Manhattan seven years ago.

Bingo, I've got it right. I leave a message on Sam's voice mail. And now, to dig in.

---

## Family scrapbook: Photo #4

*There's a crack down the middle of the picture, slightly diagonal, and around the grey image a deeply yellow border is delaminating. The woman's lips are pursed. She's wearing a turban. Her skirt is long and shapeless, the roaring twenties mean nothing to a Hungarian Jewish immigrant in Pennsylvania. Her eyes are narrowed against the sun, and her shoulders are softly sloped, but her pride radiates across a full century.*

*Her last name before she married Ernest Persil was seized by her father as they struggled through Immigration at Ellis Island, a decade earlier. "Where are you from?" Her father gives the name of a county in Hungary. "What's your last name? I can't read that!" Desperation, as her father clutches the hands of his two daughters, aged six and eight. His name is long and unpronounceable, with accent marks and unlikely consonant combinations, and in his own country, blatantly Jewish. He blurts the name of his county again, sweating. The older girl's eyes narrow, her lips purse. Her mother, may her memory be for blessing, would have corrected him. She opens her mouth — even now the girl despises inaccuracy — as the immigration officer sighs and stamps their papers. "Welcome to America, move along."*

*They pick up their bags, all they have are the two little rug bags. Everything else had been looted by armies of Croats, Serbs, Slovenes, in turn. She'd watched as her mother was dragged away, their little house burned to the ground. She and her little sister had hidden in the water cistern. Two days later their father had finally made it back to the village and pulled them out, wet, hungry and terrified.*

*America was the promised land, and she would learn to live with inaccuracies.*

*In the photo she's holding a bundle in her arms. She holds that baby in front of her, in the bright light, raising her reason for living to meet the sun. It is her victory. It is my father.*

# Chapter Ten

# Monday Evening
# Still Going Down

We're at the dessert stage, with the Texas Sheet Cake front and center, when Lilly's phone goes off. She leaps from the table to grab it. I know she's jumpy after the burglary, but her alacrity surprises me. "Francis!" she says, breathless.

In the week I've been here her son has never called once. That may be normal for her other two boys, and not just because they're step-sons, given that they're as close as any birth-child could be to Lilly, but because they're in their late twenties or early thirties and one, William, has a real job. She's had a great relationship with her boys, and even with her various exes, except Connor who was a creep and we all knew it from the start.

All that is by way of distraction because Lilly is so excited to hear from Francis that she knocks over her wine glass, and while she rushes to her bedroom to talk to him, I start to mop up. I don't get very far, just through the first round of paper towels, when Lilly comes back out.

"I'm putting you on speaker," she's saying, so "auntie Zara can hear."
I look up. After not hearing from her beloved son for at least
a month, and more, according to her, she's sharing him? "He's gotten
a call from Jeanine," Lilly says.

"Hi, auntie Zara," Francis Xavier says over the speaker.

"Hey, Francis X," I say. "How's Chicago?"

"It's um okay," he says, and I recall that scared voice from a few
years ago, calling from Vermont, trying not to panic, when his mother
was missing.

"What's going on?"

"Like I was just telling Mom, I got a weird call from this lady, she
said her name was Jeanine, said she was Grandpapa's nurse when
he died, and she threatened me, and told me I needed to tell Mom
to give her a deed or something, and otherwise she would turn her
over to the police. So I'm calling and I don't know what the fuck is
going on, sorry auntie, and I wish you guys would leave me out of
your weird shit."

*Well!* Not like we dragged him into our weird shit. But his aggres-
sive tone masks some real fear. And Jeanine is claiming she was
Dad's nurse? News to me.

"Hey, not our fault, Francis," Lilly's already saying. I hold my hand
up, but Francis is already answering.

"Well it isn't mine either, and I don't want anything to do with
anything there."

It sounds like the fissure between them is more than superficial.

"Okay," I say loudly, to get in the middle and stop the mother-son
waltz. "Francis, I'm sorry that Jeanine called you. This was the last
thing we expected. Do you know who she is?"

"No, and I don't give a flying —"

"Francis Xavier," I say sharply. "Let me talk for a minute, and then
you can make up your mind how much more you want to hear." He
grunts, and I take this as assent. This is so far from the Francis X I
know and love, I can't help but wonder what's at the root of it. But

that's for later.

"First, Jeanine is Trudy Semple's daughter. Trudy was the lady who took care of Grandma before Grandpapa died."

"I know who Trudy is. I live in New York, remember? Or I did."

I raise my eyebrows at Lilly, but she shrugs.

"Okay, so Jeanine is her daughter. Trudy's dead. Covid." No reaction that I can hear from Francis, so I go on. "It turns out that Trudy and, apparently, Jeanine, were with Grandpapa when he died. So he wasn't alone after all. Which is good," I say, sugar-coating things a little. We all had felt terrible that he'd been alone, with only an unknown hired nurse with him.

"Uh huh," he says. "She says she was his nurse. Big deal."

Lilly and I look at each other. I wonder if it's true.

"But before he died, at least according to Jeanine, he gave Trudy what's called a life-estate in the New York apartment. That means — "

"I *know*," Francis says impatiently. "It means she can live there til she dies, and then it goes to someone else. I'm not stupid."

Most people have absolutely no idea what a life-estate is, and they aren't stupid, but I let it go. I do file in the back of my mind the question of how he knows this.

"No, you're not. Which is why you need to listen to this next part. If you were stupid I wouldn't tell you about it. So, as you point out, after the person with the life-estate dies, the property goes to someone else. If it's true that Grandpapa gave Trudy a life-estate in his amazing, fancy — "

"Expensive as shit," Francis interrupts.

"Yes, expensive apartment, but Trudy died a year ago, the property belongs to someone else now. I don't know yet to whom, since everything in New York moves at a snail's pace."

"And everyone says we New Yorkers talk and walk so fast, and the City never sleeps," Lilly says.

"Except during a pandemic, when everything stops," I go on. "But I've ordered a report, and I've gotten the preliminary results, so I'll know soon enough about the life-estate. And the person who gets it after that, who is called the remainder, or remainder-man."

Francis snorts out a laugh.

"So we think that the remainder is not Jeanine. Though I'm still not entirely sure why Grandpapa did this, or how it was being financed, though there is an account open at Citi, where he banked, and so I'm pretty sure that's it."

Lilly makes an O with her mouth.

"So, your mom and I met Jeanine a couple of days ago, last week, and she demanded that we do two things: she wanted us to give her over the deed, so that means she isn't the remainder-man, or woman, or person, or whatever," I'm hoping for another laugh from Francis but I don't get one, "or she wants us to do something about the mortgage, which means the account it was being paid with is out of money, or, for some reason, she wants the menorah we got back — "

"*I know* which menorah, auntie Zara." He sounds totally exasperated.

"Well, what you don't know, probably, is that your mom's house was burglarized earlier today, and the place was trashed." At this I do hear an intake of breath. "And, to top it all off, that pretty menorah that you decorated with ceramic tiles to look like the one from the family, the Cost Plus one, well, that's what they took."

At that, he truly lets out a guffaw. "Are you serious? Hey, Mom, maybe I really am a legit artist. Maybe my stuff *is* worth a shitload of money!"

I file *that* away too.

"So, now that you've got the context," I say . . .

"And Sherlocke bit the robber," Lilly adds.

"We don't know that," I say.

"Cool!" I can almost hear a smile in Francis X's voice.

"Now, tell us about Jeanine's call."

"Thanks for the fill-in, auntie Zara. Puts things in perspective."

Lilly rolls her eyes as if to say *it's not like I didn't try.* "So the phone rings and I don't recognize the number but it's got a New Jersey prefix, so it could be someone I know. When I answer her, she says her name is Jeanine, and she's a friend of Mom's and says that you, Mom, you've had an accident. I'm like, *Oh my god,*" I see Lilly's face change, almost like she's going to cry, "and I'm suddenly terrified. Like last time. I say, *What??* And she says, get this, she says, *Not yet. But she will.* And that Grandpapa gave her a deed, she was his nurse at the end, but that my mom and my aunt control it now. *So maybe you tell your mama that she and her ugly little sister* — sorry auntie, that's what she said — *give over the deed, or I'll go to the newspapers and tell them that all that fuss about the menorah, well it's a fake.* So I'm all what are you talking about? And she says, *And you can tell her that her museum-lover, well he's not going to be happy when he finds out that the menorah's a fake. And we all know what he can do.* And she hangs up. So I called you."

We sit in silence for a moment, stunned and more than scared.

"Excellent recall, Francis," I say. "Verbatim?"

He says *yup,* right at the same time as Lilly. "He can do it too."

We all can. Lilly, Francis and I. It's the world's weirdest skill, being able to repeat a conversation word for word, and Mom could too. It's useful for me in my investigative work. It haunted her.

"Tell you what, Francis. Can you write out the whole thing and put it in an email to me? It may be useful. Also the number she called from."

"Sure, auntie Zara. Ok, gotta go."

"Call me again soon," Lilly says, but he's hung up.

And *that* too I file away.

---

"I'm going to kill her," Lilly says.

I don't blame Lilly. If someone involved Angie in my life in this scary way I'd be murderous too. "I'm wondering if we should report this extortion to the police," I say. I wish Sam were here. "Or at least tell Alan Seskin about it. It's beyond our little circle now."

"What does Sam think?" Lilly asks.

"He's so behind in the story that I'd have to catch him up on everything since this morning. I mean, I feel like we've lived a lifetime in twelve hours."

"You haven't been in touch?"

"I tried, but he hasn't called me back. That happens when something's up at the Coalition. And we've been online, so whatever that might be hasn't hit the news yet."

"Secret Agent Man, Sam I am," she says.

Old joke.

"You know who we should definitely tell? Phil Caravaggio. The DOJ would have a serious interest in the extortion threat, especially since it's tied to Rosen now. Or sort of. I don't know. Jeanine was clearly our burglar, or at least behind the burglary. But I can't really see her climbing through a window, can you?"

"Actually, you know, she's as tall as I am, and if she really is dad's daughter, she could be athletic... or like you, not athletic."

"Hey, I got a black belt in tae kwon do!"

"Fifteen years ago. But anyway, I've gotten in through that window when I've locked myself out. And like it or not, a middle-aged blonde white lady isn't going to attract negative attention in this neighborhood. It's such a safe area, anyway, that the window, even if it doesn't lock right, hasn't ever been a problem before."

"It is now."

Lilly nods. "I'm scared, Zara. She threatened Francis. She's been in our house. She's somehow involved or knows about Rosen. I mean, she said that he and I were lovers, so she knows that, and that wasn't in the article, and she knows that he's dangerous, and that wasn't in the article, so somehow she knows more than she let on at that meeting."

I'm scared too. "Is Lev coming over tonight?"

She nods. "He said he could be here after dinner. He was eating with his sister, they do every Sunday but he missed yesterday, so they're going to eat at the nursing home with their dad, even though he doesn't know who Lev is, most of the time."

"Been there, done that," I say. Lilly shoots me the look. "I know," I say. "You sure did it a lot. I'm really grateful, you know. Really, truly."

She only nods. It will always stand between us.

"You're the one who was there. For Dad too. Though he never said he appreciated it, I know he did. And Mom definitely did."

"Yeah. But when you showed up from California, it was the big deal. *Zara's coming!* With me, it was always, *Lilly, how come you're not here at my command?*"

Since what she says was true, there isn't too much to say.

"Francis sounded good by the end of the call," I say, hoping to steer the conversation away.

Lilly looks at her hands. "I don't know what happened. We were so incredibly close."

"Maybe he just needed some space, some time to grow up."

"What, I wasn't giving him space?"

She can take up all the space in a mansion. But that wouldn't be helpful to say. I think back on the conversation. "How long has he been gone?"

"Eight, nine months. He went to Chicago to see his dad when things opened up the first time, then Chicago went on major lockdown and he said he didn't feel comfortable traveling home, even though I've got antibodies, and he probably does too. And he was staying with his dad, and, I don't know. After we all got vaxxed the first time, in the spring, I thought he'd be back. And now there's the variant. He says he's working, but I don't know at what. It's so weird, I knew his every inhale, his every exhale, for twenty years, and now I don't even know where he's working."

"When did you talk to him last, before this?"

"Actually talk? Not since the fourth of July. He sent me a text, just, you know, *happy birthday USA*, and a flag emoji or a GIF or something. So I called him and said didn't he have anything more personal to say, and he said, *what did you want, an Amazon gift card?* so I yelled at him that he was a shallow, ungrateful asshole like his dad, and he hung up. We've texted since, but he won't answer my calls."

Wow. I let this sit a minute. "That's tough," I say gently. I'm not a therapist, but the problem is pretty clear to me. "And what's his father say? I didn't know that you thought he was an asshole."

"I don't. I was just mad."

"That's why I married out," I say.

"None of my husbands were Jewish."

"I mean out of the insane asylum."

"The silent treatment is like his dad. When we'd fight, he'd withdraw. But Francis and I always had it out. And now, he won't talk to me."

I want to say, *I know how he feels*, but I also get the pain of a child's distance. Angie and I are having a little distance issue ourselves. And yet, I don't feel like I can say that to Lilly.

She didn't used to be that way, she was never sarcastic, rarely got angry, only said what she thought. If that was painful, so be it. That was *before*. Before Rosen, before the damage and isolation of the pandemic, before she got Covid, alone at a time when she most needed support. She's a different kind of Covid casualty.

Now, it seems like she goes through phases where she searches out others' vulnerabilities and skewers them. "Did you say anything to him about art? I mean, is he trying to pursue an artistic career?" I chuckle. "He seemed pretty taken by the idea that his decorated menorah got stolen."

"I thought he was studying online to be a paralegal," Lilly answers. That at least clears up how he knew what a life-estate was. "I told him, he needed something to make a living at, that I couldn't support his dabbling in sculpture like some rich kid. His thing right now is that art's only for the rich. If they want to diversify what art gets seen, what art gets sold, they need to pay artists. He can go on a three-hour rant about that."

"It's true, and you're both right. But maybe *dabbling* isn't the right word. After all, he's been sculpting since he was ten."

Lilly shrugs. "Yeah, maybe it was a little harsh. But still, you can't make a living at it."

"Unless your art gets stolen. Maybe this is his big break!"

We both smile.

And then we both jump, as we hear footsteps at the door.

---

"It's only me, from over the sea," Lev sings, and Sherlocke goes wild. "Hey, little heroine!" he says, scooping her up.

"We don't know that for sure," I say.

"Oh, she's a little trooper," Lev says, putting her down. "She's bit me a few times. Nothing much, her mouth is the size of a dime, but she did snag my best pants once."

Sherlocke is still dancing around Lev's legs, almost as if to demonstrate how she'd do it again, given half a chance, but her tail is wagging madly.

"She needs to go out," he says, and tosses her out the back door. "So they took my book, huh?" he says, kissing Lilly on the head. She's sitting at the table, making that action possible. Usually he kisses quite a bit lower.

Lilly nods. I guess she's already told him all about the break-in.

"Looks like you cleaned up pretty good. From what Lilly said the place was a mess. You missed a spot," he adds, pointing to a blood drop on the floor. "Hey Lilly, is Sherlocke spayed?"

"Lev…" I say.

"Yeah," Lilly answers, still distracted by the photo on her computer.

"Just asking," Lev says. "We had a dog when I was a kid, her name was Sugar, and she got into all kinds of trouble until we spayed her. Christ, that dog never stops."

Sherlocke is making a racket outside, and Lev goes to let her in. "Sorry," he calls up to the neighbor next door.

"She's been nuts all day. Especially after Lilly's sister got through the window," the neighbor says.

"What?"

It's that he can't hear from far away, but the neighbor takes it otherwise. "Yeah, the cops came by, and said there'd been a break-in at Lilly's, but I told them, no, it was her sister. Lilly told me last week that she was coming out from California. A blonde gal, and she got in the window. The dog was going ape."

Lev can't hear all of this, but I can. I go outside. "It wasn't me," I say. "Quiet, Sherlocke!"

The neighbor, an older man with a scarf around his neck despite the temperate weather, gives me a good up-and-down look. I'm standing by the window, and he nods. "You're right. You're too small. The other blonde lady, she was tall like Lilly. And she waved at me, she wasn't, you know, dressed like a burglar, she had on those nice pants the ladies wear for yoga, but they only came a bit below her knee. I like those pants."

He's hollering from his window. I go over to the property line, and he says, a bit quieter, "She had those long, long legs like Lilly, now I see that it sure wasn't you. But she had blonde hair, kind of like yours, but she was, shall we say, shaped like Lilly, but not as nice. I notice those things. I used to be a dancer. Years ago." He winks at me. "I guess I shouldn't have told the cops that she was Lilly's sister."

*Criminy.*

"Thanks," I say, "we'll sort it out." Now we know who the burglar was, though. "Come on, Sherlocke. Leave it." She's worrying a piece of trash on the ground. I pick it up. It's a scrap of black stretchy cloth.

"If this were CSI, we could get that analyzed," Lev says.

But it's not, and the cops already think it was me. And that will be more than enough to keep them from investigating. "Good girl, Sherlocke. Well done," I say. And then I notice that there's a bit of blood on the cloth. "You *are* a little hero, girl," I coo. "This is definitely from the burglar, and if that's Jeanine, then it should have similar DNA to ours. Weird, right? I mean, if she's actually our half-sister."

"You'd think you'd be more excited to find family," Lev says. "It's not like you have a lot."

"If this new family member weren't an extortionist and a burglar I'd be more excited."

We go inside to show Lilly our find. "We can get it tested," she says right away.

I mention the sisters thing. She wrinkles her nose. "I don't want to be related to that bitch," she says. "Or Trudy. Worse yet, Trudy. Taking care of Mother and fucking Dad."

It is disgusting when put that way.

"I'm glad we made copies of my book," Lev says, "but again, Marcia is going to kill me. I mean, this is the third thing of Dad's I've lost. The menorah, the goblets, the book. What the hell is she going to think?"

I put my hand on his shoulder. He's quite muscular, I notice. "We'll do everything we can to get it back."

"I wonder what it says," he adds.

Lilly gets a copy out. "Here, Zara, you can read Hebrew, right?"

"One, not really. Two, this is like script, and it doesn't look like anything I know how to read. Three, it isn't Hebrew."

Lev clears his throat. "Um, I can sound out this script." We stare at him. Dyslexic, concussed, and deaf, Lev spent his whole school years getting into trouble. Until he was actually doing jail time no one even knew he was part deaf. The only thing he was good at was math, and he used that to cook books, embezzle and pass bad checks. Not anymore, of course. Or not recently. Not any more recently than three years ago, when he was fired from his part-time job as book-keeper for Temple Shmuel, for taking a few *small loans*. Which he paid back from the menorah's insurance money, he asserts.

"I didn't want to say it before, because I can see these words aren't in Hebrew, but I can sound it out. My dad taught it to me. It's called *soletreo*. It was like a secret code, my own private writing, so it was mathematical to me. But this is so serious, I'm worried about you, Lilly. So I'll try." I've never seen Lev so serious. "I don't know any Hebrew, except what we say at services, but this is not Hebrew. Or Yiddish, either, though there are words of each in here."

"And French," Lilly adds. "And German.

"My dad was a polyglot," Lev says.

"Like our mother," Lilly replies. Aurora spoke seven languages fluently. As she used to say, it saved her life. Like the other things that saved her life.

He nods and picks up the photocopies. "Okay, let me sound it out... here it starts, *Mi amigo se pedryo. El me dyo muezes i ojas a komer. Esta friyo i pedrimos muestro anser beg.*"

"That's Portuguese!" I say. "I mean, part of it is. Or it sounds like it. Some of it I don't recognize. The last couple of words... But the rest, read it again. *My friend is lost. He gave me... what, nuts?... yeah, that's it... nuts to eat but I can't see him in any place. It's cold and we lost...*"

"*Our way,*" Lev says. "That's Yiddish."

"Or German," Lilly says.

"Ladino!" I say. "I bet it's Ladino. They wrote it in Hebrew letters, a lot of time, not always, and it sounds like Spanish and Portuguese and Hebrew in a blend. It was spoken by the Sephardic Jews of Spain and Portugal, like Yiddish was by the Ashkenazi, who went to parts of Mediterranean Africa and Greece, then it kind of died out, but is not completely gone."

"Look at you, fount of knowledge," Lilly says. Is she jealous, since she's the super-linguist, like Mom? Or sincere? I let it go.

"I learned about it in school," I say. "I learned Portuguese, we of course speak Spanish," I add to Lev, "and I was studying the Crypto-Jews so I learned about Ladino."

"Crypt-O-Jews? Dead Irish Jews?"

"Crypto Jews," I say, but that's funny. And I never even thought of it. "Jews from Spain and Portugal, who fled after the Inquisition, mostly went to Morocco, Amsterdam, and some to England. Some even went to Poland, and that's where Lilly and I get our Sephardic part. From my mother. But some pretended to convert, and either stayed in Iberia or went to the New World, where they stayed loyal to the old Hebrew religion, but were outwardly Christian. They were in Peru and Mexico, but eventually found their way to what's now New Mexico, and some to Texas and Florida."

"Professor Persil-Pendleton, I have a question," Lev says, raising his hand.

"I'm that kind of pedant," I say.

"You like little kids?" Lev says, horrified.

"Pedant. Boring know-it-all teacher," Lilly says. "Not pedophile."

"Whew!" he says. "You had me worried. I mean, I like a little financial crime here and there, but nothing like that..."

"Why would your father know Ladino?" I ask, getting us back on track. "Even those Jews who went to Amsterdam from Spain didn't use Ladino. Never mind France."

"He wouldn't. He was Alsatian. Not anything from the Spanish area. All German and French."

"Maybe if we read the rest we'll find out."

"And hopefully, we'll get the original back. It sounds like something that should be in a museum or historical archive," Lilly says.

I shoot her a look. "Like the ledger pages."

## Zimmerman Family scrapbook 1942:
## Henri et Zacarias

*Mi amigo se pedryo. My friend is lost, I haven't seen him in two days. No, I am lost, he has gone. He left me nuts and leaves to eat. I'm cold and afraid, but the shelter we built will keep me safe. I pray. Zacarias will come for me, I know. He won't leave me to freeze, to starve. If he can. If le bon dieu wishes.*

*He left me this book and two leads to practice the secret language. The language he learned from un juif marrocain. I can read Hebrew, mother dear mother made so sure of that, blessed be her memory. I will practice daily, I swear. This way I will remember mother, I will remember Ruta, I will remember papa. I will try to remember papa but that is so not clear. I only remember his smell, his pipe, his beard. So many years, four. I remember maman.*

*So today I write, Zacarias I pray for your safety, ta bonne chance, I don't know how to say that in our words, may le bon dieu have mercy on you.*

*I'm very hungry. That is the first thing I learned to say in our secret language. It sounds like French, fomo, j'ai faim. I can also say, these leaves are good. They are. They are like the oseille maman made soup from. Today I eat leaves and I find more nuts. The leaves of soup, maman, I miss you.*

*Every night I dream of you, maman. I try not to wake screaming. Zacarias taught me to smother my voice in my dreams, so when they come and find you, and they pull Ruta from behind the bed,* and they—I can't. I don't have the words and in French it would be death for me to write it. It would kill me. Death. Kill. Zacarias taught me those words first, before hunger.

Vo eskrivir la estorya de Zakarya. Si ya se muryo, la djente ke se akodren de el de esta manera. El nasyo en Amsterdam. I will write the story of Zacarias. If he has died he will be remembered this way. He was born in Amsterdam. He is like us, one of us, but not the same. His great three times grandfather or mother came from Portugal, and they ran far (fuir) from those who would kill them for being—them. Like now. He has black hair, dark eyes, and skin like molasses bread. I remember molasses bread and can't write. Fomo is faim. I know that word every day.

Zacarias speaks German, only it's called Nederlander, and it's different. Soft and beautiful. He says German is beautiful too, not the people but the language. If the language is beautiful the people must have been too, quelquefois. Zacarias says all the beautiful good tova people of Germany went to nederlander to live and now the German Nazis want them back. It makes no sense but nothing of this terrible time makes sense. It will always be this way. It will never end.

He lived in Amsterdam. He was safe until they came. His family is still hiding, and he came to the forest to help the—I will write his story but if I die will he be remembered? It will fait rien if we both die. He came to help the men who are working to ess pi eye tzel. They are nederlanders und alsaciens juives et cristiens fighting to learn the nazi moves and send that to the army. They will die if they are found.

Zacarias found me in the forest after they shot maman and took Ruta, my sister, my sister, my sister. Even an eleven-yarz boy can help he said. After what you've seen, you can help. But I have not helped yet. I only eat the nuts and leaves and wait for him to come back.

*I told him about them, how they took Ruta, and all our pretty plates they broke and broke my sister. I will wait for him. I will pray for him though praying didn't save maman, didn't save Ruta. She could be alive. She would want to be dead. She is only thirteen.*

*I can draw, that is something I can do. I draw the forest, the leaves, and I draw the plates. I write down all the words I know so if I need them they will be there. I will kill them if they come. Maman, Ruta, I will kill them if they come, I couldn't kill them when they came. I was the man, I am désolé.*

---

"I can't read anymore," Lev says.

I can't translate anymore, and Lilly is crying, so it's a good time to stop. "Look at the back," I say. "I know this is hard, we'll work on the rest, but can you go to the lists, in the back?"

The original book, now in the hands of our burglar, is a leather-covered but otherwise old-style copybook. Lev is reading from a photocopy he took, and we're looking on with our set. At the back there's a list of items, in several languages, and prices. Even I recognize Hanukkia written in Hebrew, and the word appears on the list several times, in print letters. It may also be in script elsewhere. Lev scans the list, pointing out three that I recognize as Hebrew, and one that I don't, being in script.

"Tell us what those say," I say.

"One: gold hanukiya, red stones, am of, 400.

"One: gold menora, seven, sol am, 200.

"One: gold cover, detallé en bleu, deu ___, — I can't make out the word — 500 menora.

"Two: cups silver, hanukiya, deutche con 300.

"So maybe the second word there is *con*, which is French and I don't need to translate it," Lev says. "I don't know what the other short words mean."

Lilly looks at the words a minute. I may be good with language, but she's stellar. "I think they're abbreviations," she says. *Deu* could be God, but it could be short for Deutche, obviously German. And then where it says *deutche con*, that's German cunt. Or prick. The French are liberal that way. Also asshole. All of the above. So yeah, the word that's scrawled, that's *con* again. So those two menorahs he bought from a German whatever."

"Sounds about right," Lev says. "That's what he called them."

"Like us in Spanglese," I say. "Lilly and I spoke a mix of Spanish and English to each other, like a lot of kids in Texas and the Mexican border cities. Your dad spoke Germench!"

"Yeah, also known as Alsatian," he replies.

"American officer," Lilly says. "That's what the *am of* is. There are other places where it's more spelled out. In English. *Sol am* would be *soldat americain.* American soldier. See, here, and here, it's written out more, in partial words. So he bought some items from Germans, some from Americans."

"And the dates make sense," Lev says. "They start as early as 1945, around the time of the liberation of Paris, and end in mid-1947, when he left France and emigrated to the US."

"I wonder if any of these are ours," I say. "He could have bought it later, once he was in the States."

"No," Lev says. "The menorah was special, and he bought it in Paris. That I know for sure. I can only guess that it's the one that says, *gold cover, blue details, from a German prick for 500 menorah.*"

"If the five hundred is francs, in late 1945, let me look it up," I say. "I know that they devalued the money after the end of the war, and it was, here it is, yeah, about one hundred twenty francs to the dollar."

"Look at you," Lilly says.

"I remember that the US tried to get them to use dollars, or something. Charles de Gaulle stopped that right quick," I say.

"US Occupation Francs," Lev says. He surprises us all the time.

"I wish we could ask your dad," Lilly says.

"I wish I could ask him lots of things," Lev says. "Including I wish he knew who I was."

Lilly puts her arm around him, and kisses his cheek tenderly. I look away.

"Don't be embarrassed, you child!" she says to me. I can't tell her that I'm sick with jealousy. She used to love me. *I'm so greedy*, I think. Here I have Sam, and Angie and Meghan, and I'm jealous of Lilly giving any affection to Lev. She who has no one. Not really. Even Francis Xavier has turned against her.

"Anyone want some seconds on cake?"

<hr />

It's after eleven, Lev and Lilly have gone off to bed, and I'm just about to turn in as well, having been here long enough to adjust to New York time. The little guest room in Lilly's basement is sparsely decorated. There are two single beds, and I mean *single*, not twin, the narrow mattresses favored by dorm rooms, in addition to that desk that sheltered me and Sherlocke from the thunder, and a rack on wheels for clothes. Lilly hasn't exactly splurged, and the sheets have a faint moldy aroma from being in the basement. Although the room is below grade, it's also somewhat warm, probably from the humidity, but I don't want to leave the door open because I can do without Sherlocke's messy kisses early in the morning.

One thing I can say for the room, with the door shut the sounds of the rest of the house disappear. Not so with the door open, and as I cross from the bathroom to the room after my shower (*my only advice for marriage is to shower before bed*, Aurora had told me the night before my wedding, even though I'd been living with Sam for three years by then) I can hear Lilly and Lev talking in her room.

It's not pillow-talk, either.

*But we can't give back the money*, Lilly's saying. *It's spent.*

*All of it?* Lev asks.

*No, not all. But you spent some of yours too.*

*Why don't we each give back half? This adds up to fifty grand. Alan's negotiating, and I think he thinks they'll take that.*

*Zara says there's another way. She says if it's worth a hundred, there's no problem.*

*But how can we convince them? I put fifty on the valuation, and I thought that was high.*

*I've got a friend. I think he'll say it's worth a hundred.*

*Another one of your friends,* Lev says. I don't hear her answer. He laughs.

My cell phone rings, it's Sam, and I shut my door.

<hr />

"Thank goodness! Where've you been?" I ask. "Hell's a poppin' here."

"Flying."

"What? Where?"

"I'm driving up from Kennedy. I'll be there in less than an hour."

"Here?"

"Where else? Things have gotten too nuts from your messages and emails. So I got on a plane and here I am. Or will be."

I'm glad. But also not happy. "Why didn't you tell me? Or ask?"

"Ask? What — for permission to come to New York?"

True, it isn't like I own the place. And I actually wanted him to come. I would have asked him to. But it's infuriating, and he'll never understand why. "Good, I'm glad. But I wish you'd at least told me first. I'll go tell Lilly. I mean, it is her house."

"I thought you'd be pleased. I can't believe you're acting this way," he says. "I thought you'd like the surprise. And things sound like they're going to shit there." He sounds petulant, which is not his normal reaction to things.

I sigh, and realize that his defensiveness is almost an acknowledgement that I'm right. "I'll see you when you get here. Everyone's in bed already, so just text me and I'll open the door for you."

After we hang up I text Lilly. Even though she's right upstairs from me, I don't go up, since Lev's there. She just texts back a thumbs up.

I'd told her in the text that I'd make up the other single bed, so I go back upstairs in search of sheets and towels. Everything in this house is above my head, and that includes the sheets in the little linen closet off the hall next to Lilly's room. Unlike the orderly way Lilly keeps the rest of the place, the sheets and blankets are all upside-down and topsy-turvy. Maybe the burglar hadn't missed this closet, and had messed up the sheets. The burglar, meaning Jeanine.

As quietly as possible I pull the ottoman from her living-room so I can get up on it to get down the single sheets without bringing all the linens down on my head. The top of the sheet is caught on something, and I can't pull it loose. There's something there behind the sheets. Something hard and metallic. I reach back behind the sheets and when I pull forward, whatever they were stuck on yields, and the sheets come tumbling down despite all my care. The metal square comes with it. There before me is a brass spice box. *What the heck?*

I climb down from the ottoman and examine the find. It's extraordinary, even more elaborate than the menorah, but brass, not gold, enhanced with the same turquoise enamel as my ring and the menorah, and with tiny stars of David instead of little planets. On the bottom there are little blue and gold birds. It's got tarnish on the one side, and grotesquely, what looks like a streak of dried blood on the other. And I see why. The top of the container, where the lid would attach, is sharp, like the lid had been torn from its hinges, and then replaced. I didn't cut myself only because I was pulling it from the bottom.

The container is about six inches top to bottom, counting its little legs, and there's something familiar about it beyond the use of that rare turquoise enamel, but I can't place it. I pick up the sheets and another item, much smaller, tumbles out.

It's the bird spice container, gold with rubies, from the website of never-recovered objects.

I hear my phone ringing. I grab the sheets, toss the contraband back on the top shelf with some other linens, and run downstairs for my phone. I expect it's Sam, though I told him to text when he gets here, not call, but it's not. It's Francis Xavier. I toss the sheets on the cot.

"Hey sweetie," I say, out of breath. "What's up?" His calls are never good, and there's no such thing as a good call after midnight.

"Auntie Zara," he says, and he sounds a little drunk, "I need to tell you something. Something I couldn't tell my mom when I called. Can you talk?"

"Uh, sure, Francis. What's on your mind?" Probably the last thing I need, I think.

"Two things, really. First one, when that lady called me, she said some real shit things about Grandma and Grandpapa. Real shit. It made me really mad. Like that Grandma was a whore in Germany, that she screwed German soldiers for food, and that she kept right on going once she was married."

"Oh for god's sake!" I say. "What's wrong with that woman? No, Francis, that's not what happened. And I don't know why she'd say that to you. What good would that do her?"

"I dunno, auntie Zara. I don't know. She kept saying that Grandpapa, though she called him Poppi, he loved Aurora, as she said, *Poppi loved Aurora, she never loved him back, and he loved her anyway. And my mom* — this was what she was saying — *she loved Poppi and took good care of him and never left him.*"

"She's a basket case, Francis. She's a nut. Put it out of your mind. Your mom and I will deal with this."

"Don't tell her! She'll go ballistic! She always says Grandpapa didn't love her, and that's why she couldn't stay married to my dad, she didn't know how to love any man..."

*Why would Lilly be laying that on her son?*

"And that's why I'm scared to tell her. About...about me."

"What about you, Francis?" I knew. I knew but couldn't say.

There's a thick silence on the line, then a sob, and a hiccup.

"I came out in Chicago. Dad understands. He says, well, he says he felt that way sometimes too. About guys. I knew that in my bones. So I went to Chicago so I could come out. Mom will kill me."

*Of course.*

"No, sweetie. She won't kill you. She'll be fine with it."

"But after what that lady said about Grandpapa, and all that, it's...well...I *had* to tell you. It explains everything. It's all my fault, but it explains everything." He's crying, and this all comes out in gulps.

It's all I can do not to say, "No shit, Sherlock." Or Sherlocke. Instead, I say, "Of course you're gay. I knew that. Your mom probably knows that. And she's fine with it. And so am I. And none of this is your fault, and the fact that Grandpapa didn't show love to his daughter, and Grandma didn't show love to anyone, and that your dad has always been a little mixed up on that score —"

"Hey, don't say my dad's mixed up."

"But none of that has anything to do with you. You know that. Read up on it, join a support group or something. But nowadays, it's no big deal, really."

"Not to anyone except the person who has to deal with it."

"True, Francis X. You have a point. But really, it's going to be okay. Just go to bed, and we'll talk in the morning."

"Goodnight, auntie Zara."

My text goes off just as I'm saying goodnight to Francis X. Sam's out in the driveway, and he's sorry he sprung his trip on me.

I *heart* him back, and go open the garage door.

# Chapter Eleven

# All Together Now

"I'm sorry," are the first words Sam says to me. "You're right. I should have told you. It was meant well, but I get it."

I kiss him. "You already texted that. I'm glad you're here."

"I thought of staying at a hotel in the City, but that didn't make any sense either," Sam says, and I've rarely seen him so disorganized.

I marshal my thoughts. "I have a lot to fill you in on," I say finally. "But first, come in, get yourself settled. It's only nine in California, you're probably starving. Lilly has a bunch of weird food in her fridge. Do you want a sandwich? And I made a Texas sheet cake, the one where the icing caramelizes on top. It's amazing with coffee." I'm babbling. It *has* been a long day.

Sam shakes his head. "I'll leave the sweets to my sweet," he smiles, "and take that sandwich. And a beer."

He settles his bags into the small bedroom and joins me upstairs in Lilly's kitchen. "Her bedroom is right there," I say, pointing, "and Lev's with her, so let's take this downstairs to her TV area, and we can talk."

Once he's set up, I ask him, "And why are you really here?"

"You've been married to me for forty-some years, so I'm not surprised you guessed. Yes, there are problems that it would be good for me to be in New York to help sort out. Remember how they were about to sell some major Trump assets last fall, but held off because there was too much uncertainty? Well, it turns out that there's some covert Russian debt on some of the most important properties in both New York and San Francisco, and the Coalition doesn't want this to go unnoticed."

"While the Coalition itself goes unnoticed," I say. It's a complicated financial and political web, right up Sam's Coalition's alley, but not the sexiest issue on earth.

"Obviously. But that got me into a bunch of back-room banking systems, and we were able to track almost all the debt, and while I was there, guess what I found?" I'm afraid to ask. "A notice of default on your dad's old apartment, showing that payments haven't been made on the unit for, well, about four months. And not just that, but the building itself, since it's a co-op, which is similar to a condo back home —"

"With some pretty significant differences," I say. "For one thing, the co-op corporation can get a mortgage on the whole building, unlike a condominium association, but the buyer of a unit has shares and a proprietary lease, and a loan against the shares that isn't exactly a mortgage," I say.

"Exactly. And unfortunately, guess what? In your dad's building, some of the shareholders are part of that syndicate that owns the properties that Trump and his buddies are trying to unload. And that may or may not belong to the Russians. So..."

It's almost one in the morning. Maybe that's why this is all leaving me in the dust. "Why couldn't this be simple? But that has nothing to do with me or Lilly. Or ultimately, who owns the apartment."

He pulls me toward him. "It does, sort of. I was worried about you. Now that I know that there's some political, and Russian, involvement in that property your dad had, and that his, um, other daughter is up to something and wants it... And most important,

I got the copy of the shares document. Congratulations, Zara. You and your sister are now the proud owners of an apartment in New York City, complete with a loan in default, maintenance In arrears, and a Russian connection."

"We are? Wow!" is the first thing I say. I am learning the meaning of *nonplussed* first-hand. "You waited to tell me this?"

"I flew to New York to tell you this!"

"And to play Captain America. But okay." I'm still thinking slowly, I'm having a hard time taking it in. "So Lilly and I are the remainders?"

He gets up and pulls his phone from his pocket. "Here you are. Lilly's not going to like this." I peer at the small screen, and see that indeed we're the remainders. But not equally. I'm ninety percent, Lilly's ten percent.

"He never quit, did he? Why did he do this? Why didn't he make Mom the remainder? That's strange. He left everything else to her."

"Well, with Trudy having a life-estate, and her being almost ten years younger than your mom, who was already ill, he must have figured that Trudy'd outlive Aurora. And, of course, he wouldn't want Aurora to know that he'd bought an apartment with marital property money. Right? And left it to his mistress…"

"Good point," I sigh. "But now I own that fancy, outrageously expensive apartment?" I shake my head. "Wait until I tell you the rest."

I fill Sam in on everything I can think of, from the break-in to the spice containers, to Sherlocke, and last, to Francis Xavier, including his awkward, teary, and likely booze-fueled coming out to me.

"No surprise there," Sam says.

"Only to himself," I say. "Denial is an amazing thing. And now, Rosen's left the hospital, and is nowhere to be found, and no one is overly excited about the fact that there's a deranged killer on the loose. And how did Jeanine know he had Covid? And are they connected?"

"Well, now that we know she's a nurse…" he says.

"If she actually is."

"Easy enough to find that out. Hold on." Ten minutes later, Sam shows me her license. Is there anything he can't find? "An LVN. Licensed vocational nurse. So, not an RN, a few levels down. We call them Licensed Practical Nurses at home. Hard, hard work, none of the pay that an RN gets, but it only takes a couple of years of schooling, especially since she's been licensed since 1980."

"Where did she work? Any way to find that?"

He clicks a bit. "NYU Langone, for several years, nothing I can find after 2014."

Makes perfect sense to me. Langone is two blocks from Dad's apartment, that was where he went after his heart attack, for the bypass surgery. And 2014 is when he died. I start to shiver. I'm actually unbelievably angry. Sam wraps his arms around me, and I'm reminded of his solid, comforting steadiness. A rock in a stormy ocean.

"Can you see if Rosen was there? There's apparently no record of his being in any hospital. Caravaggio says that he disappeared, but not before continuing his own trial with the court. We know he can do magic with computers, but this is unparalleled."

"He may do *magic*," Sam says, and I have to smile at the annoyance in his voice, "but he leaves a trail. Every time. So all we need to do is follow it. I can't do that on my phone, though. I'll take a look tomorrow, after my meeting."

"You have a meeting tomorrow? You just got in, it's already after one in the morning. What time is this meeting?"

"Unfortunately, around eight. So I'll leave here at seven or so. I'd better get to bed, I guess, though I'm not tired — it's only ten thirty at home."

"Yeah, but you'll have to get up at six and that will be three a.m. at home. More or less your bedtime."

"What do you have going tomorrow? I should be back by about two."

"Nothing. But the phone rings all the time, and things are changing by the minute. We've got to figure out what to do about Jeanine, now that I know about the co-op. I'm scared that she's going to come back. I'm pretty sure she was our burglar, but what's her connection to Rosen? And somehow, I need to talk to Lilly about those spice holders, get the ledger sheet back to the FBI agent, and not run into Rosen. Sort of your basic day."

Sam is up and gone, and I'm sitting in Lilly's kitchen drinking her good coffee, and looking out the window at the beautiful blue fall sky. When Sam and I moved out West there was very little I missed: Mom, real rye bread, and the autumn. I begin thinking about bread, and look up a recipe for a sourdough rye that I once made back home. I can improvise a starter with milk and yeast and some rye flour, and let it ripen a couple of days, and by Friday I can make real rye. Or, I can start some flour, water and onions now, and add some yogurt for a quick starter. Or, I think, as I slice the onion, since we're in New York, we can just buy one.

Lilly emerges from her room, stops short when she sees me. "What are you doing up?"

"It's eight already," I say. We both laugh. I'm never up at this hour in New York, no matter how long I've had to get over jet lag. "No, actually, even though Sam got here late last night, he had an early meeting this morning, so he had to leave at seven."

"Secret Agent Man, Sam I am," she says. "Well, I hope that I didn't disturb you too much last night."

"Hint hint? Didn't hear a thing. But did we bother you?"

"I heard you get the sheets...oh. Uh, you got the sheets?"

I nod. She fiddles with the coffeemaker, humming a little bit. Almost like Winnie the Pooh, humming a little tune, hoping not to be noticed. I only last a few moments before I break down and ask.

"What are those spice holders doing in your closet? They're on the list from Lev's dad, aren't they?" She nods. "And you were playing dumb with the bird one that we saw on the Polish Unrecovered Art site, weren't you?"

Lilly bites her lip. She has beautiful lips, full and red, and she looks like Sophia Loren in a pout. "I, um, shit, Zara."

"Yeah. That about sums it up. Where did you get them?"

She doesn't answer. I can't believe it.

Lev comes out of her bedroom, wearing only boxer shorts. I don't even care that he's lovely. He grins and waves, and heads to the bathroom. "Not so fast, buddy," I say. He stops and turns around. "Where'd you guys get the two spice containers?"

He blinks his cobalt blue eyes at me, raises his eyebrow at Lilly, and walks away. The bathroom door shuts, locks.

"Son of bitch, Lilly. Don't tell me. Don't tell me that you guys, oh for god's sake…"

Lilly shakes her head and goes back to doing unnecessary things to the coffee maker. "It's not a great story, but they are his, after all. So he's entitled to them."

I close my eyes. "Okay, Lilly. That's enough. Don't tell me anything else, okay? I don't want to be complicit."

"Complicit? *Complicit?* You're more that complicit. You're practically the problem. You'll run right to the cops, to Caravaggio, to the fucking FBI, won't you. You'd turn your own family in, just so you can be *right*. So of course I couldn't tell you."

That was an abrupt change of mood. Sort of the thing that can only happen to a long-married couple, or to sisters. "So we're back to that. But where did you find them?" I say, very softly.

"I didn't. Lev, well, he got them from, well…"

After we stumbled into breaking up Rosen's artifact-stealing career, only Lev's — or our — menorah was recovered. Or so I thought. At least now I know why Lilly didn't want Lev to contact Sheila, Rosen's tiny assistant. Though she was on the right side of the law, this four-foot-eight admin knew everything that had been in the collection, everything that Marie had stolen, and what had and hadn't been recovered.

"How did he get them? When?"

"When Marie came out to Cranford that night, to give Lev his heirlooms back once the insurance claim had been made, Lev was supposed to meet her at Temple Shmuel. When he got there she was dead. We know this, right? Okay, but the items she was supposed to turn over to Lev? The menorah, the goblets? He found the spice containers in the bushes."

"Why is this the first I've heard of this?"

"Because, Zara. Because he didn't tell me. If you must know. He brought them here after the insurance company paid up. Because he was investigated for insurance fraud, remember? And if they had a warrant and searched his house, they'd find them. So, about two months ago, he put them here."

What can I say? I asked. Now I know. No wonder they both freaked when the Feds came to arrest Lev at Lilly's house.

I could just see it, both of them praying, *Sure, arrest Lev, but please don't search the house, please don't search the house!* "How much did he get for the insurance on them?" She doesn't answer. So I ask the follow-up. "And how much did you get?"

"I'm done talking about this," Lilly says.

So, what was a simple insurance fraud scheme — should such a thing exist — is now a living, breathing nightmare. What else could go wrong?

I get another cup of coffee and go downstairs. I don't want to sit with Lilly, and I'm curious about the co-op question on Dad's apartment. I also realize that I haven't told Lilly about it, or about it being in the portfolio of properties Trump is trying to sell to manage his billions of dollars of debt, and most of all, I haven't mentioned that we're remaindered on the apartment, in vastly different proportions.

I open my email. And of course, Agent Skordall of the FBI would like to see us. Today if possible. Tomorrow if not. Or, of course, they can come to us.

"No way," I say out loud.

"What?" Lilly has appeared behind me in the TV area.

"Agent Skordall, her gorgeous self, would like to see us today. Or tomorrow. Or they can come here, which is what I just said *no way* to."

Lilly comes and sits by me on the couch. "Hey. I'm sorry. I really am."

I'm still fuming. Why is it that I have to forgive on her timeline? But then again, why not? "Okay, but for what?" At least I should get to know what the apology is for. I can think of so many things that would warrant it.

"It's been a hard year and a half. Hell, it's been a hard bunch of years, ever since Mother died."

I know that. It's been hard for me too, though if I truly parse it, it's been a lot harder on Lilly. A broken leg that left her with a limp. A scar on her chest in the shape of a part of a swastika. Money problems. Issues with her most cherished son, the extent of which she still doesn't know. Having a convicted felon as a lover, who, personable as he is, apparently hasn't changed his spots.

I've had my own issues, but nothing like hers. "I get it."

"No, I don't think you really do." There went the apology. Though I don't say it, she must have heard my thoughts. "But regardless, none of this is your fault, Zara. I can't stand that you're so judgmental, but I've certainly given you things to be judgmental about. And then I've lashed out at you, before you could even judge. Because obviously, I'm judging myself. And for lashing out at you, I'm sorry."

Even her apology is about her. But it's an apology, and it's a recognition that she's lashed out. "I know I'm judgmental. I wish I weren't. It's like your — " I stop myself before I say *your lack of ethics.* "It's like your willingness to go along with other people's schemes, even though you eventually get snared by them. It's something we do. But I don't want to be enemies with you. We're all we've got left of the original family."

Lilly puts her hand on mine.

"Though not quite," I add. "We've just gained a half-sister."

Lilly laughs, and we're united in our outrage for a moment. And then I think, *wait until she finds out how this is remaindered.* I don't want to tell her, but eventually I'll have to. Besides, there's so much more to tell her about the apartment: The co-op; the loan; the default; the association of the building with the now-non-President, may the Lord be thanked.

"Well, what do you want to do? Should we go see Agent Skordall and give her the ledger sheet? Or do we have anything else to do today?" I ask. I think about the onions I sliced before Lilly and I started going at each other.

Lilly ponders for a moment. "I guess we should just get it over with."

"Yeah. We can call it an honest mistake. But don't say anything about, well, anything, ok? Maybe I should go alone? But then, you're the one with the ledger page..." And I don't want to be blamed.

"No, let's both go together. It's down towards Wall Street, isn't it? Near the Freedom Towers?" I nod. "That's a long haul."

"Last week was the twentieth anniversary of 9/11. Maybe I'd like to see the Towers."

"I'll go with you. We can leave Lev at Grand Central and he can go home. Better away, I think."

I nod. "Definitely."

I hear Lev coming down the stairs to join us. "Hey Lev," I say, turning to face him, "have you heard anything on the charges against you? Have they been formally dropped?"

Lev answers from the foot of the stairs. "Not yet. But Alan says it just needs some signatures."

"If Lev can get off, there's no reason to think that you'll be indicted," I say to Lilly. "Though it still seems pretty weird, Lev, that they arrested you and released you and dropped your case all in about five hours."

"Yeah, I thought the wheels of justice were supposed to move slowly," Lilly says.

*But they grind exceedingly fine.*

<hr />

While we're on the train, the three of us, my mind churns with terrible thoughts. I finger the toothbrush I've rolled into a change of underwear, tucked in my purse. I mean, what if they arrest us? Why would they, I remind myself, but still, I've brought supplies. I wonder if I'd be allowed to keep them. *Stop that, you lunatic!*

Chiding myself doesn't help: my next thought is only barely better. Did Lev sell out Lilly? Is that how he got off so quickly? Did I dare ask him? And would he even tell me?

That would be something to ask... someone else. Caravaggio? Could he find out? He was prosecuting Walter Rosen, not Lev. Maybe Agent Skordall would know, but I couldn't ask in front of Lilly.

It would break her heart.

I glance over at Lev. They're sitting across from me in a four-seat combo, him with his good ear next to her, and he's holding her hand with one hand while using the other to scroll on his phone. Lilly is reading Vanity Fair, turning the pages with her free hand. She's wearing a teal-blue long-sleeved tunic over black leggings, and silver and black ballet flats. Her dark hair is in a side pony-tail, no adornments necessary. She's wearing bright red lipstick, something she deeply missed during the pandemic.

She lifts her reading glasses from her eyes, perching them on her head. "Smooth your hair a bit," she says, and I know she's feeling normal. "I like the sweater."

It's cooler today than the first day we went into the City, and there won't be sundresses and tank tops this time. I'm wearing my brown and gray sweater with gray jeans. Nothing special, but she's gone out of her way to say something nice.

I go ahead and spoil the moment. "Hey Lev. When you were at the station after they arrested you —"

"Sh!" Lilly says. "You want the whole world to hear?"

I have a very quiet voice unless I'm in court, so I know I was discreet. Sort of.

"Yeah. What?" Lev says. He's looking right at me with those beautiful blue eyes, his black hair slicked away from his forehead, the gray streak emphasizing his thick curls. He tilts his head inquisitively, and though I know it's to turn his hearing side to me it looks charming and sincere.

"What did they ask you about Lilly?"

He raises his eyebrow, and I note that it's on his good side. "Nothing. Or really, very little. Why?"

"It just seems strange that it was so quick, the turn-around and next thing they were talking about indicting Lilly. I was wondering what they asked you."

Lilly's mouth has dropped open. She knows exactly what I'm saying. And so, apparently, does Lev. "No, I didn't sell her out, if that's what you're wondering."

Should I deny? I leave the question out there. I don't want to lie, but I don't want to appear to be the suspicious, heartless bitch that I realize I must be.

"Of course he didn't," Lilly says. "I can't believe you'd even think that. How does this stuff even occur to you, Zara? It's sick."

"Hey. Look, you two. I'm a lawyer, and this is an obvious question. And all I asked is if they asked you anything about her. Not what you said. Not whether you volunteered anything, or sold her out, or anything else. All of that you came up with on your own. So no, not sick. But now that you mention it, what *did* you say about her?"

*Stop yourself. Stop yourself.* But I need to know, and if it's unfounded, then better yet.

Lev takes a deep breath. "They let me go because they're not dismissing the case. Alan suggested I agree to a charge of over-stating the claim on the menorah, and agree to pay any difference back on the value. But they don't have it, and they know it isn't mine anymore, I had to give it up to you under the Restoration Act. So it was a compensation issue and nothing more. I promised to try to bring the menorah in for valuation, but that it now belonged to Lilly. I think the whole *indict Lilly* part is to scare her into letting them get the menorah valued. They don't know that she got part of the money, and I didn't tell them."

"How are you going to pay the difference back?" I ask.

"Until I know what it is, I don't have a clue. And neither do they."

"And Andres hasn't gotten back to me yet," Lilly adds. "So you can stuff your nasty suspicions. Christ, Zara."

I shake my head. "They weren't mine. I was just asking."

Lilly picks up her magazine. "Well now you know."

• ⊹ ⫷●▶◁●⫸ ⊹ •

We pull into Grand Central, and I realize that I haven't even seen what I was looking out the window at, I've been so distracted. My hands are cold and damp with nerves, and I wipe them quickly on my pants before picking up my purse. Lilly has the ledger sheet in her handbag, in its plastic zip bag, but we took care to scan it again on her phone before we left, and she emailed it to me. "Hey," I say. "The spice jars aren't on the ledger, right?"

"Out of the blue, Zara? You are so weird. No, they're not. At least not on the page we have, which would have been what they took from Mother. They were wrenched violently from some other terrified woman's hand."

The train is slowing, with the screech of metal wheels on metal tracks, and the smell of the train tunnel enters the passenger car. I always associate that smell with arriving in New York City, and it's an exciting odor no matter how often I experience it.

"No, but that means we don't have to tell Skordall about them," I say.

"What brought that up? And who *would* bring that up?"

"I'm just worried," I say, as the screeching stops. "If they don't know about them, you can't be charged with harboring missing artifacts. The bird one is probably worth a fortune, if those rubies are real. And it's on the Polish Unrecovered Art website. That means that it's something that would be recognized. And there it was, per you, at the museum, in plain sight. My mind is just following a path here. Just let me think this through. And just don't say anything, okay?"

"There you go again, telling me what to say. I'm not stupid, you know. Bye Lev," she adds, kissing him.

"See you on Friday," he says. "Zara, you'll still be here, right?"

"My return flight is right before Yom Kippur, so yeah, I'll be here. Good lord willing," I add.

"GLW. Remember our acronym," Lilly says to me.

"GLW. See you Friday," I say to Lev. It's a relief to have him gone. Who knows what other gems he'll turn up with.

As soon as we get up to the sidewalk level, I'm again overwhelmed by the combination of how many people there are, and how few compared to pre-pandemic days. I turn right out of the doors, and Lilly grabs my arm. "This way, silly." We go left to Park to grab the Four train. "The same as you used to take when you were here. "

We're standing at the corner, waiting to cross the street, when Lilly adds, "Now that Lev's gone, tell me what you found out about the apartment."

◆ ⊷ ⊷◆❍❂❍◆⊶ ⊶ ◆

I try to start at the beginning. "Bear with me, even if I tell you things you already know. We need to think this through in order. Slow down," I add, as she strides across the street. "So, we start with Dad getting the apartment. Why? Because he wanted to be near the hospital and clinic where he was supervising residents. But he only did the clinic one day a week, and Mom was sick, so that's kind of specious. I always figured he wanted to get away from the sickness and despair one or two nights a week, and didn't blame him.

"He always took such good care of Mom, and I felt sorry for him, watching the love of his life deteriorate before his eyes. Even if it got way worse afterwards."

"But then we learned the truth, right?" Lilly interjects. "He got Trudy to help with Mother, that's so disgusting, I guess he was sure Mom wouldn't recognize her from fifty years before, and when Trudy wouldn't do it anymore, he started staying at the apartment more and more."

"Yeah, I guess, to be with her, but she was no prize by then."

We go down through the train turnstile, and it's a different smell, the unique aroma of New York Subway. Thank goodness it isn't summer. We walk partway down the platform, and though it's midday it isn't crowded. "This really took a hit. No one wanted to be in the trains or the station if they could avoid it. It was all essential workers risking their lives just to get to jobs where they could risk their lives," Lilly says.

"So, yeah, he gets the apartment. At some point, this is the early new century, the building goes co-op. Now I don't really know too much about this, because we don't do co-ops in California very much. It's like a condo, but different rules. It's cheaper to buy into a co-op, and the corporation can get loans, which is something that condo associations can't do."

"You're losing me, Zara. Is this important?"

"No, but it's fascinating to me. And a bit of it is significant." I take a deep breath. Even through my mask I smell train tracks, body odors, pizza. "So Dad buys the apartment when it goes co-op, but I don't know this. His payments are less than the ridiculous rent he was paying, but unbeknownst to me, he opens a new account to pay on the loan he gets to buy the co-op, along with the maintenance. So I never see it."

"Unbeknownst. You're the only person I've ever say that out loud," Lilly says. "So you knew all his other accounts?"

"Yeah. I was actually a signer on them, too."

"Wow, what temptation!"

I glare at Lilly. "No, it wasn't. Never."

She shrugs. "I guess that's the benefit of being married to a bread-winner."

Or of being financially ethical. "Anyway, so Dad buys into the co-op at the insider price. And since it's a co-op, they can vet anyone he sells it to or wills it to, based on whether they decide they want that person living there, which I never have heard of. What a playground for discrimination. But anyway, he's in. And he lives there two days a week."

Lilly nods, glassy-eyed.

"Ok, fast-forward to summer, 2014," I continue. "He has the heart attack, and he comes back to the apartment to recover from the bypass. By all accounts, especially his, the operation goes well, and he tells me to not to fly out. You're in France that summer, and he doesn't tell you *not* to come back from Paris, but he doesn't tell you to do so, either. So, unlike his usual demand for all the attention all the time, he's telling us it's no biggie. Why? Because he's got Trudy there with him, and, it turns out, our new-found half-sister, if she really is, Jeanine. Whose middle name is Emilia, by the way."

"Son of a bitch!" she says. "He always said he would have named me Emilia if I'd had a dimple. Instead, I got Lilliana. After our grandmother. And he goes and lets Trudy name Jeanine Emilia."

The subway stops suddenly, and we pitch forward. "Hold on!" I say.

"It's nothing, it's just being itself," Lilly says, and sure enough it starts again. My heart is pounding wildly. I've been at home too long. "You know the picture she sent you? That's Dad after the operation. He's got that heart pillow they give the patients when they release them. And Trudy's holding the shares certificate. I guess Jeanine took the picture. It gives Trudy a life estate. Trudy died, and Jeanine says it was during the second wave of the pandemic, so probably November-December of last year." I take a deep breath. "But here's the kicker. You and I are the remainders. We inherited it."

"We own an apartment in the middle of Manhattan? Woohoo!" Lilly cheers.

Even in New York City that will draw a two-second glance from one's fellow riders.

"Hush, yeah," I say. I don't go into the fact that I'm ninety percent and she's ten percent. But Jeanine knows this, and that's why she needs me to sign off. "What Jeanine's been doing is living in that apartment rent-free, and now apparently Dad's account, the one that's been paying the loan and maintenance all these years, is out of money. So the loan's defaulted about four months ago, but since it's a co-op, it's harder for a bank to start foreclosure, since the corporation that everyone's a shareholder in — I told you this was a bit relevant — has to approve any new purchaser."

"Geez, better you than me, understanding this. Did Sam help you find this out?"

I nod. "Some of it. So now you and I own a co-op with a delinquent loan, a squatter tenant, and, to top it all off, Trump is a part owner of the building and he's selling his interest, or trying to, to pay his huge debts. And Jeanine wants the apartment given to her, probably so she can sell it, or somehow, I don't know how, get a new loan since there's no way she can pay the loan and maintenance on a nurse's wages."

Lilly blinks at me. "This is complicated as shit." She used to never swear, pre-pandemic, but she barely teaches anymore, so she doesn't have to watch her language as much. "But wait. Jeanine's really a nurse?"

"Yeah. An LPN so she doesn't earn like an RN."

"She probably made plenty during the crisis," Lilly says.

"Yeah, that probably kept her afloat, maybe she has enough to get a loan, but she can't start paying on Dad's loan, because it was automatic on his account. And the minute the bank finds out he died, I mean, that was a long time ago, but they actually probably don't know yet, they can call the loan. And they sure won't take payments from a party who's not on title."

"And we're on title!" Lilly crows. "But what do we do about Jeanine? Can she make us give her the apartment?"

"Nope. She can blackmail us, she can tell the bank and they'll foreclose, she can threaten, but legally, it's ours. And that's what we tell her. Just, simply, *no*. The hard part will be getting her out."

◆ ╫ ◈▶◐◎◑◀◈ ╫ ◆

The subway lurches along, and Lilly is silent. I assume she's thinking through what I've said. I know I am. Now that I've put it all together, at least this far, a bunch of niggling questions arise. For example, who signed Dad's death certificate? If only Trudy and Jeanine were with him when he died — I'm betting that Jeanine is the "nurse" that was present — then how, exactly, or why, exactly, did he die after a successful operation? He certainly doesn't look at death's door in the photo Jeanine sent.

"I think Jeanine sent you that picture to show you how happy Dad was to give Trudy the co-op," I say, "but he sure doesn't look like he's *al punto de muerte*."

"I'll bet she did him in," Lilly says, unafraid to voice what I'm thinking. "Her or Trudy. But we'll never prove it."

"Spoken like a lawyer," I say.

She smiles. "You're not the only one with a brain," but she doesn't say it unkindly. "We could get the doctor on the death certificate to tell us what he thought the cause of death was..."

"Probably too long ago, I mean, eight years almost, and all the doctor's record will show is that the patient had gone through a coronary by-pass, and the nurse attending him at home called 911 when he stopped breathing. I guess. What about that insane funeral director we had to deal with? Remember her?"

"How could I ever forget? What a nightmare. Neither of us saw the body, and he was cremated within a day of dying, and then Mom had no idea what to do, and she called me in France, and that's how I found out Dad had died."

"That horror show was something for a noir movie. I'll never forget your call. And then trying to get the ashes from that funeral harpy, she was crazy. *Your father wanted it this way. We're going to do a funeral.* I kept yelling at her, *My mother will be in charge of his funeral, not you!*"

"I had nightmares for a year afterwards," Lilly says. "Trying to make phone calls that don't go through, arguing with people who don't seem to understand my words."

"A couple of my favorite nightmares too," I say. I had them after Aurora died, until Aurora started to appear when I was awake, too, in my visions or hallucinations or whatever they are. "At least Dad doesn't haunt me, like Mom does."

"Did you have any premonitions that Dad was going to die?"

I shake my head. "No, only dreams of drooling mad dogs, but I have those anyway."

"Jesus, Zara. Well, I'll always be grateful for your star turn with the crazy funeral lady. *He was Jewish! You can't give him a quote decent Christian burial unquote!*"

"I usually try not to think about it, but now, it's all important. Just think, if Trudy or Jeanine killed him, and then set this up with the crazy funeral lady, that would be something we could try to track down. But meanwhile, there's no way on God's green earth that Jeanine is going to get even a dime out of that property."

"What about the disinheriting the daughter argument?"

"Well, she'd have to prove she was his daughter, and even then, he didn't disinherit her mother, so that would suffice. Just like he left everything to Mom, not us. And Mom could have left us a grand each and given the rest to the ASPCA."

The subway stops at last and we start to make our way out. My stomach sinks. We still have to face Agent Skordall.

---

## *Family Scrapbook: Aurora — Visions in flash, 1953*

*The line is long for the name-changing window at the social security office. I have my papers, my marriage license, my passport. It tells everyone everything. Carrying these documents is like walking naked through the streets. No one is looking, but they all can see.*

*On my passport, a picture of a terrifyingly thin woman stares back at me. Her dark hair is lank and won't take the curl, it's too thin to set, and the color — I know the color — is without shine. In the black and white shot it shows as matte black. It gives my real name. Even my middle name, the dead giveaway, Juditya. My last name, my father's name, is there too. It's the last time I will ever use that name.*

*My mother's last name was Sephardic, and in most contexts is a fractured-Spanish-or-Portuguese-turned-Polish name, not a Jewish one. In the years since I last saw my mother I've had so many names. Zosia, Aurora, Wanda, Mika, Aurora again; Warszavska was my chosen last name, the girl from Warsaw, closing my eyes to the last cries of my father, the sorrowful tears of my mother.*

*Protect yourself. Protect your family. No matter what, they come before any outsider.*

*The line inches forward and it's my turn. The woman behind the little window barely glances at my passport. Another refugee. She asks for my residency card, as I am not yet a citizen. I hand it to her, and she holds it next to the passport. My hands get clammy, but I stand straight, look her in the eye. I hand her the marriage license, and she raises her eyebrows at that. I'm twenty-three, I'm an orphan from another country, I've married a citizen, and I want to change my name. On the application for the marriage license I gave my real name, and he gave his, and included the fact that at twenty-four he's already once divorced, the prior marriage having ended for Indignities to the Person.*

*The woman looks up at me from behind her spectacles. You sure you want to do this, honey? I stare. He is my husband now, and family comes first. She shrugs and stamps the papers. I have yet another new name.*

———————————————Y———————————————

She had no way of knowing it, but on Mom's death certificate her mother's last name will be incorrectly listed as her father's, her mother's name will be listed as *unknown*, and her original name will appear nowhere on the document. She had become yet another new person, and this is who she was until the day she died.

◆ ⊪≡✦⊙◑❂◐⊙✦≡⊪ ◆

"Zara? You with us?" Agent Skordall asks, not exactly solicitous, but a bit alarmed. It's the first real emotion I've seen in an FBI agent. Like them or not, they're well trained. Agent Skordall is wearing a beige cable-knit sweater and black slacks, and her blonde hair, which I know from the time Sam and I met with her is almost waist-length, is up in a twisted bun. Lilly's hair, equally long and far thicker, is down, and the battle of feminine secondary sex characteristics is on.

Lilly is more buxom, longer legged, and has a prettier smile. Skordall is blonde — which is always good for extra points, has actual hips, and wide-spaced blue eyes. She's not quite as tall as Lilly, and thus gets the height points without the slouch or the freakishness of a female six-footer. She's also in charge.

I shake my head, not *No*, but to re-engage with reality. "Sorry, it's warm in here, and it's a bit cool outside, so I think I just faded out there...jet lag, you know."

"She's been here over a week," Lilly chimes in.

Ok, I don't kill her on the spot. "Yeah, that's kind of when it sneaks up on you," I say.

Skordall gives us both a look that's half amusement, half contempt, but I let it pass. Less said the better, I figure. She's not masked, and neither is Lilly. When we walked in, she informed us that she'd been vaccinated in the *first responders* wave, and that we needn't wear ours with her if we were also vaxxed. Lilly doffed hers instantly. "Vaccination *and* antibodies," she'd said.

I guess that makes me safe, so I lower mine to below my chin, in modern pando-fashion. I take a deep breath and that helps.

"Would you like some coffee or something?" Skordall asks, clearly not convinced of my recovery.

I nod, and she leaves the cubicle for a moment. I know it's going to be hideous coffee but to decline would just make her come to even weirder conclusions.

"Jesus," Lilly and I hiss at each other simultaneously. That makes us both laugh. "Stop freaking out," Lilly says.

I'd made her stop at the ladies' room before we went into the FBI offices, in case we didn't get another chance to use a clean restroom later. *You're nuts*, she'd said. *I'm just being careful*, I'd answered.

Now, sitting in Skordall's office, I still feel ready to barf. I look at her little work-space. Metal desk, no photos, an Audubon Society calendar like you get if you donate, and, out-of-sync, a black and white paisley lamp on the desk. No files or papers are visible, except a yellow pad with our names written on it, and 11:30 AM. Spartan to the max, and with no personality other than that lamp.

I take out the ledger sheet in its plastic bag, and put it on the desk. "Just like that?" Lilly whispers. I nod. The simpler the better. The agent walks back in, a steaming paper cup with a corrugated cardboard holder around it in her hand. She puts it in front of me. I take a sip.

I don't spit it out, but it's actual, real, office-coffee, that's been sitting on a burner, probably since eight this morning. And it's got some sweeter in it, and worst of all, some sort of powdered creamer. It's horrible, but I swallow it down.

"I didn't ask how you take it so I just made it regular," she says, pulling out her office-chair-on-wheels with a whiny squeak.

It's the second time I've been caught out on the New York "regular" which involves milk and sugar. Otherwise, specify black. My bad. "It's fine," I say, and take another sip as if to prove it. "I figured you being in the FBI you'd know how I like my coffee."

She rolls her eyes. Obviously not the first time she's heard that. She looks down at her desk and picks up the plastic-covered ledger sheet. "Ok, we know a lot, but not how you take your coffee. Or how you ended up with this. Or why you're bringing it back now. But you can tell me."

"Quite frankly," Lilly starts and I cringe internally. Agent Skordall looks at Lilly with big, sympathetic blue eyes that say *yes, go on, tell me more, your secrets are safe with me.*

"It's quite straightforward," I say sharply. The agent looks amused. "Really. When Sam and I brought in the other ledgers, we left the one with our mother's items with Lilly. She didn't know we were turning everything over to you. She took the page, as it listed the last things our mother had before the Nazis tore them away from her. Then when I took the last ledger to you, it was missing a page. I didn't know it was missing, and Lilly didn't know that there was anything wrong with taking the page, since after all, the ledgers were…" No, I couldn't say *ours*, or even, *rightfully in our possession.* Agent Skordall waits, in classic investigator mode, using silence to urge the remainder of the confession.

"So I took out the page, so I could show that the menorah was mine, in case anyone disputed that, if we ever found it," Lilly says. The lawyer in me cringes — she's saying way too much, but I don't stop her. This has to be done. "And now, with the art thief Walter Rosen going to trial, we figured it would be good for you to have the complete set."

We both breathe a sigh of relief. There, it's out. "But of course, now that Rosen is back on the loose, there won't be a trial, but if he gets caught again, we want you to have the complete books," I add. "But why isn't anyone as worried about his escape as we are? Remember that he killed a girl in New Jersey, and cut up Lilly. And you're just letting him run free!"

She takes the page and holds it up. "Just took a straight-razor to it?" she asks.

That makes it sound awfully deliberate, but Lilly's cool. "Sculptor's knife." Skordall's eyes widen. Score one for Lilly, and there's a tiny look of respect.

Skordall's wearing a bracelet with keys on it. With one of the keys she unlocks the drawer and places the page inside. She returns the bracelet to her wrist after she's safely tucked our ledger page in.

"We are aware of his escape," she turns back to me. "And we're definitely aware of the danger he poses to society and to you. I promise you that. Thank you for bringing this in. I'll have to have you sign a declaration about your possession of it, but that can be typed up quickly in a few moments. Meanwhile, tell me about Jeanine Emilia Andrade Cruz."

Oh my. I didn't expect that.

"Quite frankly," Lilly begins.

---

It's a tough choice: do we spill the whole story or just enough? I have a feeling she knows more than she lets on, but Agent Skordall is patient. Too patient, in my opinion.

"So let me get this right. When you and Mr. Pendleton came in with the ledgers, Rosen was still on the loose, nothing had been recovered, and you, Lilly, had been brutally attacked. You left four out of five ledgers with me, but you, Zara, had kept back the fifth, leaving at in Lilly's house. After you returned to the scene of the kidnapping, you dug up a small cache of artifacts that Rosen had allegedly buried, and — "

"Hey. Not allegedly. What do you mean by that?" Lilly, as the principal victim, has the right to be outraged.

"Well, we didn't see him do it, did we?" she says. "At any rate, you dug the things up, you say there were only a couple of plates and your menorah. And then he attacked you again, this time at Zara's apartment — how did he know where to look?"

I glance at Lilly. "He's a computer whiz," I say. I'm not going there.

"Okay, well, yes, that's true," the agent says, and glances down at her notepad. She's not written anything down. "That's when we nab him, thanks to your quick thinking."

"Actually, no," I say. "We hadn't dug anything up by then. We did the following weekend. It was warm, and there was no snow."

She raises her eyebrows, but says nothing. I don't fall for it. I wait. I think I'm going to break Lilly's foot if I step on it much harder.

"Hmmm," Skordall says, but when we don't say anything she goes on. "All right, we arrest Rosen, you dig up the items, and then you and Mr. Pendleton bring in the final ledger. Missing a page. That you don't realize. Tying the menorah to your family."

"Uh, right."

"So, tell me all about Ms. Cruz."

"Who?" Lilly says.

"Jeanine," I say. "Why?"

Agent Skordall seems to be weighing her answer when a junior officer comes in with a paper. She looks it over, nods, and thanks him. He gives Lilly a covert glance as he leaves the cubicle. He can't be more than twenty-five for crying out loud.

She hands the document to me. "Here, sign it. Then you," she adds to Lilly. I read it through. She's done a very good, careful job. All we're attesting to is that the page came from the Nazi ledger, and in the process of turning over the other book this page was left out. We were acknowledging that the page belonged with the books. That's it.

I sign. I pass the paper to Lilly and nod. She signs. It's done.

Agent Skordall takes the document back and again, the key bracelet comes off, the declaration goes in the drawer, and the bracelet goes back on. "Ok, why did you leave the page out?"

*Whoa, trick question.* Before Lilly can say *Quite frankly*, I jump in. "It tied the menorah to our mother. The menorah was stolen from her. She was only thirteen. She went through exactly the hell you imagine a beautiful young Jewish girl would be put through during the war. We wanted to keep her memory."

It's true. It just leaves out the insurance issue. "Okay, okay," Skordall says. "Fine. Let's leave it at that for now. Back to Ms. Cruz, Jeanine if you prefer. Who is she, and what's her connection to Rosen?"

"In all honesty," Lilly says and I try not to wince, "we have no idea what her connection is to Walter, or if she even has one."

"She has one," I say. Lilly stamps my foot this time. "She claims she's our father's extra daughter, with his girlfriend of a long time ago. We don't know if that's true, because we just met her. She's been living, she says, in our dad's apartment since he died almost eight years ago, and now she wants us to deed it to her. It's apparently in our name. And we think she broke into Lilly's house and stole the menorah, or thinks she did. She took a fake."

"A fake menorah?"

"Well, it's a real menorah, just not *the* menorah," I say.

"My son's an artist, and he made a pretty menorah with similar patterns, but not the real thing," Lilly adds. "That's why we had a sculptor's knife lying around." I'm proud that she says he's an artist, without her usual added *wannabe*. That will help down the road.

I miss a few words, having gotten distracted by the thoughts of Francis Xavier, and pick up as Lilly is saying, "She sent me a threatening email, and called Francis and threatened him too. But we don't know what the connection to Walter is."

I wish she wouldn't refer to him as Walter.

"I want to know where he is," I say. "Why isn't anyone upset about his escape?"

"Don't worry about it," she says again. "We're on it."

I sigh. "Lilly was brutally attacked once. I don't want to be a sitting duck."

"About Ms. Cruz?"

"Oh yeah. So she's after something from us. But we're thinking that her mother, who was our dad's first wife, but was his mistress off and on the rest of his life —"

"Charming," Skordall says. I roll my eyes.

" . . . either killed him or hastened his death, right after he gave her a life-estate in his co-op apartment. But we have no way to prove it. Just that . . ."

*Just that he was doing fine, then suddenly he was dead. That we didn't even know he'd died until the crazy funeral director who'd picked up his body, without even someone accompanying him, and had him cremated, and then, only then, called Lilly. That our mother was too out to lunch to act. That Trudy was with him, and that Jeanine was a nurse, and somehow, as soon as that deed was signed, he was dead.*

"I don't know where to begin…" I say. I give her the short version.

"And Jeanine says she found you because of a photo of you, Lilly, in the paper holding the menorah in a human interest story about art theft?"

"Right. And meanwhile, Rosen was in the hospital, allegedly with Covid-19, and somehow escaped, but not without first finagling a continuance of his trial."

"Uh huh," Skordall says. I wouldn't believe me either. "And he happens to find Ms. Cruz, randomly, and she's your half-sister or whatever, and she wants your father's apartment, so she breaks into your house and steals the wrong menorah, and then what?"

I'm stymied. I look at Lilly. She shrugs.

"I think we're done here," Agent Skordall says, rising.

Lilly stands too, looking straight at her. "Okay, you're done. But you've lost your thief, he's a murderer, and we're the target."

Skordall colors a bit. "Don't worry. Take my word for it. We've got this."

We make our escape into the sweet, sweet air of freedom, lighter by one ledger page.

# Chapter Twelve

# It Hardly
# Seems Fair

The high of release doesn't last. The wave of anticlimax and self-recrimination overtakes me.

It's too long a walk, so we head back towards the subway in silence. There was a time, before Lilly's injury, that fifty blocks would be nothing, but now she's maxed at twenty.

"We sounded like fools," I say when we stop to rest Lilly's leg. "Like children! We're sixty. What the hell."

"It's because she's the authorities," Lilly says. She leans on a parking meter just a bit. A bicyclist swerves around her, swears and speeds off into the crosswalk. "*We've got this*. Really? Tell us how."

"And how does she know about Jeanine?"

And, I don't add, I was ready to spill my guts, so grateful was I that the ledger-page issue went so smoothly. So easily. So suspiciously simply. "And she was so cool about the album's ledger sheet. Like, no biggie, sure, just slip it to me and I'll lock it in my drawer with my key chained to my freakin' wrist. Why?"

Lilly shrugs, "Maybe you were just paranoid and overthinking this."

I wasn't. I know I was a bit over the top, but it was a real risk. Lilly either won't see it or won't admit it, and there's no percentage in pushing it. "I still don't get her interest in Jeanine," I say instead, and as if summoned by telepathy, Lilly's text goes off, and it's Jeanine.

"Speak of the devil and the devil appears," I say.

"*I think we can resolve this equitably. Come to the apartment. I'm here all day.*"

"I didn't know she knew words like *equitably,*" I mutter.

"Don't be such as snob. She may be a grifter but that doesn't make her stupid. For all we know, Dad put her through Harvard."

I control myself, barely. "I don't come when I'm called," I say.

"Contrarian. But I'd want to prepare for a meeting, not jump into one," Lilly says, taking on my usual caution while I boil. *Great, Lilly* texts back, *but not today. We'll get back to you.*"

We descend into the bowels of the city. We pick up the first train that comes; it's a local but we're in no rush.

But when the subway approaches the 33rd Street stop I go for it. "Come on, Lilly. We've got to do this."

She doesn't argue, she just follows me out, and it all comes back to me. Dad living large in the apartment, with views to Kingdom Come, and that smell, that odor of, now I know, Trudy. But I was "on the list" and had the right to go in. All I had to do was check in at the desk and they'd send me up.

"We're going to see Jeanine. If she wants to talk, we'll talk. We're going to tell her she can stuff her demands up her derrière," I say. I'm still seething from my sense of powerlessness at the FBI, and I'm heedless in my anger.

Now that I've realized that Jeanine has no property rights, I want her out. Then what? Who knows. Sell the co-op, probably. Surely. There's no way I want to be stuck with a payment like that. A renter would cover it, if the co-op board would let me have one. And values are still going up like mad. I'm walking so fast I'm almost running.

"You on this planet?" Lilly asks. She's keeping pace by virtue of her long strides, but I'm panting.

"Sorry. Here's the deal. This is ours. Don't text her. We'll just walk in, stop at the desk and say — no, we just walk in and go right on up."

"What if she's not home?" Lilly asks. "We just said we'd come another day." How practical of her.

"That's when I go back down, and get let in."

"Don't you still have a key?"

"No, tossed it years ago. We're just going to make this happen."

"Sounds good to me," Lilly says.

The building's wide driveway sweep is unique in the area. It provides a luxurious, gracious entry to the two connected edifices, a place for a cab to let its passengers descend, a doorman to open the door. The sheltered parklet that we sat in last week is fuller today, residents taking their seasonal enjoyment of the outdoors, right in the middle of screeching Manhattan. The regular produce cart is at the corner, the pretzel guy is out too, and I can smell that somewhere nearby the Halal Guy is selling gyros.

We walk in, and turn left. Inside, I never get lost. No one stops two nicely dressed white late-middle-aged ladies. I push the floor selector and we get our elevator letter. I like that, it makes sure that the doors only open at the specific floors. It seems safer.

We emerge on the eighteenth floor, third from the top. "Dad was pissed that there were two more floors above him," I say.

"What are we going to say to Jeanine?" Lilly asks, uncharacteristically nervous.

"I'll give her verbal notice of eviction," I say, knowing that's nonsense. Maybe she won't know.

I'm excited and my hands are sweating when I ring the little doorbell. We wait. I ring again, and knock too. Nothing. I put my ear on the door, but it's one of those metal security doors and all I hear is my own heartbeat.

"This isn't going to work," Lilly says. "I'll be right back. You stay here." She strides back to the elevators, leaving me standing there at the door.

The elevator door opens and I hear voices. I pull myself straighter. Anyone coming down the hall would wonder what someone was doing out in the hall. I school my face into relaxed interest. But whoever they are stop at another apartment well before this one, and don't even give me a second glance. So much for security.

I lean against the apartment door. What if Jeanine comes back and I'm without my defender? But the door doesn't seem quite right, and as I lean back in I quietly lift the handle. It moves, and the door is unlocked. I hesitate — my entire body is rigid. I don't dare break the rules, enter uninvited. I realize how much I depend on Lilly in these moments. I close my eyes and push.

As the door swings open a scene of devastation greets me. It echoes Lilly's house last week, but this can't be Jeanine's work. She wouldn't trash her own or semi-own apartment.

It isn't a large apartment, but it's beautifully laid out, with a small foyer, and then the kitchen to one side, the hall closet to the other. Then the living/dining room opens out to enormous windows that bring the greatest skyline ever into the room. On either side of the living room there's a bedroom with en-suite bathroom.

Every cabinet, every drawer, every canister has been opened in the kitchen and dumped out. In the living room a plant has been knocked over and dirt is tracked on the rich, cream-colored carpet. Cushions have been pulled from the two chairs that I recognize from my parents' home. A curio cabinet that my parents got in Japan twenty-plus years ago stands open, and it looks like the little objects were swept by an angry arm onto the floor.

And on that floor, on the tile that covers the entry, is Francis Xavier's art-menorah, its decorative pieces scattered about, its central candle holder, the *Shamash*, bent sideways.

A sound comes from the bedroom. I suppress a responding squeak and scurry back to the hall. I'm breathing hard as I silently pull the door closed. I shut my eyes as I hear the latch click.

Almost immediately I hear Lilly coming from the elevator, cheerfully telling someone about a show she's been streaming, the one about the Crown. "I'm rewatching season four," she's saying.

"I just loved Diana," the woman with her replies, and around the corner they come, Lilly towering over a youngish woman with a long dark pony-tail, glasses, and a tight green polo shirt with the address of the building.

"She was so classy," Lilly answers. "Hi, Zara," she frowns, taking in what must be my look of terror. "This is Philomena, she's going to unlock Dad's apartment for us."

Just like that.

"Hi," Philomena says. "Your dad was a really fine guy. I know it's been a while but I'm sorry for your loss." She unlocks the top lock first, then the bottom. "When are you moving back in? You know that you have to arrange the movers through us — holy Mary Virgin Mother of God!"

I follow her gaze as she takes in the mess. "Holy shit!" Lilly says. "Jeanine's gone on a rampage."

She tiptoes carefully across the room, gingerly stepping over the trashed menorah without comment, to the window. Her feet leave tracks of dirt and something else, it smells like fancy dusting powder. I look down and I realize that I've tracked it too, even though right now I'm still standing at the door. I glance behind me and quickly step backwards, into the hall.

"Where are you going?" Lilly says.

"Just checking the latch," I reply, mingling my new steps with my prior ones. Rule-followers may not be brave, but we think of the details. "Don't go in."

Philomena is speaking into her phone, but it's not 911 she's calling, it's the management office by the sound of the woman answering. She's asking about damage, not danger.

"No way she did this to her own place," I say, entering again. The sound comes again from the bedroom. Lilly and I both look up from the floor and our eyes meet. She raises one black brow, and without comment pulls away from my hand and walks through the living room to the bedroom. She throws open the bedroom door. It hits the wall with a bang. From around her shoulder I see more disarray, a king-sized bed with the linens pulled off, a dresser with drawers hanging ajar, clothes dumped everywhere. But no person.

"The bathroom," I whisper.

In contrast to the slamming open of the bedroom door, Lilly opens this door slowly, stopping part-way when the door hits something. Being thinner than either of the other two, I am able to slide through the opening. I'm not even scared, I'm not even breathing. I've got Lilly.

There, on the floor, Jeanine is sprawled, blood covering her face and hands.

"Oh my god," I say, edging back out. I drop to the floor and reach around the door, grab hold of her leg, which is stopping the door from opening, and push it forward. She moans again, but I push far enough that Lilly can open the door.

"Jeanine," Lilly says. "Hey! Can you hear me?"

"Mrs. Cruz," Philomena says.

I straighten up and move past Lilly and Philomena back into the room. My hand is wet, and when I look at it it's covered in blood.

I hear Philomena calling 911 now, and it flashes oddly that she'd call management first. But the room is going gray, the edges waver, and I am close enough to the bed that when the room goes black, *I'm reaching for my father's waist and I don't know if I get to him, his face is melting like wax and the room is spinning and I wake on the nurse's cot, sweating and nauseous.*

"Zara! Don't you dare pass out!" Lilly grabs my arm hard, and shakes me. "Don't you dare!"

I sit down on the bed and put my head down. Lilly presses against the back of my head and I press my head into her hand, and the feeling ebbs. She hands me a corner of the sheet and I wipe my hand. "Sorry," I whisper. All I want to do is sleep. For some reason the weight of exhaustion is unbearable. I barely realize that I lie down on my dad's old bed, and there's no scent of him after seven years, and close my eyes.

The next thing I know police are at the door.

———— ✦∙⟨●⟩∙✦ ————

I pull myself to sitting, avoiding Lilly's glare. There's only one cop, heavyset and bristling with a belt of implements. He throws me a glance but I'm not as interesting as the colossal mess on the floor and the groaning woman in the bathroom. He pushes the door wide open, speaking into his shoulder for an ambulance.

Kneeling next to Jeanine he reaches a gloved hand out to her neck. Her eyes flutter, she takes a ragged breath and limply raises her arm. "No..."

"It's okay," the cop says, surprisingly gently. "Ambulance is on its way."

She opens her eyes, this time with what looks like consciousness. "You're okay," he says again. "What happened to you?"

Jeanine tries to move her head, emits a small cry, but she's shifted her glance enough that we watch her take in Lilly's presence behind the officer.

"She! She...it's her fault!"

The cop glances over his shoulder but Lilly spreads her hands wide in a gesture of innocence.

Two paramedics appear at the bedroom door and I point to the bathroom. They move expertly past Lilly, me, Philomena and the cop; their only focus is Jeanine.

"What hurts?" one asks.

"I fell and hit my head," she slurs.

"Bullshit," the cop says, taking off his hat and wiping his perspiring face. But she's able to sit up with help, and the EMTs help her onto a stretcher — *protocol, ma'am, sorry* — and take her out of the bathroom.

"Free to leave?" the EMT asks. The cop nods, speaks into his recorder, no hand-written notes here, that the victim has been escorted out by the meds. We all watch in silence as they carry her out, obliterating all the tracks on the carpet.

"Now, ladies, tell me what you're doing here."

Briefly I outline that we are the actual owners of the apartment, and while Philomena opens her mouth to interrupt she clearly thinks better of it as soon as her boss appears. Her supervisor stands at the doorway, and his face is gray with dismay.

"We were set to see the place, as it's going to go on the market, and Jeanine didn't answer the door for the inspection appointment so we got the management to open the door. And there she was."

"Did you touch anything?"

"No, it was in disarray, exactly as you see it, when we walked in," Lilly says.

Philomena opens her mouth again, and closes it.

"And the blood all over your hand, ma'am?"

I don't look at it. "I bent down and pushed Jeanine, Mrs. Cruz's leg out of the way to open the bathroom door, because we heard a moan, and my sister tried to open the door, but her — Jeanine's — leg was in the way."

"And she wiped it on the sheet," Lilly chirps. He gives her a funny look, but doesn't follow up.

"We'll send someone to look at the footprints," he says.

Finally, Philomena speaks. "The ladies told me that they were the owners, but the owner was their father. And Mrs. Cruz and her mother lived with the owner, until he died. And then his wife and daughter stayed on, which is permissible under our co-op rules. But we were told that Mrs. Persil inherited the co-op, not these Mrs.

Persil, but Mrs. Cruz's mom, so that's why she stayed, but now these Mrs. or I guess, Ms. Persil they own it, so we had to let them in…"

"Thanks, Philomena," the supervisor says from the door. "I think the officer is concerned with the intruder or whoever hurt Ms. Cruz, not with our co-op rules."

The policeman looks from one to the other. "I'm sure it's important," he says, "but your safety is what's most critical. Did someone other than these women come up to see the victim?"

"I'd have to check," Philomena says. "We keep a log of all visitors who don't have keys," she adds.

Of course, we'd walked right up, and that's not lost on her boss. Or, after a couple of seconds, on her.

The cop wipes his face again, then takes an actual notebook from his pocket. He looks right at me. "Name?" I give him my information. As soon as I get to the California part he stops writing. "Oh really?"

"She's visiting me," Lilly adds, and gives her address.

"So you're all related?" he asks. "All family?"

Lilly starts to answer but I cut her off. "Distant relatives."

Philomena chimes in. "She, the lady who was hurt, she lives here. They don't."

"We own it," I say.

"Their dad did, not them," Philomena insists, "and then his wife and daughter. Mrs. Cruz, the lady you just took out."

"Not his wife," Lilly jumps in.

"Not his daughter," I say.

"Ex-wife." Lilly.

"Her daughter." Me.

"Yes she was." Philomena.

"Life estate," I start.

"Wait a minute!" the officer says. We all fall silent. He turns to me. "Life estate? What's that?"

Oh no, I can see where this could lead. I make myself as pedantic as possible, despite the literal blood on my hand and the talcum on my shoes. "Our dad owned this co-op. He left it to his ex-wife, the injured woman's — Jeanine Cruz's — mother, in a life-estate. After his ex-wife died, the property passed to me and Lilliana. Ms. Cruz was still living here but she wasn't on title."

Contrary to my expectations, the cop's eyes don't glaze over. "So now you two own it, and were going to sell it?" I nod tentatively. "So what happens to the victim when you do?"

"She moves out!" Lilly says brightly.

"Especially with a little encouragement from you two," he says, looking pointedly at my bloody hand.

"I'm a lawyer," I say stiffly. "I'd only offer legal encouragement."

The cop shrugs, puts his notebook back in his pocket, sighs. "Don't leave the state without telling us," he says. I know he's got no authority to demand that, and I can see that he knows too, but it sounds convincing. I nod. "Let me know if you have anything else to add," he says, and gives Philomena and me his card. *Add?* We'd told him nothing. "But now, I'd like you all to leave, and we're going to ask that the door be secured," he says, addressing this last to the supervisor, who nods.

"I'd like to look around and see what's been taken," I say.

"Okay, but make it quick. If you aren't the resident, we'll need you out," the supervisor says.

"I'm the actual owner," I say.

"Well, when you get me a certified copy of the shares, and permission from the board and the tenant, you can come in," he answers.

It's *or* not *and* but I don't feel like arguing. I walk right over to the other bedroom, which dad used as little office. I'm hoping for some papers, something that will explain this whole mess. But the room has been turned into a sewing room, complete with cutting table, machine, and shelves of cloth, yarn, threads and bobbins.

And it hasn't been trashed.

I quickly open everything. Nothing seems to be of any interest. But in the bottom drawer of the cloth bin, a cheap, metal and quilted plastic affair with drawers and wire baskets, there's a little photograph, framed, face-down. I turn it over. It's a wedding photo, and in it is Dad, about twenty, in his army uniform, and a small, beautiful blonde woman, smiling radiantly, happy, and holding a single white rose.

I slip the photo into my handbag. As we leave, Philomena is telling her boss, "There was nobody up here before I let Mrs. Persil, um, that one, into the unit," she points to Lilly. "Except her," she adds, looking over at me. "She was waiting here in the hall."

"So how'd the short one get up here without signing in?"

"I don't know," Philomena wails. "But I gotta say, I'm really sorry Mrs. Cruz got hurt. She really loved her daddy. She was with him to the end, unlike the other two. He always said she was his favorite daughter."

---

Back out on the street, I ask Lilly, "Is Sarabeth's open yet?"

"Who cares, Zara. The one you knew, on Madison, is closed for good, and the Central Park one is about a million blocks away. I'm exhausted."

"Oh. But it's only a subway ride. Please?" I draw out the *pleeeeese*. I need solace. I need comfort.

It's been two and a half years, and I've missed their lemon curd with a vengeance. Even if it's a different branch, they're my special place. I can make lemon curd, and I can make darned good scones, too, but there's something about being here in Sarabeth's culinary embrace.

Except that it's going to be inside.

"Never mind," I say, "let's just go home."

"Come on, Zara. It's safe. It's huge, this branch, not like the one you remember. And they'll only let a certain number in, almost everyone here has either had it or is vaccinated, and the windows will be open. And we've certainly been up close and personal with a whole bunch of people today." Now she's the one pushing for it.

We get on the subway, and the train goes tearing uptown, screeching and growling. It's not a long ride, but it's too loud to talk, too full for me to even be willing to breathe. I decline a seat, it's too close to other people. Lilly plops herself down and pulls a plastic bag I just realize she's been carrying onto her lap. I stand near her and look down at the top of her head, something I can rarely do. Her gray roots are peeking through, she's less gray than I am but it shows in her dark hair, and suddenly I see how vulnerable, how tired she is, how hard she works to keep it all going. I hold back the impulse to stroke her head, to kiss her forehead. Just barely.

We screech to our stop and she stands, once again the force of nature that she is. "Left, Zara, this way."

---

It's wonderful. We sit at a little table by the open window. Central Park is in early fall glory, its wider avenue shaded by trees just beginning to show edges of color. The narrower paths are aromatic with leaves; slender women push strollers and have excellent dogs on leashes; pretty storefronts are decorated for the changing season. It doesn't have the charm of my beloved Upper East Side, nor the vibrant intensity of the West side, or the cool factor of the Village, but it's a beautiful part of the City.

I wash the bits of blood off my hand in the ladies' room, and when I return to the table our coffees have come, and soon, the scones, with lemon curd for me and butter and jam for Lilly. I close my eyes, and it all fades away except this table, this moment.

"I snagged the menorah," she says, showing me the poor, abused art-project she'd been transporting in the plastic bag.

"I never even saw you pick it up, never mind bag it. Well done!" I say. I'm not ready to show Lilly my find, it's too explosive and will damage the moment. Instead, I bite deeply into my scone.

My reverie is short-lived, as my handbag almost vibrates off my lap. Sighing, I check my phone. Sam has texted about six times, increasingly urgently, this last, the first I've noticed, in all caps: DON'T GO HOME.

My heart has its own crazy rhythm, and I show the message to Lilly before I take the phone outside to call him. I quickly scroll through the others, but they're not informative, just requests to call him, text him, something. "I'm okay," I say, as soon as he answers. He breathes. "I'm at Sarabeth's with Lilly. What's going on?"

"You're all the way on the Upper East Side?" I correct that, and he continues. "Stay there. Don't go back to Katonah. In fact, stay there until I meet you."

"What's going on?" I ask again.

"I don't want to go into it on the phone, but we've tracked Rosen's computer activity. Like I said, he leaves a signature trail. He obviously had plenty of time on his hands in the hospital, but it looks like his Covid result was faked, the email from the doctor to the head warden was manufactured, and your friend Jeanine was allowed in as a private security nurse. We can't read what he writes until we trace the individual threads, so I don't know what they've got cooked up, but she knows where Lilly lives, so now he probably does, and he's a loose cannon. So at least wait for me before you two go home. I'll drive over now."

"We haven't finished our scones," I say.

"Zara! This is serious." As if I don't know.

"Jeanine is not a problem right now," I add. "She's in the ER." I give him the short version of the scene at the apartment.

"Oh my god, Zara. You went to the apartment? Sit tight. I'm driving. It will take at least twenty minutes, if not more, for me to get there. Don't go anywhere. I'll text from the street."

He hangs up before I can remonstrate further. I go back in to tell Lilly the news.

"Oh for fuck sake," she says. "So we sit and wait for your knight in shining armor to come and get us? And then what? Does he have a bazooka or something?"

"Huh? Oh, Sam, you mean. No, I don't think he's armed. But yeah, I guess we wait for him. Why do you think Agent Skordall kept saying that they had Rosen under control?"

"No clue. She didn't seem to be upset that he was out running around. No one seems to care. And I'm the sitting duck." Now she's on the other side of the argument.

My phone goes off again. Sam texts: *change of plans. Take the train home. I'll be there ahead. Traffic unreal to get crosstown. Im stopped. If I get on the HHudson I'll be there before you be very very careful.*

"Looks like our knight in shining rentacar is stuck in cross-town traffic and is going to meet us at your house. We can linger as long as you'd like, and head on back on the train."

She checks her watch. "If we take the Three Oh Five we'll be home at four. Yes, please," she adds, as the waitress refills her coffee cup. "It is decaf, right?"

"I still don't get the connection," she says, wiping the crumbs up from her plate with back of her fork. I do the same. Every crumb is delicious.

"Well, Dad and Trudy were always connected. I mean, I guess we accept that they had a kid together...so I guess Jeanine was always connected with Dad too. Remember the text Dad sent me, that Thanksgiving where he didn't go home?"

"I remember that Thanksgiving all right," she says. "I and Francis and Carlito and, who was it, Jacques, right? They and I had Thanksgiving with Mother, I bought most of it but she could still do some, she made her great stuffing with apples and sage — I've never gotten it right — and it was the most peaceful, pleasant Thanksgiving we'd had in years. I knew Mother was unhappy, but she put on a good face especially since Carlito was there, and I didn't get to see him all that often after Gilberto and I divorced, and Mother had taken to him like one of her grandchildren from the moment I married Gilberto and well after the divorce. It was wonderful."

"And Dad sent me that text, like he was justifying his behavior, even though we didn't know about Trudy being there. I mean, I figured he was with a woman because of what he said, and because he wouldn't want to be alone, well, ever. But he said that Mom had constant affairs, including with Henderson, the poet not the baseball player, and that he put up with it because she couldn't help herself after the trauma of the war. I think he called her a nymphomaniac."

"Yeah. The next week they were together again, all lovey-dovey and kittenish. It was disgusting. But there was something about them, I don't know…"

"Mom once told me that it was okay to fight with your husband, as long as you loved the reconciliation. I told her Sam and I preferred not to fight. And she said, *You're made of ice, Zara. And that's good.* I'll never forget it."

Lilly looks at me with big sad eyes. "We're so different, you and I. I've fought with every single man, husband, lover, boyfriend. But unlike Mother, I hated the reconciliation. Which is why there weren't many. Until after they were gone, of course."

I touch her hand. There isn't much to say.

We pay up, and head back down to Grand Central for the train.

---

## *Family Scrapbook: Photo #5, 1968*

*Daniel and Aurora are sitting close. An empty cocktail glass to Aurora's right catches the light of the flashbulb as she looks with soft eyes into the camera. Her dress, a quintessential evening gown in floral design, plunges deep at the neckline but rises to wide*

*straps at her broad shoulders. Daniel's suit jacket is open but his
solid-colored tie is still tightly knotted. The camera has caught him
about to speak, his lips slightly parted. He does not look angry.*

---

The strap has slipped off Aurora's shoulder. It has always seemed
that Daniel's hand is near it, in the moment before he raises it back
up her arm. But looking closely it's an illusion, and the hand is the
waiter's, behind her, holding a small tray.

No one is there to catch the falling strap.

---

"Do we have time to stop at Zabars and get rye bread?" I ask.
I can't believe I'm pretending this is in any way a normal day. "It will
be quicker than if I make it, and there's nothing like New York rye."

We get to the shop, deep in Grand Central, and the overwhelming
number of breads almost brings tears to my eyes. "You really love
your carbs, don't you," Lilly says.

I give her a look that says *but I don't show it.*

"Ooh, pumpernickel," she says. "Let's get one of those too."

"Remember when Mom used to say, *do you mean it or are you just
pfumphing through the nose?*" Lilly grins. "Turns out pfumphing, or
whatever, means *making wind,* so she was saying *are you farting out
your nose!*" We're both laughing, and she orders a pumpernickel as
well as a rye, sliced.

"So, since *nickel* is like, Old Nick, or the devil, it's Devil's Fart
bread for us!" Lilly says.

Rye with the germ and seed coating left on is what's used for
pumpernickel, I tell Lilly, so it makes sense that it probably does
give a little gas.

"Pedant," she says.

The train is practically empty, and we get a four-seat set to ourselves. "I hope that whatever we're walking into at home isn't Rosen," Lilly says.

"Sam will be there first. And guess what I just realized? If Trump has an interest in the building where Dad's apartment is, and that's being sold to pay his debts, then it will be listed as one of the properties in his syndicate. That's how someone could track down...well, I guess it's still in his name, so that wouldn't get...unless the life-estate was recorded...Or you Googled *Persil* and got the notice of default because of the Trump sale...or vice-versa..."

"You're muttering," Lilly says.

"No, that's it. Deeper than just a search like you or I could do, but if someone with real deep computer skills found the connection between us, the apartment, Dad, Trudy, and therefore Jeanine, then they would know about the default, the apartment, and once they pinpoint Jeanine, she's a nurse, and she can go into the hospital, and yes! It starts with that goddam article about you and the menorah in the paper. It's a tautology, but the connection is clear as day."

"To you. And no one uses *tautology* in casual conversation, you pedant."

"That's how he did it," I say.

"Who?"

"Rosen, you idiot. Sorry. Not what I mean. No, really, sorry." Lilly turns away. "Please, I didn't mean it. Listen. This is the entire thing."

She doesn't answer. Too many years of Dad calling her stupid, Mother calling her impulsive and emotional, me condescending.

"I'm the idiot, Lilly. I'm really sorry."

"It's okay. When I think of all the horrible things I've called you over the past two months, *idiot* doesn't begin to describe it."

"Stop. No kumbaya on the train. Now listen. This is how Rosen found Jeanine, and us. It starts with the article. He sees the article in the paper. Realizes that we did indeed find the menorah. Because remember, he didn't know. He's all, *oh shit, they're going to convict me.* Even though the ledgers don't show the menorah, since you took the page linking it to Nazi-stolen art, the museum theft is almost enough. Of course, that implicates Lev — without the insurance issues — and that's why they arrest Lev. I'll bet when we talk to him he'll say that he told the Feds about the ledger page."

"No! He wouldn't!"

"Lilly, they let him go right away. He gave them something. That's what it was — I'm sure of it. And once they knew, they threatened you, hoping that you'd come clean. It's not about the insurance fraud. That can be worked out. But it's about the Nazi-art-theft conviction. But they can't just go to you and say *your boyfriend says you have a missing page of a valuable ledger, so turn it over and no one gets hurt.* Because probably, as part of the deal, he made them promise not to do that."

"Mighty nice of him. I think *that's that* with Lev."

"Hey, we're speculating, remember? So when we turn it in, Skordall is practically doing cartwheels, but she makes me look emotional and warm, so she doesn't show it."

"You are emotional and warm, Zara. Really. Somewhere under there, you are."

I guess that's a compliment. "Anyway, where was I? So Rosen sees the article, starts searching, and comes up with the apartment, and Dad, and the default, and probably even the shares certificate. If Sam found it, Rosen found it. And from there to Jeanine it's just a birth-certificate. So he engineers his fake Covid result, they put him at NYU Langone, he contacts Jeanine, and does his Rosen thing. And it's perfect, because there's no more money for the loan on the apartment, so Jeanine is going to be evicted if she doesn't come up with a way to pay for it. And trust me, it's a lot. Less than the rent was, I'm sure, but the rent was almost seven grand a month."

"SEVEN GRAND A MONTH?" Lilly shouts.

Even on a practically empty train that's too loud.

"Hush! Yeah."

"And he wouldn't even lend me a grand for Francis's wisdom teeth. Son of a bitch."

"But he found you the best oral surgeon in New York. And he arranged for Francis's trip to Poland. And he gave you his car. So, yeah, it was extravagant, but... anyway, so Jeanine jumps at the chance to get in league with him, I can just imagine."

"Yeah, she's got big tits, too."

"I wonder if she's actually our half-sister."

"She's probably mine, anyway."

"Hey!"

"Sorry. Though maybe it'd be better if he weren't your father, no?"

*Family Scrapbook: Who's your daddy? 1967*

*I'm getting my first blood test, before my tonsillectomy, I'm seven years old, and I watch the blood go up the needle into the tube. I'm going to be a doctor, like Daddy. He always says I will be. Never, even in the early sixties, does he ever say I can't because I'm a girl. "You're smart like your mother, and good at science, like me," he says. The blood goes into the needle, up into the tube and I stand up, all done, no tears. He smiles at me, then I watch his face melt, like a candle. The room is gray, the edges are fading, it gets dark. I reach for his waist, I'm so small and he's so tall, I don't remember if I get to him, but the world goes black and I come to, lying on the cot in the nurse's area, nauseous and sweating. "You fainted," he says. "Now I can't be a doctor," I start to cry. "I fainted too, at my first dissection," he says. I don't know what dissection is, but I hold his big, dry hand, and I'm comforted.*

"No."

"No what?" Lilly asks.

"It wouldn't be better if he weren't my father."

"That was five minutes ago. Have you been thinking about this the whole time? You're weird."

"You know what else is weird?" I say. Lilly rolls her eyes. "No, really. There was a syringe in Jeanine's bathroom. In the trash. And no one, not the cop, not the EMTs, no one noticed."

"She's diabetic, remember?"

That image from my memory, of my first blood test, wavers back in. "That's why I fainted. The blood, plus the needle. Dad wasn't diabetic, but Trudy was, and Jeanine is too." Something is rattling me.

I pull the photo from my bag and hand it to her. She gasps and holds it away a bit to see it better. "Holy shit," she says. "Holy, holy shit."

After a minute she says, "Well, that pretty much ices it."

"I never doubted that he'd married her. And I have the divorce certificate. It's just, did he really have a kid with her, eight years later when he was married to Mom?"

Lilly reaches into her bag. "I thought I'd nabbed the only thing worth taking," she says. She hands me a pile of plastic laminated IDs on lanyards. They're Jeanine's nurse's identification badges for NYU Langone. Looks like they renew them annually. Dad was there. Rosen was there. There's one from 2014, when Dad died. And another one, and it's current for 2020-21.

## Chapter Thirteen

# The Lying Kin

The train pulls into Katonah, and we walk the six blocks through a post-card town of small shops and stately Victorian homes, from the station to Lilly's home. I notice that she's hardly limping at all, which, after all this walking and commotion, is good. I see a low-end late-model American car parked in front of her house, with its discreet rental sticker on the bumper, and I breathe a sigh of relief. No one but a renter would be driving a Dodge Charger with nothing at all — not even a box of tissues — in the interior.

The front door is unlocked, and we go in. "Sam?" I call out.

"Not quite." And there, coming out from behind the door and looming over me, a face I'd hoped never to see again in my life, is Walter Rosen.

He's nearly seven feet tall, his white-blond hair longer and less styled than when we last met, and his blue eyes are more faded. He's wearing a hospital gown, mercifully he's also wearing green scrubs pants, and those nasty little slippers they give you at the hospital. Over the gown he's wearing a long white lab coat.

He slips behind me, pulls me into him with an arm across my neck, and he has the nerve to rest an elbow on the top of my head.

"Hello, Walter," Lilly says. "Nice outfit." And *I'm* made of ice? I'm standing stock still, not ready to struggle. He's big, and I need the element of surprise. I also have started to shake.

"Lilly, *mein Schatz*. Come give me a kiss." Lilly, to my shock, comes over and gives him a kiss, right on the lips. She even stands on tiptoes when she does it. She doesn't even look at me.

He drops the arm from my neck, turning to pull Lilly to him instead. Quickly I bend my knees and duck out from under his elbow. He stumbles slightly and I take the opportunity to flee into the kitchen.

I've dropped my bag at the door when Rosen startled me, so I don't have my phone to call the police, but I can get out the back door and start screaming. Maybe that nosy neighbor will call the cops for me. And I need to head Sam off so he doesn't walk into this. Unless he does have a bazooka.

"Don't move, little sister," Rosen says.

I look back and he's got Lilly held tight against his chest, and he's got an ugly kitchen knife at her throat. My mouth goes dry. He would use it, we both know that. "Okay, but put that down before you hurt someone," I say.

"My, such bravado. Who knew? Though I do know you've got a nasty little kick in you. I'll be taking my revenge for that a bit later. But first, let me enjoy my lady." His hand moves to Lilly's breast and I want to kill him. Her eyes glaze over and I know she's letting her mind transport her away from this. It's how I get through things. I didn't think she did. She's a doer.

"I saw what you did to Jeanine," I say. I want him to stop pawing Lilly. Why did she go to him? Why didn't she stay back? "We got the ambulance in time."

"Don't know what you're talking about." He's concentrating on Lilly.

"We went to the apartment. Looks like you trashed it pretty thoroughly," I say. "Still looking for your stupid little menorah?" I can't just leave, and leave Lilly in his hands.

"Shut up, will you?" he says, his free hand making its way to her other breast.

"Leave her alone and I'll tell you where it is."

He looks up, across at me. I can see that he's trying to pull his focus from his lust. He's not the sharp villain he was two years ago. Time in jail will dull a person. He wants Lilly, he wants her badly, but he wants his gold menorah, too. "Where's the rest of the stuff?"

"Didn't you find it at Jeanine's?"

He finally focusses on me. "Dumb bitch got the wrong thing. Some ceramic tchotchke worth nothing. Well, she paid for her mistake. You saw that. At the hospital they'll never even notice her ketone levels — fools, all of them — just like they didn't notice your daddy's." Lilly jerks her head up, but Rosen presses the knife slightly and she glazes over again.

"What about my dad," I say, trying to keep his attention.

"Stupid woman, can't stop talking." Does he mean me? Apparently not. "*Just let me take my medicine* she says. And she shoots herself up with insulin. Right in front of me. Disgusting. Her little knife cuts, the blood? All theater. Souvenirs. I gave her her medicine all right. She'll be dead in no time. Just like your Poppy as she called him, after he signed over the shares. Enough insulin to take down a big guy like your dad, sick as he was, *strong as a horse*, she said. Or to take down an ox like Jeanine."

"She's going to survive," I say. "You're toast."

He laughs, a dry little laugh. "Then so is she. But if you two cooperate, one of you will survive. Take a guess which one?"

He pulls Lilly sharply back into his chest, and moves the knife down, until it's right under her left breast. He puts his mouth to her ear, but says loud enough for me to hear, "You, my sweetest delight, you will live. You'll come with me, we'll go to Europe, no one will find us. *Nicht var?*"

He's lost his mind. It's scarier than the brilliantly calculating giant he once was.

"Of course, darling," she says softly. "Of course we will."

"Unless your stupid little sister does something, well, stupid," he adds. "Then, alas, you both will have to stay here. But then, I still will let you live, my love, so that you can always remember me."

I shudder, but Lilly stays still.

"No, really," I say. "I have all the things you want. I mean, the beautiful pieces of art, the menorah, the spice containers — "

His head jerks up at that. "What? You have the containers?"

"Ow!" Lilly says. In his excitement he's scratched her with the knife.

"*Och.* Sorry, *liebchen.*" He thumbs the little drop of blood. "Not too bad. You!" he says to me, then, to Lilly, "what's her name again? Yours I will never forget, my Lilly, my rose, but hers?"

"Zara," I say. "My name is Zara. Short for Zarathustra." I don't know why I say that. It was my funny-pedantic thing in high school.

"What a pedant your sister is," he says to Lilly. She and I both laugh. Mine's a little hysterical, but Rosen is surprised. "What is so funny?"

"Oh, just that everyone always says that about Zara," Lilly says. Somehow, the tension is broken by this, even though the situation is exactly as it was. "Family joke."

"So, now I'm in the family," Rosen says. "Speaking of family, that idiot, Jeanine, really is your half-sister? She says she is, and that her mother was his wife, then his mistress? What kind of a man does that?"

He's babbling, though he's asking what Lilly and I have been asking ourselves.

He's still talking. He must have been lonely the past two years. "Then after she and her mother helped him die, she got his gorgeous apartment. Dumb as day, but she was obviously pretty at some point. Not as pretty as you, my delight," he adds, to Lilly. "And not as beautifully voluptuous."

Now we all know the family secrets. This is my last chance. "So, Mr. Rosen, did she tell you all this? And you believed her?"

He chuckles. "Let us sit down, and I can enjoy the delights on offer." He pulls Lilly towards the couch, and I edge towards my handbag. He puts her on the sofa and snuggles up next to her, pinning her with his weight. His stomach growls loudly.

"Hungry?" Lilly asks. "Want some dinner?"

"I want you, my sweet pastry."

"Of course," she answers. "Besides, I've told you Zara's the chef in the family."

"Zara is the ugly, skinny chef!" He laughs. "Zara! Lilly says you're a good cook. I haven't had a decent meal in two years. Cook me something, not that I will fall for your shellfish trick if you try it. If I like it, maybe we'll let you live too."

"Gladly," I say, but before I get to my purse he says, "And don't touch your bag. I would hate to spoil my fun with Lilly before I have it. Now get in the kitchen. Meat with noodles and gravy. With carrots. Cook!"

"Okay, okay," I say. If I can stay in the kitchen, I can edge out the back door, get help while he's with Lilly. Poor Lilly.

I clatter a pan on the counter, open the refrigerator and grab the onion I'd sliced what seemed like years ago, this morning. I see a package of minute steaks. Minute steaks, I haven't seen those in years. An onion, a beer, some sour cream.

"Want a beer?" I say. He's bent over Lilly. No answer. "Hey Rosen! You want a beer or not?"

"No! I don't want a beer. I want a meal, and I want my beautiful art pieces and I want my Lilly. I can tell you, Zara, Jeanine was nothing like your sister. Nothing. No charm. No energy, no imagination. Just lay there, grunting. No wonder your father divorced her mother, if that's how she was. Big tits, but no style at all.

"And no artifacts. So she wrote up the order for me to leave that hospital, their system is laughable, I put the order into their computer system myself, and she escorted me out. As if I was going to go back to jail! Fools..."

"How did you find her?" I ask. I put onions on to sauté, it's the best way to fake a dinner. Where the hell is Sam?

"Mmmm, smells good. Come, Lilly, should we go to the bedroom? Away from your scrawny sister? Let her cook. And if you do anything, anything at all, Zara, I will kill you. Do you understand?" His voice is icy and suddenly completely unaccented.

"I do," I say, very small. "But first, tell me how you found Jeanine. Please?"

"Better, better... so easy, Zara. It's all on the internet now. Even a chimp could do it. That lunatic ex-President, yes, I agree with you on that, he's a shareholder in the co-op. He needs to sell his shares, and everything else, to pay his billions of debt. I read it in the news. And then, sweet Lilly, your face was in the papers, with my menorah!"

"Ow!" she cries.

"Yes, a little pain for that. But I'm grateful, because from there, to searching for your name, which I did every day, every day, Lilly, I saw that Persil had an apartment in the co-op, but that your daddy's loan was in default. No big trick to find out the man passed away in 2014, and then, the deed showing the life estate in Mrs. Semple, and then the remainder in you. Nothing to it, to find out that Jeanine is the current resident, the building's system is only slightly more secure than the hospital's." He laughs. "Idiots. Come, Lilly."

He pulls her to her feet, and holding the knife tight against her neck again, frog-marches her towards the bedroom.

"My dinner, Zara, or your pretty sister won't be so pretty anymore."

⁜

His back is turned. There's no time to waste. I grab the frying pan full of hot oil and onions, and scurry up behind him. He has the knife against her neck, he's almost two feet taller than I am. I only have one shot.

"Hey, Walter! How about a threesome?"

He starts to turn.

I'm holding the pan handle with both hands, I swing it fast over my head, centrifugal force keeping its contents in, and smash it against the back of his neck. Hot oil and onions pour down his back and the blow makes him lurch forward, the knife moving away from Lilly. She grabs his arm and shoves him down, falling on top of him as she slips on the hot oil. She's no light-weight, and the air whooshes out of him in a rush.

I raise my foot and bring my heel down, hard, on his nose, and blood spurts into the air. I have no desire whatsoever to faint, and I pull Lilly away from his flailing arms. She rises to her knees, drives one shoulder into the forearm with the knife, and collapses on top of him.

"I think I re-broke my leg," she says.

"Come on, let's get you away from him," I insist, trying to hoist her. She shakes her head. "I'll keep him pinned."

I pull the knife from his hand, his arm safely pinned under a lot of Lilly. "Beat the shit out of him," I say. "Less PTSD that way."

She takes my advice.

I grab my phone as soon as I'm sure she's safe and pound in 911. "There's a rapist," I say. It's simplest and will get the response I need. "He has my sister." I give the address. The dispatcher is calm, asks me for the damned cross-street and the town. I'm breathing hard, and I'm trying to whisper. "He has a knife. Send someone." She offers to stay on the line. I say I can't, and I click off.

It feels like forever but in less than a minute I hear the sirens, and in no time I let the police in the front door.

It's our duo from the other day. They give me a look and then see Rosen and Lilly in the hallway. The male, I remember his name is Bruno, draws his gun.

"We've got him," I say softly. I really don't want to see that gun go off.

"Get away from him," the female officer says. Lilly tries to get up, but we all realize at the same time that she can't. Including Rosen. He grabs at her, and holds her against him like a shield.

"I have his knife," I say, pointing to the weapon on the counter. The cops walk directly up to Rosen, and pushing Lilly aside none too gently, they cuff him. I reach for Lilly and help her, as best I can given the size differential, and she hobbles to the sofa.

"At least the bone isn't sticking out this time," I say. She just glares and lies back against the cushions.

"Do you need an ambulance?" Bruno asks.

"Yes," I say.

"No," Lilly says at the same time. The cops look at us. "No," Lilly repeats.

I hear a yipping in the back bedroom. I'd wondered where Sherlocke was. I go to let her out, but Rosen is sitting handcuffed on the floor of the hall.

"I'm going to need to take your statements," the female says. I squint at her name tag. Fazzinga. I should have known. Growing up, the place was crawling with Fazzingas. She made good — for any family, but for that one, definitely.

"I went to school with someone from your family, I think," I say.

She smirks. "You and the rest of the county. So you say, this guy was trying to rape one of you? Which one?"

She makes it sound unlikely, as in *who'd rape a woman your age?* Not a good attitude for a cop, especially a woman cop. But this isn't the time. "And you two seem to know him."

"We do. He's escaped from the Federal jail in the city, via the hospital. He attacked Lilly three years ago."

She shakes her head and takes out her phone, opens the dictation function. "Ok, start over. Start with your name, and then who this guy is and how you know him. You sure you don't need an ambulance?" she adds, to Lilly.

"I'm okay," Lilly answers. "I want to see this asshole arrested. He tried to rape me at knife-point. It's only thanks to Zara that he didn't succeed."

"So he's a fugitive from the feds?" Bruno asks. "Wow!"

"She offered me a threesome," Rosen says. He still looks dazed. "She even brought out the oil." The cops, fortunately, ignore him.

"And the onions," I add.

"The little bitch, she attacked me with food again. It's what she does."

It *is* funny, a little bit. Officer Bruno looks over at me. "It's a long story," I say, "not relevant."

Officer Fazzinga is typing into her phone. "Where do you say he escaped from?"

I explain again. "No record," she says, and Rosen laughs.

"You still need to arrest him for assaulting Lilly!" I'm outraged.

"Looks like *you* assaulted *him*," Fazzinga says.

"Are you kidding? He brings a knife, he attacks Lilly, I defend her, and you think I assaulted him? Are you kidding me? Look at him!" By now I'm shouting. I'm feeling lightheaded. "I'm half his size! He's wearing hospital clothes!"

"Hmm, so he is. Well, nothing comes up on any of the databases. I guess we could take him to the station." She's still hesitating, looking at her phone. "Ms. Persil-Pendleton, looks like you've been in some trouble earlier today in the city."

*That* is coming up? But Rosen's escape isn't? "Oh, for crap's sake," I say.

"She's a thief, too," Rosen says.

"We know that," Fazzinga says.

"Look who's talking," Lilly says from the couch.

"Ok, we're done here," Fazzinga says. "You all can sort this out."

"No!" Lilly and I shout at once.

I hear voices coming up the walk. Sam. I hear Sam, and a woman, and someone else. Please God let them be able to convince the cops.

Better late than never. The first through the door, being a professional, I suppose, rather than because the other two are gentlemen, is Agent Skordall. With a gun. A big gun. Everyone, cops included, take a giant step back.

"Agent Leticia Skordall, FBI," she says. She takes in the situation. "Well, fuck me."

That breaks the stalemate, and the cops lower their weapons. I notice that Skordall doesn't until theirs are holstered, and she doesn't holster her weapon, just holds it pointing down. Sam comes up behind her, glances at me and frowns. *What? I didn't wait for you?*

Bringing up the rear is Lev. I will him with all of my telepathic brain to turn around and leave. I have no telepathy left, evidently. He more or less saunters in. "Stay out of the line," Skordall says. I assume she means the line of fire, but I'm thinking of the lineup. Clearly my brain has lost all control.

"Everyone okay?" Sam asks. We all nod, except Rosen, who spits on the floor toward Sam. Sam controls his smile but I see it on the sides. To show anger is to lose face, and both men know that. Rosen has cracked first.

"There's no record of a fugitive," Officer Fazzinga says. She's going blonde to blonde, ignoring the rest of us. "These ladies tell us that the perp is on the run from you guys, but I don't see it."

Sam starts to explain that Rosen's talents include gumming up the systems of institutions, even those with high security, such as, say, the Department of Justice. Skordall cuts in, "Yeah, but we've got him chipped."

It's almost theatrical. Everyone in the room except for her gasps. Actual, radio-play-worthy gasps. Rosen, sitting on the floor in handcuffs, in a hospital outfit with a white lab coat with blood from his nose all over it, looks up at Skordall. "Bullshit."

She shrugs. "Nope, not at all. That's how we knew you were here. We tracked you to their dad's apartment, then here."

"You knew he was there and didn't tell us?" I shriek.

"That's why I called you six times," Sam says. "That's why I told you to stay put when you finally answered."

"Goddam traffic on the West Side Highway," Skordall mutters.

"Don't you have, like, lights and sirens?" Lilly asks.

"We were in Sam's rental, which is not at all protocol, but it was the quickest way to get here."

"You too?" I ask Lev.

He shakes his head. "No. I just got here on the train, saw Sam and the lady coming up the walk, and joined the party."

Always where the action is, that's our Lev.

"It's our third call to this house in a month. Second time this week. False alarms on two out of three," Fazzinga says.

Skordall looks over at me. "Not false," I say. "This officer," I gesture at Fazzinga, "thinks I broke into Lilly's house and trashed it. It was Jeanine, at Rosen's command."

"The neighbor ID'd —"

I cut her off. "She's blonde-gray, like me, but about six feet tall, like Lilly." I swallow hard. "She's our half-sister."

Fazzinga and Bruno sigh at once. "So, should we take him in or do you want him?" Bruno asks. First words of sense in the entire debacle.

"What do you have him for?" Skordall asks.

"Breaking and entering, attempted rape, assault," Fazzinga says.

"Onion Fu...like Kung Fu," Bruno adds, shrugging.

"No, that was me," I say.

"Second time she's tried to kill me with food," Rosen says.

"Take him in," Skordall says, "and we'll send some of our guys to pick him up later. Onion Fu?"

"Can't you smell it?" I say.

"Never got my sense of smell back."

"I thought you were vaccinated," I say.

"I was."

"Attempted rape?" Sam says. He looks at me again.

"Not me, Lilly," I say.

"Your wife did offer me a threesome," Rosen says to Sam. Before anyone can react, Sam steps forward and kicks Rosen in his already bloody face.

"Sorry, I tripped," he says as Officer Fazzinga lunges between them.

"Okay, let's move out of here," Fazzinga says and she and Bruno lift Rosen by the arms. "Christ you're tall," she adds.

"Hold on to him" Skordall says. "He's very, very slippery."

"Especially with the oil on him," Bruno adds.

"Fucking Keystone cops," Sam mutters under his breath.

"Watch it, bub," Fazzinga says. "That was assault, and there are plenty of witnesses."

I rarely see Sam lose his temper, but when he does it's terrifying. Usually he turns pale, and his right hand twitches a bit. I glance down, and sure enough, there's that little movement. Fazzinga puts her free hand on her holster. He looks right at her and his mouth is tight. "I don't see your body camera," he says softly.

She flushes pink. At that moment Rosen wraps his long leg around Officer Fazzinga, knocking her to the floor. One hand has slipped out of the cuff, thanks to the oil and his oddly artistic hands, and he pushes himself off the floor and bolts to the door.

I put my hands over my ears, my panic move, terrified that someone is going to be shot. But Skordall is too quick for him, and with a smooth move knees him in the crotch. I think I scream as Rosen goes down, and Skordall pins him to the floor. All three cops have their weapons drawn. "Cuff his feet, too, next time," she says to Bruno. "Like I said, he's slippery."

"Can someone get Lilly a glass of wine?" Lev says. We pull our attention to Lilly, who's slumped on the sofa.

Bruno and Fazzinga take the break to haul Rosen out, handing a contact card to Skordall as they pass. I hear Sam exhale. Lev pushes by to get to the liquor cabinet. I go to Lilly. I know Sam too well. It wouldn't be good for me to say anything to him.

Skordall is not as wise, but she's not his wife, either. She puts her hand on his arm. "Easy, cowboy. You've got him in the cross-hairs with the evidence."

"I know, Leticia. I know. But that son of a bitch..."

"I know too," she says, her hand still on him. He looks at her hand, and she drops it to her side.

As she said when she walked in the door, *Well, fuck me.*

## Chapter Fourteen

# The Scrapbook of Dead Relatives

We're sitting around the dinner table, Lilly and Lev, Sam and I, eating the minute steaks as a faux Stroganoff. Waste not want not. Lilly's leg isn't broken, just sore, and she has it perched on an ottoman while we eat. Sam and Lilly have killed one bottle of wine and are opening another. Lev and I aren't drinkers, but even we have a glass each. We all deserve it.

"So," Sam says to Lev, "I hear that your father's notebooks have quite a story to tell."

Lev pulls the copy from the shelf.

"We didn't find the original in Jeanine's wreckage of an apartment. I looked," I say as Sam leafs through it.

"Remind me to ask Leticia to keep an eye out for the original. They're getting a warrant for a search of the premises tomorrow," Sam says.

"Leticia? Aren't we cozy." Lilly hasn't missed it, and I wonder if she saw the hand-on-arm bit.

"Can it, Lilly," I say. "In California we're a lot more informal, that's all."

"You're in New York," she counters. "And why do you think I staged that collapse? I wanted *Leticia* to get her hand off you, Sam."

So she didn't miss it.

Sam looks from one of us to the other. "I'm not going to discuss this." I give Lilly the hairy eyeball. *Don't.* She shrugs.

Sam turns back to me. "So why the hell did you walk into the house after I told you to wait?"

"Hey. Easy. I thought you were here. There was a rental car out front."

"Zara, you know I would never, ever, ever drive a Dodge, no matter who was renting it to me."

It turns out it was Rosen's rental, charged, of course, on Jeanine's credit card.

"When are we going to talk about Jeanine killing Dad with insulin?" I say. Lev and Sam stare. "I was just figuring it out, then Rosen told us. And she's diabetic."

"Rosen told you..." Sam says. "Now *there's* credibility." Now it's my turn to glare.

"Actually," Lilly chimes in, "Jeanine almost told us herself." She relays the comment at the café, from our first meeting. "Remember how red she turned when she said she was diabetic, *like Poppi*, and you said, *no, Trudy was?*"

"I'm sure she talked herself into thinking Dad was, so she wouldn't be a murderer."

"And Rosen?" Sam can't get past that.

"He gave Jeanine a huge insulin shot, and she went into a seizure or something. She probably did fall and hit her head, like she told the cop. The blood all over the place was just Rosen's signature, decoration, or icing on the cake," I add.

"Well, she survived it," Sam says, "once again. Thanks to you."

"Barely," I mutter and get up to clear the table.

Lev leaps into the silence, opening the copy of his father's book. He picks up the story of his father in the woods, right where we left off, but Sam says, "Skip to the lists. Tell me what's on the lists of the things your father bought in Paris, and afterwards."

Lev flips the pages. "Aye aye, Cap'n."

Sam chuckles. "Sorry, long day for everyone."

*He* gets an apology.

Lev goes to the list, and reads. I translate when it's Ladino, Lilly or Lev when it's French or German, or that combo that is Alsatian. The menorah, the spice jar, the plates, the goblets, the mezuzahs, the list goes on. "Wow."

"Quite a rescuer," Sam says. "And all of those items were lent to the museum?"

"Oh god no. Only a few things. Most of the rest he's sold a long time ago, to Jews. He was careful. Only to Jews. "

No mention of a ruby-encrusted spice container.

"How do you feel about keeping these things?" Sam asks. "Some of them belonged — all of them must have belonged to people who yearned for them."

"Not my call," Lev says. "And it's my patrimony too. These were stolen from my people, and my dad bought them back. He got them into the right hands, and when he couldn't, he kept them or sold them to others who never got their own treasures back. No, I feel fine about it."

I'm tempted to raise the issue of the spice container. In effect, he's received stolen goods, since it was stolen from the museum, and further, it's on the Polish Unrecovered Art site. Odd that no one has put those two facts together yet, but with the volume of items, perhaps it's not as surprising.

And if it was acquired during Rosen's tenure at the museum, he could be completely aware of its provenance, and never have reported it. He could have blessed it personally, had Marie steal it, and made off with it himself. Except that Lev got it, so no, that couldn't be it...

When Marie stole the items from the museum, the plan *had* to have been to give Lev back his pieces. But the rest? Was she going to give most of them to Rosen, keep a few things for herself, and let the insurance reimburse everyone? I must raise it.

Lev won't meet my eyes. Sam looks astonished. Lilly gets up and hobbles to the bathroom, letting Sherlocke, who once again has gotten stuck back there, out. Sherlocke bounds over to Lev, and he picks her up without looking at her, puts her on his lap and pets her.

"You need to tell them," Sam says. "Otherwise you really are receiving stolen goods."

"It's probably worth hundreds of thousands of dollars," Lev says.

"But it's on the list of Polish Unrecovered Art. You'll never be able to sell it," I say.

Lev nods. "I know. But it's so beautiful. And all the other stuff was mine. It's the only one that wasn't." I don't challenge him. "I'm sure the museum made money on the insurance claim…"

"Not the point," I say. "But I'm sure that's what Rosen was after. That's probably what he sent Jeanine here for: the menorah, the spice containers, the ledger sheet. She obviously thought your dad's book was the ledger sheet, and Francis X's menorah was the true one. He must have been furious."

At that, even Sam laughs. "Where is this spice box now?" he asks.

The term *pregnant silence* comes to mind. I look at Lilly. Lilly looks at Lev. Lev looks at Sherlocke. No one says anything. Sam looks at each of us. "Okay," he says, "was it something I said?"

Lilly breaks first. "Quite frankly," she starts.

"Oh my god, don't lie about it!" I screech.

"Honestly," Lev says.

We all start to giggle. "It's not a laughing matter," Sam says.

Sherlocke jumps off Lev's lap and trots over to the linen closet and starts to yip. "What is it, girl?" Sam says. "Is Timmy in the well?"

I get up and walk over to the linen closet. Lilly limps after me as I open the closet door, and the spice containers tumble down onto my head. "I had trouble reaching the sheets on the top shelf that I needed for Sam's bed, and when I found the spice containers, I just tossed them back up, and shoved some sheets against them," I say.

Obviously not well enough to keep them up there, since they were up too high for me to do a good job. Which tells me that Lilly knew they were up there, since Lev is only an inch or two taller than I am, and it really takes a six-footer to do a good job of hiding them. Unless he stood on the ottoman, like I did, which, for some reason, seems like too much pre-meditation for him.

Lilly carries them over to the table, and I fire up my iPad to the Polish Unrecovered Art page. We scroll through to the spice container with the rubies. It's not exactly the same, I note, so maybe it's by the same artisan but not the exact one claimed. That would be very, very helpful in the defense of Lev's prosecution.

"We need to tell Phil Caravaggio about these," Sam says.

"And have Lev prosecuted for receiving stolen goods?" I ask.

"And me?" Lilly adds.

"I'm still here, folks," Lev says. I suppose no one likes to be talked about in the third person. "And though I agree with Sam, we need to tell Alan first. He'll know what or how to tell Caravaggio."

"I still don't get it," I say.

"After Marie took the artifacts, she was supposed to give me back my stuff. She and Rosen were going to split the rest up somehow, none of my business. I got a few other things Marie took from the museum, but only because when Marie met Rosen up at Temple Shmuel for the handoff, she must have known something terrible was about to happen to her, and she threw all the items she could into the bushes. Including some of my father's pieces.

"She threw them into the bushes," he repeats. "One of the containers is mine," he adds, pointing to the brass filigreed one, "and one isn't. But it is truly beautiful. If it belongs to someone, we can return it."

Lilly sighs. It would be a beautiful thing to own, and a valuable piece to sell, but it's not ours. Or his. It's someone else's, and the museum needs to find out whose it is.

From whose hands was this spice-holder torn, the container that held the aromatic consolation, the spices to reanimate the heart for the start of the week? Whose life was shattered with the theft of this beautiful holder of the last moments of Shabbat peace?

"There are rewards," I say, forcing myself back to the present, "for recovering stolen Judaica. And you should be entitled to one. They actually have mediators that negotiate between current owners and long-ago theft victims. There should be something there for you."

Lev shrugs. "I got my father's stuff back. That's the most important thing. And we got the…the insurance money for the menorah. And Marcia won't kill me."

"Who's Marcia?" Sam asks.

"My sister. She's the one who takes care of my dad, I mean he's in a memory-care facility, but she goes every day, and she would absolutely slaughter me if I didn't do the right thing. She's bailed me out of practically everything in my whole life, as much as she could, and visited me in jail, and sent money to my ex when she needed surgery. Marcia is the best, but she's a demon when she feels wronged."

"How'd she do with the menorah?"

"Joint custody. Lilly has it some of the time, I've got it the other."

I clear my throat. "Hey. I was the one who recognized it. I was the one who claimed it, who found it, who spoke to Mom's ghost about it. Lived for it. I thought *I* was sharing it with Lilly."

"You are," they both say at once. "You and I are the same," Lilly says. "Joined at the hip. In fact, it's your turn to have it this year. As soon as we get it back from Andres."

"Who's Andres?" Sam asks. "How out of the loop am I?"

---

The next day, Sam again has to go into the City, but Lilly and I have no appetite for further adventures. It's overcast and cold, and she puts a log in her fireplace. I sip coffee, she puts her leg up and drinks mulled cider, and we read the previous Sunday's unread *New York Times*. I do the crossword and start the acrostic. She reads the fashion supplement. "At least there's some hope of being able to go places this fall, and wear this stuff," she says. "Look at this jacket. Gorgeous."

I glance over and nod, and go back to my acrostic, but first I key in the BBC Scottish Symphony Orchestra website and put on the watch-and-listen series. They're doing a series on Bartók, the Hungarian composter. His wild, crazy and romantic music feels just right. *Gypsy with a touch of Disney*, Dad used to say. I am at ease.

At two o'clock the phone rings. "Let me put you on speaker," she says. "It's your new boyfriend," Lilly whispers to me.

"Hello, beautiful ladies," Andres says through the speaker. I roll my eyes.

"Turn off the music," Lilly says. I pause it.

"No, that was lovely," Andres says. "Bartók, no? How perfect for today! So, I've got a valuation for you. It was difficult, you know. This is an important artistic piece for a number of reasons." His voice is serious now, devoid of the ridiculous flattery he's been laying on. "First, as you know, it's a piece of stolen art. These can be very important, not just for the families, like yours, but for their historical contribution to understanding World War II."

"We know," Lilly says. I put my finger to my lips, *hush*, and turn on the voice memos on my phone. I know it's illegal to record a conversation without permission, but this is something I want to preserve for my own use. Even I will break the law, sometimes.

"You may need me to issue a report," Andres says. "It will be useful to you with the insurance company."

"Thank you," I say. But I keep the recorder on.

"So, as I was saying. There's the personal value, and there's the historical value. There's the moral value of having something returned to the family, the descendants."

I see the light wavering, the room taking on the green-gold shine of an impending hallucination. *Not now,* I say to it, *I need to hear the report.* The aura obediently recedes.

"But there's the financial value as well. And that sometimes doesn't comport with emotional or historical value." I make a face at Lilly.

"But in this case, the technique of the turquoise enameling is a rare, lost art. It's not cloisonné, which frankly is a dime a dozen, but actual turquoise, and with gold designs on it. Like your ring, Zara. The menorah itself is, amazingly, pure gold, except that the base is filled. But the remainder is valued, even on its metal alone, without the workmanship, at over one hundred thousand dollars. With the history and the workmanship, I would put the value between one hundred and fifty, two hundred."

I exhale hard. "Wow!"

"A hundred and fifty-two hundred?" Lilly asks. "What kind of a number is that?"

Andres and I both chuckle. "One hundred and fifty thousand dollars to two hundred thousand dollars, Lilly," he says. "You've got dyscalculia, *bella.*"

"Well, I speak five languages," she says huffily.

"That's excellent," I say. "We'd really like a report. And I get that there's a cost to that."

"Ah, the business-sister," he says, and he adds something in Italian that I don't catch. "Naturally. The phone report, I give for free, because you are both such charming girls, but the written reports, well, that's much more formal."

"Of course," I say. "I look forward to getting it."

Lilly takes him off speaker and goes off to her room to finish the conversation. I text Sam. *Looks like the menorah is worth at least*

*150K. That gets L and L off the hook, don't you think?*

*Yeah I'd guess,* he texts back. *Call Alan.*

*What are you up to? Visiting the FBI?* He's off in the City, and while I know the issue with Agent Skordall is nonsense, it doesn't hurt to ask.

*Yeah, but not our lovely agent. This is coalition business. They're on our side now.*

Nothing a little change of administration won't do for you.

*Back by 7. You cooking?*

He knows a decent dinner is more likely that way, but I'm not. *Outside under the heatlamps. There's a really good Italian restaurant here, and I'm done.*

We sign off just as Lilly emerges. "Lev's going to talk to Alan, and then we can talk to Caravaggio. Do you mind if Andres comes to dinner with us tonight?"

"Won't Lev mind?"

"I think Lev and I are kind of cooling off," she says. "He's a little fast and loose with the law for me."

God, it's hard to keep a straight face.

I wonder if Lev knows that they're "cooling off" yet, but it's not my business. "I'm good with it. Make sure Andres brings my ring back, too."

⁕ ⊹⊱◈◊◈◁⊰⊹ ⁕

The next step is to deal with the bank and the apartment. I call Alan Seskin, give him the heads up on the value of the menorah. "Yeah. Lev Zimmerman called and told me. When can I get that report?"

I tell him we expect it within a week. "That clears Lilly too, right?"

He grunts. "She's never been indicted, but that should take care of any possibility. Close call for her, though."

I don't want to think about it. "So, Alan, what do you know about evictions in New York City?"

"Oh, god, don't get me started. A fucking nightmare. You got a tenant you need to throw out?"

I briefly run down the Jeanine problem. *She's still in the hospital, the prognosis is good. I have mixed feelings about her survival, and mixed feelings about being so conflicted. She'll probably be arrested for burglary, whether she'll do time is questionable, she might have killed my father, but maybe not if she was the "favorite daughter" god damn her, it was probably Trudy...* But Alan has no interest in my moral quagmire.

"Even if she's never paid a dime of rent, once she's in possession she's got protections," he says. "And it's a co-op so they get to decide who you put in her place. You gonna sell it?"

"For sure," I say. I don't want anything to do with it.

"Let me know how much. I may have someone interested in it, pay you good money, skip the real estate agent hassle. And I'll get you the name of an unlawful detainer lawyer in the City. It's a specialty. Not mine. But I can tell you, the best way? Cash for keys. Give the lady some money, and out she goes."

<hr />

Sam gets back early, just before it starts to thunder. "Holy shit, what's that?" he says, then laughs. "I forget."

"Me too," I tell him. "I dove under the desk the first time I heard it last week. I guess we'll have to cancel dinner."

"No way," Lilly says.

"No, we can still eat, and Andres can still join us, but at a restaurant? Outdoors?"

"Jeez, Zara. If we cancelled everything every time it rained here, we'd never get to do anything. There are tents, and heat lamps, and, God forbid, indoor dining."

"We'll see," I say.

"Don't be paranoid," Lilly says.

"Let's see if we can get a Zoom with Caravaggio," Sam interrupts. "I want to hear what the search turned up. And we can bring him up to speed."

Amazingly, he's available, and soon we are all little squares on a screen. I join from the guest room on my iPad, Sam's on his phone, Lilly on the computer, with a headset. I have to admit she looks very fetching in them.

Lev, at his own home in New Jersey, is pointedly not on the call.

"Well you certainly have been busy," he says, once we've all exchanged updates. "I'm glad the menorah is safe. And thanks, Sam, and your group, for breaking that code on Rosen's hack. It's amazing how much he did with a phone from a hospital bed."

"What gave it away was the trail he left when he was still in jail," Sam said. "His usage, of course, was monitored, since he used the Federal jail system's computers that they provide for the inmates, but he would erase his tracks, leaving only the ones that he wanted. When he did that, there was a signature, a pattern that showed up. It was pretty sophisticated, but we found it. And that's how he got into the hospital, tracked down Jeanine Cruz, and got out of the hospital. By the way, it turns out that he did have a bona-fide positive Covid test. It was probably what gave him the idea of how to escape."

"Well ,that makes sense," Caravaggio says. "In the search of your dad's apartment we found some things that tie Rosen to Jeanine, but her hospital IDs can't be found anywhere. Which is odd, because she was using one to get in and out."

Lilly clears her throat. "Um, I took them when we were there."

"You did? Why?"

"I don't know, they looked important. And I didn't know you'd do a search."

"Jesus. Do you have them?"

Lilly nods. "There are two. One for 2014 and one for 2020."

Caravaggio laughs. "That's the ticket, then. Because her license was suspended in 2014 for neglecting a patient who needed oxygen, and the patient didn't die only because the supervising nurse caught it. And she got her license back, temporarily, in 2020 during the Covid swamp. They needed everyone. Do you have it?"

Lilly gets up and gets the IDs from her drawer. She shows them to Caravaggio on the screen. "Get them over to me, would you?"

"Can you prosecute her for killing my dad?" Lilly asks.

Caravaggio's mouth drops open. I give him the short version.

"That would be the NYPD and the District Attorney, not us," he says. "Though without any real evidence...Rosen might or might not...no...but if he *did* inject *her*...I don't know. I'd take it to the DA if I were you."

Or use the threat to get her out of the apartment, I think. Extortion can be very appealing.

Finally, we tell him about the spice containers. "They were part of the theft. One belongs to the Zimmerman family, and one is on the list of Polish Unrecovered Art website for stolen Judaica. Lev found them."

"This guy doesn't quit getting himself in trouble, does he?" Caravaggio says. "We'll add that to our proof against Rosen. How do you think the museum was able to have that piece if it was on the list?"

"It's slightly different from the one shown on the website," I say. "So since Rosen was the interim director, he could say that he researched the piece and it was not on any list. If anyone called him on it, he could point to the distinctions. That would either get him off the hook completely or exonerate him for having made an error. I wonder, though...if he altered the picture somehow, so that the piece wouldn't match. It's got rubies all over it. I'll bet it's worth a fortune!"

"Can you show it to me?"

I look over at Lilly, but that's hard to discern on Zoom. She shrugs. "Lev has it."

"For fuck's sake," Caravaggio says. For a Department of Justice lawyer he sure swears a lot. Everyone seems to. Maybe it's being on remote for so long.

"Don't worry," she says, "it's safe, I'm sure."

"Art's a funny thing," Caravaggio says. "People want it, even though it doesn't produce anything, if you know what I mean. Same with precious stones. I mean, why? What's a ruby? But art, of course, gives beauty." He sighs. "You ladies have been very, very valiant in bringing this art thief, and history thief, and possible murderer, to justice. But you come from a pretty fierce line, so I'm not surprised."

"Thanks," I say. I'm surprised. "Fierce. That's a good word." Our grandmother on Dad's side was fierce. Our mother was fierce, and it was her menorah that started this all.

"I was thinking about your mom. Your mother's name was Aurora Juditya. That's a beautiful name, but Aurora wasn't a common Jewish name."

"We know. But it was pretty emphatic of her to keep Juditya when she dropped her maiden name." I don't go into details, of her father's obviously Jewish last name, and her mother's Slavic-ized Sephardic name.

"You know the painting, *Judith and Holofernes?*" Phil Caravaggio asks. "Zara, you kind of look like Judith in that picture. Four-hundred-and-twenty years ago, my ancestor painted your ancestor. How crazy is that?"

———————————

Andres leaves early the next morning. Of course he stayed the night with Lilly. What else could have happened after all that wine and him ordering in Italian and asking for special dishes, not on the menu, that were delicious beyond belief.

I hear him leave, Lilly is giggling, and I'm glad for her. She needs a little loving, and Lev can't be everything she needs.

I creep upstairs and she turns around. "Coffee?" she says.

We sit by the window, watching the day grow bright. Tomorrow night is Yom Kippur, and while I rarely fast, I always go to services. Except, of course, last year. And this year. Sam and I are leaving tomorrow morning, heading back to California. I'll be home in time to listen to the Kol Nidre on the internet.

I can't wait to be by the estuary, with the smell of the bay, the call of seagulls, and the dry September air. And my booster vaccination appointment has just come through for ten days from today. Truly a new year.

But I still have a question. "Lilly, when Rosen was standing next to me, when we first walked in the door, he was leaning his elbow on my head. Why did you come close and kiss him? Why did you approach him?"

"You don't know?"

I shake my head. "No, that's just stuck in my mind. I don't understand."

I'm terrified. Is she going to say she loves him? Or something equally incomprehensible? If she'd stayed back, he couldn't have grabbed her — maybe. He wouldn't have tried to rape her — maybe. Would everything have turned out differently? I put a worried face on, because I dread showing the judgment I'm feeling.

She looks sad. "If you didn't know, you must have thought, God, I don't know what. But I did it because he had a knife, Zara. He was pointing the knife at you, and grinning at me. He was going to kill you. And you looked so small there, like a child almost, with him leaning his elbow on the top of your head. I couldn't let him hurt you. I had to protect you. I had to."

I don't know when we both stop crying but finally I say, "Maybe he's finally out of our lives. Maybe Mom's secrets, Dad's secrets, maybe they can all go to their graves with them."

"GLW," she says, the acronym for *good lord willing.*

"They're all entitled to their secrets, heaven knows I wouldn't want Angie knowing everything about my not-very-sordid past, but when those secrets come up from the tomb like a dead hand and grab us around the neck and try to choke us — "

"Zara! Get ahold of yourself," Lilly says.

I take a breath. She's right.

"I'll get Jeanine out of the apartment one way or another. Maybe she'll still die, or I'll turn her in to the DA, or we'll have to pay her off somehow. But I'll get her out. Then we'll split what's left fifty-fifty. It'll be a nice chunk of change, I'm pretty sure."

I don't need to tell her that the split was supposed to be ninety-ten in my favor. She had to protect me. I have to protect her, even if it means another secret.

Lilly grins. "I could use it. And now that we can travel, maybe I'll go to Chicago, see Francis."

*Uh, you might not want to right away.* "Tell you what. You haven't been to California in years. Why not come out and stay with me? Then we can invite Francis Xavier, and we can all hang out!" I sound insanely chipper.

"You know what would be even better?" she says. "Since I'll have the money, why don't I come out, get a temporary rental, and do Meghan's kindergarten pod for a while? I am a teacher, after all."

"Would you?"

"I would love nothing more."

———•THE END•———

# WRITER'S NOTES

It's easier to write historical novels than contemporary ones—after all, we know how their plagues and elections turned out!

We all know the suffering brought on by the Covid-19 Pandemic. More than a million Americans, and multiple millions more worldwide, have perished in two and a half years of plague. Vast numbers were ill, some severely, and some with lasting physical damage. The miracles and diligence of science that brought us vaccines and treatments in record time weigh against the political and personal stupidities that worsened outcomes for so many. At this writing, people are still sickening and dying from Covid, but most of us are managing, with vaccines and medicines that were unavailable in 2020 weakening the impact of the disease.

But it's the malaise, the "languishing", and the emotional toll of the pandemic that haunt this book. Each individual experience has its own nuances, but we were all affected. We don't know the future, but we can look the present in the eye.

And now, a word about "truth." This is a work of FICTION. Which means that I made it up. None of it is real, but it's all artistically true. Believe what you want.

# ACKNOWLEDGMENTS

No book is born alone. I have many to thank, beginning with the brilliance of Yael Shahar and Don Radlauer of Kasva Press. One cannot have better editors and publishers! Further gratitude to poet and writer Priscilla Long (no relation) who read and critiqued an early draft, and whose suggestions made it so much better. To my IRL sister, Francesca Hagadus, whose love and support, to say nothing of a couple of knock-out ideas, make writing so fun. While I've stolen your identity for Lilly, you are far, far more sensible than Lilly could ever even aspire to! And of course, to Clyde, without whom none of this exists.

I dedicate this book to my dad. He didn't make it past February, 2020, but his spirit lives vividly in the memories of his children, his grandchildren, and even his great-grandchildren, one of whom he just missed meeting. That is our blessing.

One weekend, about a year after my mother died, my father finally told me all he could recall about her stories from the war. I recorded them as he talked, and at the end he asked me to find a way to tell her story. Unlike the father in the book, he is not only very much alive as I write this, but as a ninety-two-year-old he's as wild and engaged as he possibly could be. I immediately spit three times and make all of the other superstitious gestures to ward off any consequences of that declaration.

My real sister, Francesca Hagadus, is an amazing person. She allowed me to use our story, fictionalize it, explore it and offer it to you, my reader, without limiting what I wrote. She did, however, require that I submit to going to her hairstylist at least once in return. She may require that she get to choose my wardrobe for the book tour, and in gratitude I will submit. She cried with me, laughed and generally stared at me in amazement as we walked through the drafts of the book. My heart is full.

# BASIC
# REFERENCES

Cecil Roth, *A History of the Marranos*
*The History of Jewish Humor*
Elizabeth Rosner, *Survivor Cafe*
Helen Epstein, *Children of the Holocaust*
Leopold Staff, *The Sun*
The Jewish Museum of New York
SFJCC
San Francisco Contemporary Jewish Studies Museum
Robert Edsel & Brett Witter , *Monuments Men*
Ann Marie O'Connor, *The Lady in Gold*